BLOOD KIN

BLOOD KIN

Steve Rasnic Tem

SOLARIS

First published 2014 by Solaris
an imprint of Rebellion Publishing Ltd,
Riverside House, Osney Mead,
Oxford, OX2 0ES, UK

www.solarisbooks.com

ISBN: 978 1 78108 197 6

10 9 8 7 6 5 4 3 2 1

A CIP catalogue record for this book is available
from the British Library.

Designed & typeset by Rebellion Publishing

Printed in the US

For my parents

Emmett Tyler Rasnic
February 1921 – May 2005

Patricia Horton Rasnic
February 1928 – present

Tomorrow, and tomorrow, and tomorrow,
Creeps in this petty pace from day to day,
To the last syllable of recorded time;
And all our yesterdays have lighted fools
The way to dusty death. Out, out, brief candle!
Life's but a walking shadow, a poor player
That struts and frets his hour upon the stage
And then is heard no more. It is a tale
Told by an idiot, full of sound and fury
Signifying nothing.

— William Shakespeare,
Macbeth (Act 5, Scene 5)

"The past is never dead. It's not even past."

— William Faulkner,
Requiem for a Nun

Chapter One

WHEN MICHAEL HEARD the noise of his grandmother falling in the bathroom, he went out on the porch and sat down where white paint had gone to gray and then to bone from all the backsides that had rubbed there; he had not knocked on the bathroom door, he had not inquired as to her condition. He'd gone immediately, without thinking, to the front door and through it, to the family's traditional meditation center, that worn-out patch of rotting veranda, from where you could see as far as you wanted to see.

He might let her die. He might be killing her.

But he couldn't be sure she had fallen. He thought he'd heard the thump, the slap of bare, scrawny flesh on linoleum, but that might have been just weary feet padding over to the sink.

He'd felt a little bit of her pain, then, but he was always feeling her aches and pains. Not that he had her expertise in the family talent. She'd felt it when he'd stepped in front of that car a couple of years ago, gambling on death or disability — he didn't care which, a thousand miles away from here.

For him it had always been more subtle: a notion that someone was in trouble, an inkling of things falling apart, a vague suggestion of future or past events. Uncontrolled, maddening, useless. And before that key event with the car — no accident, more a game of Truth or Dare played with himself — there had been a collection of observations which told him he'd be returning here soon. There had been the landlady who swore he'd received a phone call from his mother (dead many years

now). And the neighbor who suddenly started calling him Jake.
And the package that had arrived full of dead leaves.

But his grandmother had grown old with that sort of feeling
into other people's hurts, and all the old Gibson cousins used to
say she was the best in the family. Which meant being cursed.

She probably wasn't badly hurt at all. She was old, and pain
came with the territory. There was no good reason to think she
was lying there dying.

Disgusting, decrepit old woman. As it was he'd never get her
smell off him. At least if she was dead he wouldn't have to listen
to, or live, her stories anymore.

The thought of her dead made him rub his arms from the chill.
Anxiety was suddenly crawling up and down his fingers, making
his palms wet and itchy with apprehension. He was getting to
be more and more like a gen-you-wine Gibson every day. Where
was his sympathy? His gratitude? He was just tired, was all, but
he was almost ashamed of himself. Almost.

He stared at the yard. Morning light left a slightly milky sheen
over the tall blades. Like moonlight, if the sky were a darker
shade. Cold light. He watched the wooden lawn furniture resting
near the house like furniture in a quiet parlor. Watched as if there
might be activity there he wasn't seeing yet. His grandmother
had had quiet rooms like that, a long time ago. Now they were
crowded with dead relatives' furniture and the fodder for more
of her tales.

The lawn furniture leaned toward the house. Cored with rot,
probably. He couldn't imagine what held the pieces up unless it
was the energy generated by the rotting process itself. Like some
people he knew. The furniture cast no shadow. The minimal
contrasts, the grayness between objects made him feel groggy, as
if he had carried a sliver of dream with him when he climbed out
of bed that morning, and now it was infecting him.

The calming green of the grass drew his gaze further down the
lawn, to the walk of ashen flagstones, dark in the morning, and

past that to the narrow dirt road which looked so damp and cool, but was neither.

And on the other side of the dirt road, across a narrow ditch invisible because of the tall thistles that filled it, so that he never could know what lay along its winding bottom, the layers of his family prison began to peel back, to the dense wall of olive and black-green trees that shifted ponderously out of the mists as the vapors moved in and out and between them, their bulk lightening in the morning shine.

And though unseen, he knew that beyond those trees lay the advance inlets of a vast kudzu sea lapping at the far edge of the woods. The restless kudzu, temporarily stymied in its march across the valley by this great wall of trees, had made itself known with the occasional bright green runner snagging Michael's attention.

Beyond that, he knew, was the glen, now four feet deep in large-leafed kudzu. A small house like an outhouse or a smokehouse was buried at its bottom, shingled in rough bark and walled with planks no two the same width.

Which held the long narrow crate with the well-nailed lid, reinforced and bound in thick iron.

Which held his death, apparently, and his grandmother's death, and perhaps the deaths of everyone in the valley if he did not understand his grandmother's tales well enough. If he could not peel all the layers away from their hearts.

He could hear her stirring in the kitchen. He wasn't sure how long he had been listening to her unawares, the pings of pots and spoons, and the soft clank of pans rising out of the sound of the cricket songs cocooning the dusk-darkened house.

He'd lost a day again, dreaming of the crate buried under kudzu, and dreaming her stories as if they were his own confession. Losing his life in the process. She wouldn't be content until he knew all her tales and had no thoughts of his own for keeping track of the time or the year.

So she wasn't dead after all. And soon she'd be calling him in to make her dinner, and then to put her on the toilet, and then to help her bones into the hot bath, and then to lift her out again so she could towel herself off, and then to listen to her long stories of a brown and gray past, days long curled and turned with their backs to the cold Virginia breezes.

And he knew that despite himself, although he was tired of it, and long past resentful, he would take all her words inside and make them his own, make another past in which he was the scrawny little cornhusk of a girl, Sadie, focus of her daddy's unwelcome attention, a young cricket playing the day out through the woods and down the dirt streets of Morrison, Virginia, that ancestral home of all the Gibsons since forgotten forebears had left their Melungeon plateau in Tennessee.

He couldn't help himself. He had been born into the feeling and the witnessing and the making of what he heard, and felt, to be his own.

The sky was almost the color of his skin now — a dusky almond. Out in the world numbers of people seemed inclined to find him and his burnished color attractive, and he had always taken advantage of that fact. Other people's feelings were only a skin's depth away, and once you knew what a person — especially a woman — was really feeling, you had her. You had the key to what you wanted — money, favors, sex, the alcohol and drugs which had become his main interests. Not much nobility in that, he supposed, but what was wrong with using what you had?

He used to wonder if maybe he was too smart for his own good. The arrogance embarrassed him now. He used to believe that if you were smart, you understood that life was meaningless. Tomorrow and tomorrow and more tomorrows still. All of it the same, all of our concerns petty. Without substance and full of dramatic, idiotic gestures. Perhaps that was true but at least now he wished it wasn't.

Here, tucked up under the Morrison Ridge, many looked at him with vague suspicion; his color had become a central fact of his existence. His confidence was damaged, but more than that, the fact that he had behaved so badly when he'd had the advantage of an exotic appearance made him feel shame. He was darker than most. He was Indian or black. He was maybe part Portuguese or gypsy, or some throwback or creature from another world. He had skin the color of walnuts or papaws or light maple syrup. Sometimes he fantasized that when the sun went down you couldn't see him, and he might slip his dusky body through a crack in your sleep and make himself a yellowed shadow in your dreams and whisper vague things to you that would disturb you and maybe your entire family forever. Quite a few people in the hills went mad; folks had to have some reason, somebody to blame. He was a Melungeon, or descended from them.

These days lots of people claimed the lineage — because off and on it was fashionable. When it wasn't fashionable, any hillbilly with slightly darker skin was accused of it and looked down upon as shiftless or lazy. But he decided to take pride in it, even though he didn't really understand what it meant, and even though some members of his own family had clearly been unworthy of the heritage. He had to take pride in something, with the things he had done, the disappointment he must have been to his friends because of all the broken promises, how he had used them.

His grandmother had never mentioned his drinking or his drug use, but being around her now, he realized she must have known.

At least he couldn't get a variety of drugs here, not good ones. The heads in the county used that cancer drug Oxycontin, hillbilly heroin. There might be some meth, but so far he hadn't seen any, and he'd never leaned in that direction anyway. The county was dry, and some of them still drank moonshine because it was cheaper than whiskey, accessible, and had a terrible kick — it tasted like some kind of fuel, kerosene maybe. You could buy some from this kid Mark Jepsen, if you really wanted to. Jepsen's family had been in the moonshine business for generations.

Michael wasn't seriously tempted. Apparently he had a window into not only other people's needs, but also his own. His rehab counselor used to say he'd never really change unless he hit bottom, but Michael never would hit bottom. He knew how to hover just above bottom, and maybe that wasn't a good thing. He wasn't using anymore, but he was far from cured. Maybe he didn't want to be cured. His addiction was his secret pill, something he could always take if things got really bad.

But how did you fill your day? That was the big question. You had to fill it somehow.

When he lived here as a teenager any one of his elderly female cousins would take him into their very similar parlors and tell him the story of the Melungeons, with little variation in the telling, except that Cousin Lillian's version was always a mystery story, Cousin Ella's a kind of heroic epic poem.

"No one knows where we come from," Cousin Lillian always began her tale, whereas Ella was likely to start off with something like, "This is the legend of the Melungeons, your forefathers and mine, their trials and tribulations, their struggle against blind prejudice, and their eventual triumph as one of the finest and most respected old families in the Morrison valley."

Needless to say, he had preferred Lillian's version, even after hearing it a dozen times. She always forgot having told him, and she wouldn't have heard him even if he had said so.

"The first Scotch-Irish explorers into the East Tennessee mountains discovered us," Lillian continued. "On a high plateau, in an area where white men had never been seen and in fact further than any civilized person was thought to have ventured until that time, they found a village of almond-skinned people — similar in color to the Portuguese or Indians — who spoke a kind of Elizabethan English. They had simple tools, and crosses, and appeared to practice a variety of Catholicism. But they had no written records, and even the oldest of them had no idea how they first came to be there."

At this point Lillian would pause as long as ten minutes to let that first part sink in. Despite himself, every time Michael was intrigued by the enormity of the mystery surrounding the origins of his people. Then Lillian went on about how the Melungeons, from the French *mélange*, "a mixture," were considered blacks or worse to early white Southerners, and suffered some of the same restrictions concerning voting and land ownership. No one ever uncovered the answers to their mystery, although the theories were many. Cousin Lillian preferred the one that said they were Raleigh's Lost Colony. Cousin Ella liked to think they were descended from Ponce de León's men. Neither cared to discuss the theories that they were descended from runaway slaves and half-breed squaws.

Grandma Sadie almost never spoke about Melungeon history. Michael wondered if she thought it useless now. Maybe she didn't think it had much to do with her. Once when he brought it up she said, "Oh, we be *darker* than that. And I aint talking about skin. We aint hardly even Gibson. We come from a *darker* branch."

And that was as much as she would ever say on the subject. Grandma's version flavored Lillian's in a peculiar way — they didn't seem inconsistent, but maybe just two facets of a complex whole. Michael imagined the day those explorers first found the Melungeons up on that plateau, and this one group hiding unnoticed off to the edges, shadows of the others, strangers among the strange.

"Mich... aaaell..." The whisper was soft like lizard husk dragged through leaves, the lizard jerking his legs slowly to rid himself of his old suit. The way her breath broke in the middle of his name... she was old, God, how she was old.

He turned on his hips and stared at the greasy oval on the

screen door. Two spots of egg white appeared, and dry lips the color of earthworm. "Michael..."

When the lips disappeared into the dark of the stain, Michael stood up and limped toward the door. The leg was better, but some mornings it still stiffened up, and fought him.

They said nothing for most of supper, although he could hear her lips moving wetly, preparing to speak. He could hardly bear it. He thought he might scream, waiting. "You heard me... fall, Michael." The whisper crackled like an old recording. She kept her head bowed, her nose hovering just a few inches above the sweet potatoes and tiny piece of pepper steak, so that he couldn't see her lips move. It was a maddening habit; sometimes he thought she did it on purpose, to emphasize her power over him.

It was as if she spoke inside his head. "Michael..."

Only his family had ever called him that. He hadn't been called that when he left here. Everywhere else it was "Mike," or "MG." "Michael" was a stranger's name.

"Michael..."

He looked at her. Why didn't she just say it?

"You want me dead..."

At last.

"I... do... understand." She said nothing more for the rest of the meal.

He did his leg exercises after dinner. Back in Denver, before he was lured here by his grandmother to help take care of her and in return live rent-free, he'd stopped doing them, preferring pain pills that numbed him just enough without wiping his memory of the stupid thing he had done. His girlfriend at the time, Allison, pretty much did everything he wanted or needed. All he had to do in return was make her feel an essential part of his life. He'd had an enormous talent for that sort of thing. Sometimes now he thought about writing her and apologizing, but he wasn't sure if she would understand why he was apologizing. He liked her — maybe someday there could be something there. But better for her if she never heard from him at all.

He couldn't get cell reception out here, and his grandmother didn't own a phone. Whoever heard of not having a phone? For a while he just used his cell phone to play games, until he got bored and put it away in a drawer somewhere. He wasn't exactly sure where.

She at least had an old TV hooked up to a small antenna outside. It got one, sometimes two channels, both of them fuzzy. Sometimes he watched the news, but the news outside seemed to have less and less to do with the world here in the hollow. Now and then he'd watch a show or an old movie, but night scenes were impossible to see on that TV, so sometimes he'd just make up where they were. It was like living in the old times, in the days before any significant electronics. And the crazy thing was she seemed to like it that way. Crazier still was that he was starting to get used to it.

It seemed inevitable now that he be here. He'd been on his way back here ever since he left. Even as the red Chevrolet bit into his lower left leg he'd known he was going home. As he flew backwards into the sculpted shrubbery that lined the street he knew his grandmother must be waiting for him, sitting up with his pain in her own ancient legs. It had almost made him feel guilty, but not quite. He'd made another bad decision.

The parlor/sewing room was stacked high with folded materials in dusty red, green, and blue, baskets full of brocade and buttons, chairs piled high with patterns and books and catalogs twenty and more years old. He found his chair by the old Singer, and waited for his grandmother.

To come in. To get on with the story.

He'd been back almost two years. Every night at this time, sometimes a half-hour earlier, never more than fifteen minutes late, she came in here to tell a little more of the family tale, her tale. The first month she had made him come in here, in that cracked voice, that unaccountably compelling way she had, and when he began resisting in earnest she just sat next to him wherever he was, outside on the porch or in his own room, and began to tell the tale again. You couldn't win against a crazy old lady.

He was thirty years old with no life, living with his grandmother. He couldn't leave here, and he wasn't even sure why. He felt like one of those women he used to date — wanting to leave, but somehow she was preventing it. And yet he kept coming back for more.

Once he'd limped out into the woods, almost as far as the resting fingers of the kudzu, and she'd followed him painfully out there, stumbling and sliding — he'd heard her protesting joints from yards away and it almost sickened him, did sicken him when he began feeling it himself. It took him an hour to carry her back to the house, and she'd been bedridden a week.

Every evening of that week he had gone to her bedroom to hear the story. She had talked and he had listened.

Now it was expected that he wait for her in this room. He almost, but told himself "not quite," detested the old woman, maybe most of all for the waiting. She was pretty much in control of everything.

After all, a rotting iron-clad crate waited for him. Or what was inside, the name he did not know or care to know for fear he'd be calling it down on him, and him so ill-prepared. Not yet. He needed more of his grandmother's tale.

He couldn't help listening. For it was also his story.

He sometimes wondered if she would ever let him clean this room, this mausoleum of old cloth and dress patterns. Since he moved in she had had him excavate relics and mementoes and trash from corners and behind stairwells and the backs of built-in drawers and cabinets all over the house, sorting through things that hadn't seen the light in decades. He imagined taking them from the dim artificial light of the old house into the more intense light of day, and watching them crumple or dissolve or rise into smoky wings circling the house before drifting into the trees. Anything was possible here.

His grandmother would examine each item for flaws, cast some — a very few — away, give others to Michael to look at or do with what he would, and put others back into the cabinets herself.

It was the items she gave him that troubled, because he never could figure out her criteria for the gift. They always looked much the same as the ones not chosen – old letters, newspaper clippings, and bits of toys, buttons, and Christmas ornaments. He would stare at them for hours trying to fathom their secrets, the secrets she meant for him to have.

Most of all, he resented the responsibility she gave him. It was now *his* decision whether to save any individual item or throw it away. Sometimes this took a long time — he'd look for opinions hidden within her expression but she was blank as stone — and, after all that, he'd change his mind. He'd foolishly scrabble through the trash searching for what he'd thrown away. It disgusted him... the power she had.

This was one of the hand-made houses you saw all over this part of Virginia. Piece by piece over the past two years he'd learned that its first owner had been a farmer, a hermit really, by the name of Jacobs. Grandma's uncle the preacher, Michael's great great uncle, had bought it from Jacobs. Or obtained it by some other means; Grandma seemed unwilling to commit herself on that point. One day Jacobs just left town on the back of a broken down mule he'd gotten from the uncle, not saying one word, just staring at the country he was leaving, not even bothering to take most of his belongings. The next day the preacher moved in, where he would live until Grandma's father finally took over the house.

Michael hadn't gone far enough into the tale yet to know what happened to the preacher. According to Grandma the present-day parlor was all there'd been to the original house. The woodwork in this room was darker and grainier than anywhere else, and the construction just different enough to show that another pair of hands had worked it. Walls and ceiling and broad, shiny floor came together pleasingly in this room, once you subtracted the clutter. The preacher apparently had made no attempt to duplicate such serenity in the rest of the house.

If Michael were to back out of this room, slowly, he would find himself in a narrow hallway that ran up the west side of the house. Back up too quickly and he'd already be in the kitchen, where walls tilted slightly away from each other so that you might very well go dizzy if you stared too long.

He knew there were a lot of other bedrooms, but he hadn't ventured into all of them. Some were kept locked. He and Grandma lived in the main part – the part which, despite its architectural eccentricities, seemed the most normal. He avoided the rest of the house as much as possible. Not all of the rooms were even equipped with electricity.

One day during his first month back he'd gone through the small door off the back of the living room. This led to a series of short hallways with doors branching off. He'd gotten only a few feet through one of them when he'd experienced the distinct sensation of the house unfurling itself into a maze, or a net, or maybe the dry rotting chambers of some great, woody flower. He'd backed out immediately and never tried to explore the place again.

It had been like falling; that memory of an endless succession of rooms dropping away to nothing made it almost unbearable for a while to open any door.

Some nights he would hear Grandma stumbling around back there carrying her kerosene lamp and he would try to force sleep to come.

Grandma told him that the preacher used to leave visitors out front, before there'd been a front porch, and walk into the house, "and it was like the house just swallowed him up. He didn't come out for days. And everybody said his skin was paler than when he went in, like he'd bleached it."

"Nobody'd follow him in there," she said. "Preacher traded for a lot of furniture over them years — for a healing, or running a funeral, or a special prayer, or a guarantee of children or that a marriage goes well – people said he got enough furniture to fill an ordinary house ten times over. But when my mother and me moved into this house it was almost empty. And them were some fine pieces too, old heavy stuff — dressers and cabinets and sideboards and paintings and such."

Sometimes it seemed to him Grandma was like this house, as was he, as were all his relatives he knew anything about. Rooms inside rooms connecting to even more rooms. And all of them resembling each other. By knowing Grandma he could also know all the relatives who had come before her.

As she told him the stories he was there, seeing the stories and being inside the stories, living them through her eyes. She hadn't told him much of significance yet, at least nothing for him to act upon, childhood memories of a lamb and playing near the cows, feeding the chickens and the goat, some anecdotes about favorite play pretties and the girl's worst disappointments, her small sins and her father's much larger sins, the vileness of his appetites, and the danger he posed to her sanity. But small things, relative to the big thing she promised would lie at the end of her tales.

He'd had a taste of it all his life — that special empathy of the Gibsons' — hearing a friend's memory related and reliving it inside his mind with a felicity so remarkable he might weep with the sorrow of it or gasp breathless with the thrill. Not that he ever did weep, or gasp, but the potential was there. But this was more. When Grandma spoke the words of her life he was there smelling the thirties air of those southwest Virginia hollows and river bottom farms, tasting the tastes of molasses and corn bread and feeling the growing soreness of this blister on her left foot rubbed against the ill-fitting shoe.

It was a perfection of memory he'd rather have been denied. Having to live your own life, however dull, was plenty; there really wasn't enough room for someone else's. All that could result from such an overfeeding was pain.

He was pretty sure she knew that, otherwise she wouldn't have lived alone most of her life. Yet she continued to feed memories to him.

He still had not learned what that awful crate contained, and he had a feeling, a sense disconnected from all reason, that his time was running out. He could hear the wind rustling the trees outside. He imagined the sound of a thousand kudzu leaves shaking in the glen.

Skinny little corn husk of a girl.

Twelve years old.

Her father's object, target of his frustrated desire.

Michael saw her shadow creeping across the leaning stacks of magazines before he heard her step. Then she was there in her rocker, that little girl suddenly struck old, voice crackling like yellowed newspapers catching on fire, speaking to him, taking him in through the doors...

Chapter Two

SADIE LEFT THE rotting gray shack with her daddy's shouts still chewing on her ears, and she didn't know how she could take much more. The man was slipping into craziness a little more each day — just like his own daddy and momma, and Uncle Jesse, too. Most of the back hollow Gibsons got that way after a certain age, at least that's what her uncle the preacher told her. Said they didn't have sense enough to use whatever powers almighty God give them, and that's why they turned sour that way.

Sadie herself didn't want no powers, didn't want to know no body that had them. She'd heard there were town Gibsons, normal folk who didn't talk about such things. Maybe she could go live with that bunch.

"You'll have to make your choice someday soon, Sweet Sister." She never could figure out why the preacher's voice was so hurtful to hear, just that it went up sharp in places, and he talked about things that made her irritable. You could get a terrible headache listening to the preacher too long, but apparently the folks in his congregation didn't seem to mind. "You'll be coming of age," he'd said, and again she found herself wishing she could stay a child at least until rabbits rode horses. That would be a fine day, she figured, for becoming an adult. She didn't understand quite yet what being an adult meant; she just knew she wanted no part of it. All the other girls in her class she knew had had their first monthly visits by now, but she was having no part of that either. She'd hold it back, at least until she was out of that house, maybe

Blood Kin

even out of the county. She knew her daddy was real concerned about it, asking every other day if she was "bleedin yet." She wasn't sure what would happen if she said she was. Maybe he'd stop touching her then, but she didn't think so. She figured it would probably get worse, although she didn't know how.

She'd stay a girl until she left here — that'd be the plan. Looking at her mother she saw what being a woman meant.

The thing about Daddy's craziness was that he played with it so much you couldn't feel too sorry for him. He spent his crazy spells drinking and betting and having a good time. Her granddaddy, her momma's daddy, was always talking about that. Her granddaddy hated her daddy, said her momma should've never married trash like that. The Morrison branch of the Gibsons being what they were, with a bad reputation among their own kin, and even with them being supposedly one of the oldest Melungeon families in the valley. So maybe she shouldn't always believe what her granddaddy said.

She couldn't really believe what any of them said. Not her daddy or her granddaddy, not even her mother. And Lord knows not the preacher.

She had to get out of that house, but she was only twelve years old. Maybe she could get married, but she really didn't think she wanted to get married, especially to some old fool been married three times already and outlived all three. That Mr. Mackey was on to her daddy all the time about marrying her, and giving her daddy gifts for it, but so far he hadn't made any promises. Right now her daddy wanted her all to his self, but that might change — he might get tired of her or Mr. Mackey might just sell that barn full of cows of his, to some feeble-minded man a worse fool than him, and then he'd have just enough marriage money to buy her from her daddy.

She heard a yelling then, looked up and figured she'd gotten too close to the fence around the Younger property, and there come Hattie Younger running hell-bent across the field toward her, a big stick raised in her hand ready to clobber. "Run, Sadie, run! I dont know I can catch her!" It was Hattie's oldest son Bill, his face red, giving it all he had as he ran after his ma because apparently he'd started too late.

Sadie took off down the road as hard as she could, but she'd never been a good runner, and Crazy Hattie was bound to catch her for sure, and beat her head in with that big stick. Hattie lost her mind about seven year ago — Momma said that just happened to folks around there sometimes — and for some reason she got it into her head that Sadie had done her a terrible wrong, and she was for sure going to even the score. It made no sense — Sadie knew Bill from the one-room school up on the hill — but she hardly knew the rest of the family at all, and didn't think she'd ever even spoke to Hattie. But Hattie was screaming at her now, and when Sadie turned her head around to see, Hattie was in the road only a few yards behind, her big straw hat flapping up and down, and every time it flapped up Sadie could see her face, and how the devil had gotten up all in her, and twisted things around.

Sadie had been wishing Crazy Hattie away, and then there was a pounding on the ground right behind her, and she turned again, and there Hattie was laid flat out, her face all bleeding and Bill sitting on his ma crying and waving Sadie away from there.

If you wished a thing to happen and then it happened, was that your fault? Sadie never got an answer.

She walked a little faster thinking about that, and pretty soon she was down at the bend where her daddy and granddaddy had that big rock fight a year ago, and they hadn't seen each other since then. Her granddaddy had been walking along there when her daddy came up in the opposite direction leading a cow he'd just bought in town. Granddaddy had said *something* — he'd said it was just "nice looking deal," but Daddy claimed it had been "one shitty deal," and it made Daddy so mad he commenced picking up rocks and throwing them fast as he could. Her granddaddy picked up a few and tossed them back in that general direction, but his arm got mashed up years ago between a crazy mule and the barn door so he didn't hit a thing. Finally he high-tailed it back the way he came so hard it put his knee out two weeks.

She wasn't sure Granddaddy always told things exact like they happened — nobody did — and she didn't much like the way he gossiped about her daddy's side of the family, but Daddy still oughtn't be throwing rocks at an old man like that, specially his father-in-law. One of them gave him just a terrible bruise on his left shoulder that lasted three weeks or more.

Sadie heard the noise, turned and saw the old wagon coming down the road toward town. The bank was high off the road here, so she didn't have a chance to get into the woods and hide.

It was Mr. Mackey racing his wagon team half to death again, with no thought to the life and safety of whoever might be walking the roads this time of day.

He pulled up beside her and stopped, the horses rearing, eyes bulging. But Sadie just walked on by. So he slapped them into a light trot and soon was keeping pace with her. Still ignoring him, she knew that if she didn't react to him soon he would be staying with her all the way into town. She kept her eyes to the ground and kept walking, though, needing to keep him going a little longer.

The horses veered closer, and soon she was walking on the far side of the road. Before she knew it the lead horse was grazing her as he trotted. She stole a glance up at his hot, heaving side, the huge and nervous eye. She was about to go into the ditch. The game was over.

She looked up, trying to look more mean than scared. "Get outta my way, Mr. George Mackey!"

The old man looked down at her and grinned. He wore a worn black tuxedo slick and bluish at knees and elbows — from too much proposing, Sadie figured — top hat crinkled a little in front but basically presentable, black ruffled shirt, in his button hole a pressed rose that was beginning to turn brown at the edges.

He pointed toward his big yellow square teeth, lips pulled back like a cow's to show them off to best advantage. "Goin to the dentist," he said, "then home."

"Glad to hear it, Mr. Mackey." She picked up her pace so that soon she was ahead of the team.

"When you going to marry me, darling?" he shouted behind her.

She turned quickly and screamed at him, "When snakes start milking cows! Now hush up your yelling at me, George Mackey!"

"Why, child, snakes is already milking the cows. Just ask the preacher." He grinned and Sadie thought that was just the awfullest smile she'd ever seen. A smile like that surely'd kill a baby.

The thought of snakes milking cows with the preacher looking on, blessing the event, made her go cold all over. Her feet began to tingle, as if a snake were crawling under them. She curled them sideways in the dust of the road, but the feeling wouldn't go away.

"Get away from here, George Mackey!" she shouted, tearfully. "Get away or I'll have somebody *kill* you!"

He looked at her then, startled and hurt. Maybe a little afraid too, her being a Gibson and all. He snapped the reins and the wagon pulled away.

Sadie was scared. She'd never seen him hurt before. She had no idea what he might do now.

The road went steep down for a time before leveling out in the bottom land. Here it flooded over all the time, but this had been a dry summer and the creek was way below what it ought to be.

They said it was a Gibson that discovered this hollow, following the Big Muddy Creek back to source. Walt Gibson, a big man. Daddy said he had to stoop to get into any house in the hollow, except his own. He built that one big, and well, and it would still be standing to this day if he hadn't requested that it be burned to the ground, with his body in it, when he died. Sadie figured that must have been a mighty big disappointment for his wife.

The hollow was full of bear, deer, and small game back then. They said Walt found the first level place near the source, cut the trees down with an axe — the only tool he had — the first day, and built his cabin complete the next.

Off by himself like that, he married an Indian woman, the first woman he saw. Then two of their children got married to each other, the Indian woman died, and then Walt married one of his granddaughters when she was thirteen and he was eighty-two. And he still bore six more children with her. Willy married Mae, Henry married Susie, and their son Jackson married the daughter of a man who lived over on Spence's Mountain across the county line. Another of Walt's sons, Orson, married Willy's daughter Cleo (her middle name was Patricia and everybody called her "Cleo Patty") and she outlasted them all. Whenever any of the older Gibsons talked about "Ma," Cleo was the one they were talking about. She was gone before Sadie was born, but any time she messed up people would say "think of your grandma in heaven looking down on you," and she did, and it always gave her an awful feeling that Grandma Cleo was this wonderful woman that Sadie never could be. Except she had that special Gibson talent, just like Grandma Cleo had.

Orson and Cleo Patty had Bobby, who was Sadie's daddy; Ralph, the quiet one who, with his wife Mattie, pretty much kept to themselves, only going to family events when they had to; Suzette, who was a scandal ("but what can you expect giving a child such a name," according to the preacher); and Jesse, the youngest. Cleo Patty died giving birth to Jesse and that pretty much fixed his place in the family and in the world for all time.

The preacher's real name was Jake, and his momma was a woman named Willa who'd been married to Henry for a brief time after his wife died. Willa hadn't been seen in the valley since the morning she dropped her day-old baby off on Orson and Cleo

Patty's porch after leaving Henry, she said, for good. Henry never claimed the preacher as his own, but most everybody else just accepted the baby preacher as part of the family, and Cleo Patty doted on the child. When Cleo Patty died people said something died in little Jake Gibson as well.

Of course Bobby, Sadie's daddy, had to stir up trouble. He was always saying that Henry wasn't really the preacher's daddy and so the preacher wasn't even a proper Gibson at all, no matter who raised him. 'Ma' was just such a nice lady she'd be nice to the devil himself. In fact he used to say the preacher was half devil but only when he was real drunk and there weren't nobody around to hear. Weren't nobody more scared of the preacher than her daddy, and he grew up with him in the same house. But not as brothers, that was for sure.

They still called Sadie's daddy Bobby, even though he was close to fifty now. Her mother was Dora Swenson, an outsider, and not fit according to most of the rest of the family. She was outside the family, and worse, from outside the valley. So she ended up doing extra chores for just about everybody except Great Uncle Jackson, who wouldn't allow her in his house.

Sadie didn't like the way the others treated Momma, but there weren't much she could do about it. Besides, she didn't know why she should care. Her momma had never seemed to have much use for her. She talked to Sadie as little as possible and Sadie didn't dare ask her any favors. It had always been like that, as far back as Sadie could remember.

When Sadie asked her momma why she let the others treat her like that, why she just didn't give it back to them, her momma just said, "Fool girl. You dont know nothin about it."

Mr. Swenson, her momma's daddy and her granddaddy, had a farm about twenty yards ahead, right at the bend of the road and the last house before you got into the town proper. He had moved from Spence's Mountain to be closer to his daughter, to a plot of land he'd bought from Thomas Gibson, her daddy's cousin. Her daddy had been mad enough to spit when cousin Thomas did that — they had a big fight and her daddy almost killed Thomas. Now Thomas lived out of the valley, on Spence's Mountain, and his side of the family had no contact whatsoever with the Gibsons still in the hollow.

Sadie liked her granddaddy very much. Her daddy said he was a rich man who walked all over other folk as he saw fit to get his loot, but Sadie never believed that. She didn't even believe he was all that rich; he sure didn't show it.

She turned off the road and down the dry ruts of the path leading up to her granddaddy's barn. He came out of the barn carrying two buckets of milk.

He was a tall old man, probably the lankiest she had ever seen. He walked as if all his legs and arms had been broken at one time or other. "What say there, Sadie?"

"Hidey, Granddad," she said quietly. She sat down on a fence rail and watched as he carried the buckets into a shed. He was out a few minutes later, fastening a padlock on the door. He turned and glanced at her, a little embarrassed, by the look of him. She stared at the ground.

"Sorry about that, Sadie. But you know if I dont lock it your daddy's likely to sneak down here some evening and take my day's milking."

"He's never been here…" Sadie felt the tears coming. "He wont even set foot here!" She was crying too hard now, so she climbed off the rail and stalked back up the path. She didn't know why she was so upset this time; her daddy and granddaddy were always snapping about each other to whoever would listen. She guessed she was just tired of it, was all. They both talked like the other was about the worst crook what ever lived, and the stories were all made up. Most of them didn't even make sense.

She could see the corner of Levitt's General Store about a hundred yards ahead of her. The town was pretty full these days — folks were moving back from places like Ohio, and even as far away as Michigan. It was that depression people talked about, but nobody seemed to understand. All those families that moved away years ago looking for jobs were back because those jobs all went away. She had a cousin or two like that, who tried to get on at the mines but the mines weren't hiring either. So they farmed — even though her granddaddy said the mountain land was the worst there was for farming. You had to have good river bottom land if you wanted to pull anything decent out of it. So people just hung around town, like something good might happen for them if other people just knew they were still alive.

Used to be she knew every face in town. Now she reckoned it was getting to be a lot like the big cities — she'd see maybe a dozen people she hardly knew and it was a little scary not knowing which one might be a friend or who was up to no good. A lot of people she didn't know were milling around in front of the store. She felt a little bit shy about going past them, but maybe it was best they didn't know her considering what she was about to do. She suddenly started feeling that excitement she always felt when she went to town — wondering who she'd see, what might happen, what she might be able to slip into the pocket of her yellow dress. She wanted people to notice her, wanted them to notice her every time she went into town. They'd be thinking, *Who is that girl in that pretty yeller dress?* She wondered how she was going to manage that this time.

Up on the left, just before you got to the store but halfway up the mountain above it, there were county wagons hauling off gravel and dirt and rock, what was left over after they plowed the rest over the slope. Mr. Levitt claimed they were going to bury his store one of these days, and the thought of that, the picture of Levitt's General packed floor to ceiling with greenish, moldy dirt, the customers and Mr. Levitt himself like mummies inside, filled Sadie with a strange feeling, like she'd looked into a grave. She wanted to peel all that stuff away, see what was really inside. Cause if you could see it, really see it, maybe then it couldn't hurt you. But something told her people didn't hold that to be a proper way of seeing things.

They had already planted some kudzu up there — that was that big vine the state people had brought in from Jap-an that everybody said would grow on anything, even your arm if you left it there too long. The highway department kept telling Mr. Levitt that was what was going to keep the bank from coming down and covering his store. The kudzu had these big green leaves that had three parts to them, and here and there you'd see these dry, papery pods. The leaves and stems grew out from these long runners the vine put out over everything.

The flowers were supposed to be big and purple, but one of the county workers said he'd only seen it flower a few times, maybe because they'd moved it from where it belonged and it didn't know how to act no more.

And it almost never made normal seed, even if it did start to bloom. It was like one of those big, sick, dumb babies that were born in the hollow from time to time. Born too big with a small piece withered here and there, and no brain to speak of, but Lord, how they grew! Those big dumb ugly babies would grow bigger than anyone else in the family, like as not.

The town was busy. Lots of folks in for their regular store-buying. A lot of horse-trading going on — men shouting at the top of their lungs, talking about how great their animals were and other men — the smart ones, mostly — sitting back and listening, nothing showing on their faces. And there was old lady Millburn, the only woman who traded animals in these parts.

Several men and Mickey-Gene, her cousin the idiot, were sitting out in front of Levitt's General. Petey Carter among them, his white beard stained mahogany from all the tobacco juice. Now and then he'd say something quiet and Mickey-Gene would turn slow and look at him, then laugh out loud like he had heard a joke. Mickey-Gene probably hadn't understood a word. He'd just heard other people laugh some time or other, and liked the way it sounded. Sadie thought it must be a terrible thing not to be able to tell when somebody was joking. People could be laughing at you all the time, like they did with Mickey-Gene. If something ever happened to her brain, well, she just hoped she would die.

Mickey-Gene's momma had been Suzette, the family scandal. She'd had Mickey-Gene when she wasn't married; nobody knew who the father was. Somehow Mickey-Gene had ended up being raised by Uncle Ralph and his wife Mattie. They pretty much kept to themselves so Sadie didn't see them much. Her daddy thought they were uppity, too good for the rest of the family. Sadie just figured they didn't like all the nonsense the Gibsons got into, and besides, they probably had their hands full with Mickey-Gene.

She caught herself staring at Mickey-Gene, his mouth opening with no sound, turning to her, his gray eyes floating to the top of his white face. She felt a sick, confused feeling, her thoughts getting their wings and flying away from her...

Sadie jerked away from his face. That kind of scary stuff had happened several times the week past. She touched her lower belly, and then pressed. It wasn't going to happen, not to her. She wouldn't let it. She could keep the blood back if she just didn't get confused by it. She had to keep her head set on that one thing.

George Mackey came out of Levitt's and just stood there, staring at her. She made herself stare right back. Then he started talking to the others and she was amazed at how they all perked up, taking him seriously. Even Mickey-Gene, struggling to make his face look serious like the others, but he only made himself look even more comical.

Only fools, idiots, and worse took George Mackey serious. She watched as he pushed back on his bent top hat, and then pulled up on his blue-black pants legs so he could crouch by Mickey-Gene and whisper something in his ear.

Mickey-Gene looked startled, glanced over at Sadie standing out in the road, his white face making his red hair look even redder.

Sadie walked on up the street, trying to keep the tears from coming. It was hard, she was so mad. But she knew these men. Once they saw a weakness, they never forgot it. They'd hit on it every time they saw you after that.

She slowed down almost to a stop as she got closer to Miss Perkins' dress shop. Although it wasn't just a dress shop no more — she had books and magazines and little statues and pictures and cards and all kinds of knick knacks in there now. She just never could sell enough dresses. But "Dress Shop" sounded real good, sounded fancy, and Miss Perkins must've figured that brought the customers in.

Some of the women up the hollow near where Sadie lived *did* seem to take Miss Perkins' place pretty serious. They'd speak in hushed tones about what nice things she sold them, what expensive things, and half the time they'd go into that shop just to admire, not really intending to buy. That didn't seem to bother Miss Perkins. Sadie figured most of those things were just for show anyway. More than once she'd seen Miss Perkins offer something for sale a whole month then wear it herself out in Morrison, probably just like she'd wanted all along. Miss Perkins would do her best to talk a customer out of it if they wanted to buy one of her nicer things. Miss Perkins' place was just for show, like a movie theatre (which the town didn't have) or a meeting hall (which they did). Women got themselves all gussied up just to go.

Miss Perkins didn't need the money no how. Her father had been one of the richest men in the valley, a dairy farmer, and when he died he left her enough money that she'd never have to work. Or so people said — Sadie didn't know first-hand.

Miss Perkins' Dress Shop was Sadie's favorite place for lifting things. "Lifting" was what they called it in that old pulp magazine her granddaddy gave her. It meant stealing. With all those pretty things lying around out in the open — Miss Perkins didn't have no glass display cases — it was hard to resist.

But now Miss Perkins watched her like a hawk every time she came in, but so far she hadn't done nothing about it. Probably too embarrassed to. Probably thought her Dress Shop was too fancy a place for anything as nasty as stealing to be going on. Lifting. Or maybe she was scared of Sadie's daddy, the roughest man by anybody's count in the whole town.

Or maybe Miss Perkins was afraid of Sadie because she was a Gibson, and the preacher's niece. That just might be. Most people in the town didn't think the hollow Gibsons were right folk at all. They were Indian or Spanish or Nigger or something. Not rightly human, whatever.

They were spirited, them Gibsons. Black nasty magical.

SADIE RAN UP the steps in front of Miss Perkins' as fast as she could, holding her arms out straight in front of her. She hit the door flat with her palms, so hard it burnt, and was quite satisfied with the explosion it made when it struck the wall. She ran into the middle of the shop, breathless, eyes peeled for Miss Perkins.

Miss Perkins started to shout something, and then Sadie saw her eyes when she recognized who it was. She looked down at her magazine again. Sadie had to hold her belly to keep from laughing.

Most of the stock was the same goods Miss Perkins had always had, long as Sadie could remember. Seemed like she hadn't sold hardly nothing out of the fancy stuff. Mostly people would buy a card or some stationery, one of the cheaper clay doodads or some ornament like a hairpin or sewing supplies or one of the dress patterns in a shiny metal box by her desk. Sadie figured Miss Perkins *had* to carry those things, else she'd never sell a thing, and pretty soon folks'd be too embarrassed to come in and browse no more. It surprised Sadie that no one else had been able to figure that out, but maybe they had, and they just weren't passing the word around out of respect or affection or more likely good neighborliness for Miss Perkins.

There were a few real nice doodads Sadie hadn't seen before, though — a little ceramic statue with a bright orange painted bear sniffing around a barrel that said "HONEY" on it. And a little angel with gold wings sitting on a bright blue mushroom. And a set of ivory-colored celluloid brushes, with mirror and a real cute soap container with a picture of a flower on it.

Miss Perkins was watching her close. She'd have to be careful.

Sadie had never been sure why she stole all the time, just that it excited her. It was something different; it seemed to add an extra tang to the day, made her feel like she was smarter than the people she was fooling, especially the grownups. She was poor, too. She supposed that might be reason enough, except she usually didn't care too much for the stuff she stole. She could have done without it.

She knew it was wrong, but that never seemed to bother her enough not to do it. There was lots of things folks in Morrison did was wrong — like giving her family such a hard time because of being what they was, and other things, things that people were dumb and superstitious about. So her one wrong thing didn't seem so bad.

Miss Perkins was talking to Alice Watkins, who'd come in to admire the ceramics lining the back shelf. Some of the finest pieces were on display there: the little shepherd with his four sheep, the scenes from fairy tales like Red Riding Hood, Snow White, and Rumpelstiltskin, the eight or nine different clowns, the twelve different vegetables. Alice Watkins came in almost every day to admire, and about twice a year she probably actually broke down and bought something.

"I have that figure of the old fat man on the ledge of my parlor window so that it catches the light just so. Do you know he just *looks* at me *wherever* I go in the room? And everybody says something about it, Miss Perkins, they surely do. It's *the* conversation piece in my house, it surely is."

Sadie had heard the story a hundred times. Alice Watkins seemed to find a way to drop that ceramic into every single conversation. But where most shop keeps would fall all over themselves trying to be agreeable with a customer like that, Miss Perkins just looked bored, or maybe a little worse than that — annoyed.

"Your daughter ever come back, Alice?" she asked, none too softly.

Alice Watkins dropped her head a second, then straightened herself, her elbows up and shoulders back. "Well, I'm afraid not. My guess is she's trying to start a career somewheres away from these mountains, some better place where they'll appreciate her talents. Then she'll probably come back with some real money, and help me out a little. My Phyllis is a very kind and generous girl. A lot of folks dont know that."

"Hmmm," Miss Perkins kept busy with her eyes, but they weren't looking at that poor Watkins lady. "If she was so kind, you'd think she wouldn't a run off without saying goodbye like that. That weren't exactly a generous thing to do to her mother. Took your best green dress with her I hear — the one you bought right in this very shop!"

"Oh, I'm sure she was just confused about it. I used to lend her that dress all the time for, for her dates. She probably just forgot and thought that dress was *hers!*"

"Maybe. Maybe," Miss Perkins said. "A lot of things get into girls these days. Lots of them get confused. It's that Confused Disease, I reckon. I heard of two more girls pull something similar this year, just took off from their parents without word one. No one seen them since. Pretty awful, if you ask me."

The Watson lady wouldn't talk no more after that, and after a while Miss Perkins put on her invisible sales cap again and tried to sell her something. She had her back turned a little, picking up individual pieces and pointing out the detail. Sadie could feel her contentment, the quiet music playing in her head.

Again Sadie had this feeling that she was doing something she shouldn't be doing. But she still ignored it. Miss Perkins wasn't watching so close now. The woman thought pure poetry when she handled her own stuff, not noticing another thing in this world in the meantime.

Sadie inched closer to the celluloid grooming set. She'd never had nothing so pretty as that; she didn't even know what she could do with it.

Her left hand was touching it, and then suddenly her right hand was just sweeping it all up into the loose folds in the front of her dress. She bunched the cloth together and ran for the door.

"Thief!" Miss Perkins shouted. "I *knew* I'd catch you at it someday!" She had Sadie's shoulder in her big old crow-claws, fingernails digging painful little holes into her skin. "No good thief!"

Alice Watkins was bustling over to help, her big body swaying like it was going to fall on Sadie, her face determined.

Sadie twisted away and hit the front door on the run, the screen slamming against somebody on their way in. She didn't know if the screech was the door or a person, but she felt the sudden flash of the other person's pain. It sickened her, and raised her fear sky high. She bit off a scream.

She stopped abruptly when she was out on the front porch, so full of panic she could hardly think. She'd never been caught at it before, and now everybody was looking. All the men down at Levitt's General were staring up her way, Mickey-Gene gaping, Petey Carter moving his mouth so fast he looked like a scrawny rat chomping away at empty air.

George Mackey was grinning like he was about to eat something all up. That slapped her awake, and made her mad, too. She started running just as Miss Perkins again grabbed the shoulder of her dress, tearing it a little as Sadie pulled away. She almost dropped the grooming set. She grabbed what she could and stuffed it all into her one good pocket so that she could run better. That pretty little soap box dropped to the ground but she couldn't stop to pick it up.

Sadie held on to her tears, but it was hard — this was her only dress that didn't have any rips in it. What was she going to tell Momma? And that pretty little soap box!

She jumped over the legs of the elderly fellow — Willie Philips, she thought — sitting out in front of the hardware, turned the corner up the alley past the Barber Shop. Here she almost knocked Elsa Peters down, her school teacher last year. Sadie's face went hot with shame, to have her teacher, who'd always liked her, know that she'd been thieving.

She was climbing the dirt road above the livery when a black, wool-wrapped arm reached out and grabbed at her. She shrieked and turned, and found herself looking up into the face of the preacher.

There were harsher things in this world than the preacher's face, but Sadie had never met up with any of them. He had a face like a stone left out in the woods long enough for the damp and moss and the tree roots and the ice to crack it in the worst way, not enough to make it look so old but surely enough to make it look wounded, deformed, messed up. Like the damage had scarred over bad and those scars were bound to ache nights when the weather was changing. Not an ache you could put your finger on exactly, what made it worse. And down in his neck right below the ends of his mouth he had these big fatty pouches, like gunny sacks full of his extra meanness. They made her think of the snakes he handled, like the pouches they kept their poison in. Her granddaddy sometimes said that meanness was a corruption and a disease. She thought about how under the preacher's terrible face the flesh and muscle must be all infected and maggoty inside like something run over and dead for days.

One of the preacher's scars — a crooked thing about four inches long that split his cheek from just below the left eye all the way to the jaw-line — looked like a living thing in the morning light, as if something awful had started growing in that crack in the rock face. But it was a tricky thing. Sadie had seen it fade back into his dusky skin when he must have not wanted folks to see it, like maybe when he was talking to some of the pretty young women around town, or somebody else he needed to charm.

His real name was Jake, but nobody ever called him that, not even the family. The preacher didn't like the name.

Where you going, child? It was like a whisper, or words you might think you heard in the wind but weren't really there. She hadn't even seen him move his lips. But you never did when he was angry or up to some meanness or other. She'd heard that only when he was preaching and singing at the snake-handling meetings did those lips become living things, terrible, scary alive things that could latch on to you if you weren't watching, chew you down right to the nub.

"Just going home," she cried, a little too loud, and he grabbed her arm so hard she thought he'd squeeze it in two.

Over the years that followed she would think a lot about what happened next — if her uncle caused what happened, or if she did, or if it had all happened by coincidence. Or if she'd just imagined parts of it. But not the slowing down part; she knew the slowing down part was for real. It happened to her all the time. Things just stopped, or slowed down considerable, and suddenly she was seeing things she ordinarily didn't see. Or want to.

The preacher pushed her face around so that she had to look at the livery. Didn't grab her exactly, at least not with his hands. But he wanted her to look that way, and suddenly she was just looking that way, without a word spoken or a finger lifted.

She looked, and what she saw made her cold. Fred Shaney, Will Shaney's eldest, was helping run some corn through that old steam-powered corn sheller. It was huffing and puffing and its rusted parts shaking side to side like it was about to explode.

Fred Shaney had had more than one run-in with the preacher. There was Fred's drinking and smoking, and his smart remarks about the whole snake-handling business.

40

The preacher was watching Fred in such a way it brought winter down on Sadie's shoulders. She could almost see the ice crystals in the air. Something was going to happen.

Fred was feeding the corn into the machine faster and faster. His hands a blur.

Her eyes were paining her. Spots burned in the air in front of her face. It started in her lower belly, and she squeezed her eyes shut trying to ignore it, but the soft ache was making her sick. She looked down; a thin line of blood had run down her leg. Sadie's hands were burning, burning.

His hands a blur.

Red spots. His hands a red blur.

Bright red over everything.

She watched as the world slowed down around her, as Fred Shaney's grin slowly widened and deepened as Fred Shaney's arms were lifted slowly into the air, bright red crepe streamers tied to his wrists.

"You have to decide soon, Sister," the preacher whispered. "You've reached your maturity now."

She watched as Fred Shaney dropped into prayer, wondering if this could be her punishment for stealing.

And the other men came to hug Fred Shaney, embrace him down to ground.

Chapter Three

FOUR TIMES ALREADY that morning Michael had had to carry Grandma into the toilet and set her on the stool. Each time she was weaker, until her feet dragged the floor, her high-top black boots bunching the rug as he struggled to get her in. It would have been easier to just let her mess herself and then clean up afterwards. But she would have none of that. Not that he blamed her. She still had her pride, and he guessed it was his job to help her maintain it. He'd been pretty ungrateful the past couple of weeks, pretty unkind. He certainly didn't like doing things like this for her, but he wanted to do a better job of it.

Of course he'd felt uncomfortable taking care of her. He'd never been good at taking care of anything. Once when Allison had taken a month-long trip his only job had been to water the plants, which he didn't do, not once. He'd been too busy watching TV, smoking weed, or hanging out at a bar with a few — well, he would never have called them friends — acquaintances. He discovered that two of the plants were dead a few days before she got back. He didn't know what else to do but dump a great deal of water into the pots as evidence that they'd been watered. They'd only died because, well, plants die, not because of any lack of diligence on his part.

But another plant had thrived, despite his lack of care. She had it in the corner of the living room where it didn't get much light. He had no idea what it was — some kind of thorny vine. And despite the lack of both water and light it had grown at least two feet in her absence, probably more.

nly reason he'd noticed it was because he'd tripped over morning coming out of the bathroom. Sprawled on the rug was able to see the pot of it there in the corner between the furniture legs. He had no memory of having seen it before. The pot was small, and yet the vine was long, sprawling. Where were its roots? Certainly there was no room for them in that little pot. He kicked the plant back into the corner. One runner of it clung to his shoe. He broke that piece off in disgust. Not knowing what else to do he flushed the broken piece down the toilet.

By the next day the plant had extended itself back into the center of the living room. Another day, Michael imagined, and it would be tapping on the bedroom door. He couldn't think about this anymore. He gathered up the whole thing, pot and all, and carried it out on the balcony and threw it into the alley below.

Once Allison was back he showed her the two dead plants and told her how sorry he was. He wasn't good with plants. After all, he'd said, he'd watered them and yet they still died. Better yet, when she said "It's okay, that happens sometimes," he'd acted upset that he'd "let her down" and said he would find four "great" plants to replace them with. She'd been impressed by his concern, and he never had to get around to buying those plants. He never brought up the missing plant and she never mentioned it. Maybe she'd forgotten she had it.

He cleaned up his grandmother a couple more times that day, helped her get into a nice dress, made her some soup. After a while doing these intimate chores for her didn't seem so bad. He was getting used to the embarrassing nudity and the smell, the mess. He thought about what it would be like if he ever got old. There was also something — "cleansing" wasn't quite the right word but it would have to do — about taking care of someone in just this way. Lifting them on the toilet, wiping their butt if you had to. Taking care of someone else's bathroom business. Someone famous had called it a "holy task." Michael wouldn't have gone that far, but he thought maybe there was some truth in it.

Last night's story had worked inside him long after she'd gone to bed. He'd sat out on the porch, the night pitch-black except for the antique kerosene lamp beside him. There were few places you could get a night like this, without street or house lights to bring detail out of the dark.

As much as possible he tried to allow the immediate sensations of her young life to leave him, to dissipate and join whatever stream of lost and misplaced sense memories must flow through the hidden layers of the world. He'd felt the sun on her face, and smelled the smell of it, that dust and grass aroma of southwest Virginia, and he'd felt the seize in her heart when the young man had lost his hands, and the blood filling her eyes, and draining her pale and shaking. He felt bad for the slow sacrifice of her youth, he truly did, but he didn't know how long he could stand to live inside her life this way.

He couldn't see across the road, but he could hear things moving out there in the woods. Small animals. Had to be. And occasionally there was a subtle change in the quality of the darkness — a shadow would be suddenly lighter or darker, the massive outline of a tree would shift against the night sky. Michael had a sense that if he had a different kind of light, a new kind of light some physicist might invent someday, he'd be able to pull back these shadows and see the past of this valley laid out before him. He had a notion that these peculiar night shadows, these dark silhouettes, were the valley's way of dreaming. And surely there must be some way to see into those dreams.

At any other time, in any other place, he'd of thought that nonsense. But not here, not while listening to Grandma's stories.

He kept wanting to ask Sadie what her choice had been, and what that choice meant, but he knew he'd have to wait for the story to catch up to that. She had her own timing for everything, and she didn't change it for anybody. When she drew her lines, she drew them firm.

When he'd been small, and lived here with Grandma, he'd hated that strictness at first. He never would have said he'd grown to like it, but he'd gradually felt safer within its confines, knowing that however badly he might mess up, it wouldn't be fatal, it would never ruin everything. Grandma would always protect him from that. With his mom and dad there was never that kind of firmness. His father, Sadie's son, had stayed away from home most of the time. Only a few years ago Michael received the phone call from Thailand informing him of his father's death. Sadie had said of her son, "People, any sort of people, were always too much for him. He got their feelings under his skin and he couldn't take that. I kept telling him 'you gotta set with it awhile and after a time you get used to it.' But he couldn't do that. I dont think he liked folks — they bothered him too much."

Michael's mother was another Gibson cousin, so it was a marriage like a lot of others in their family, not illegal, but it still made people talk. Gibsons were drawn to Gibsons. It had always been this way. Maybe they thought another Gibson was the only one who would understand them. Like so many in the family, his mother started in her thirties to lose touch. She'd spent the final two decades of her life in the State Hospital in Marion. Michael's single visit had been so upsetting he'd come away thinking that *he* was the crazy one.

Grandma Sadie had raised him until high school, then she and every other adult who cared enough to have an opinion (which didn't include his father), decided he needed to be in better schools if he was to make something of himself. So starting at age thirteen Michael had grown up with a succession of Gibson cousins spread all over the country, most of who thought he was wonderful and sensitive. He'd appreciated that, and would have liked to believe it, but most of the time he didn't know what he was. He felt so many things, and resented feeling so many things.

When he went off to Chicago for college he was sure he'd find out who he really was. He'd have another culture to measure himself against. He wasn't exactly embarrassed about being a Southerner, but he'd often found himself struggling to defend the South. Without thinking much about it he'd mention some fellow he'd known in Morrison and then he'd be genuinely surprised by the reaction. "Jesus, talk about *The Sound and the Fury*!" from a guy in the dorm, and, from the sweet-faced girl on the moonlight walk early in his freshman year, "Oh, Michael. It's hard to believe you came from a place like that!" After that he played up the country background more — the women, some of them, at least, loved it.

Something shiny across the dirt road caught his eye. Michael looked up and saw that there were a few kudzu leaves hanging from the outside edges of the nearest boughs, the moonlight reflecting off their surfaces. They gave the outline of trees a slightly furry appearance.

Michael was just accommodating. Probably no other description was needed. He told people what they wanted to hear. If they wanted sensitive, he'd be sensitive. If they wanted aggressive, he could be aggressive. They didn't even have to tell him what they wanted, usually; he felt it. But he understood that he couldn't be touched, not really. He dropped out of college his junior year. He lived with, and off of, a succession of friends and girlfriends. He worked a string of odd jobs. He always got hired easily — sometimes it seemed all he had to do, really, was smile for them. But he never kept those jobs long. People found him easy to talk to, so they unburdened themselves, they let him know all about their problems. But the thing was, he really wasn't that interested. They'd fill him up with their stories and after a while he couldn't bear them. He'd move on, and they wouldn't understand what had happened.

As the kerosene lamp dimmed, the night air yellowed like an old lithograph. The light pulled back, away from the woods, the road, and the front yard.

It was getting to be time for him to make plans for himself. With each week cooped up with Grandma he felt a year older.

The intense claustrophobia — boxed in with her memories of the complicated lives and personalities of those long dead — had become increasingly aggressive, until he was beginning to feel anxious about his own life. He knew that if he stayed much longer he'd start drinking again; he'd find some source for pills, whatever he would need to get through the day. But she kept telling him that his self-preservation depended on his hearing her story out. Her tellings were coming to some sort of head.

There was something in a crate beneath the kudzu out in that field on the other side of the woods, a crate that someone had felt the need to bind in iron, if Grandma had not lied to him. And Michael didn't think she ever lied.

She was up again at four. He could hear her stirring. He hadn't even been aware he'd stayed up all night. He thought about slipping into bed before she knew he was up, but then the ache in his side intensified as she struggled to get to the screen door behind him.

He could feel her thin lips begin to move.

"We'd best get back at it. We lost last night." He waited. "There's little time left, Michael."

The wind was suddenly in the distant kudzu, and the thousand green leaves of it pushed against the wall of dark trees until they swayed.

Chapter Four

SADIE DIDN'T WANT the preacher walking her home, but she didn't know how to stop him. She didn't even know how to talk to him, didn't want to. The preacher wanted something from her, seemed like most everybody wanted things from her lately: her daddy, her momma, George Mackey. But she was sure that whatever the preacher wanted would put all those other wants to shame. The preacher hadn't said a word to her for some time, but he didn't have to. Although they were walking together he was leading her, just like he did everybody in the hollow. Some people said it was because he carried our Lord with him that he was such a natural-born leader, but Sadie knew it was something else entirely. She couldn't have said exactly what it was; she didn't even want to think about it.

With her trembling left fist she clutched the back of her yellow dress so that it fell down in folds to hide the blood from her period, praying her thanks that she was so skinny and that the dress had always been so loose. But she kept thinking about that blood on her and she couldn't help thinking of it as Fred Shaney's blood, too. She kept seeing Fred Shaney's hands flopped down in the dirt like pale fish.

She kept trying to think of a way to explain it away. She wasn't ready, and she didn't even know what it was she wasn't ready for.

But the preacher knew.

"They killed him last night," the preacher said, his voice slow and watery.

"Who?" Again she thought of Fred Shaney. Who had the preacher done away with now?

"John Dillinger. Shot him down outside a theater in Chicago. Heard it on the radio down at the store."

"So? He's a criminal, aint he?"

"Depends on how you look at the thing."

Sadie wasn't surprised by his attitude, but it made her curious all the same. "Why... you're a preacher. How can you say that?"

"John Dillinger was an outsider, an outcast in an evil society. He just did what they forced him to do."

"He killed people."

"Sometimes you have to. You'll be learning that, Sadie." She almost shook her head. *Not if it means cutting people up like that, like poor Fred Shaney.*

They descended into a bottom where the creek came up almost to the roadside for a time. A soot-streaked shack on the opposite bank, eaten out over the years, leaned like it was about to fall into the water. Gazing at the wide spaces between the boards gave Sadie an achy feeling. A pleasing dampness filled the air; light shone between the trees like a wet silver ribbon.

Dying vegetation caked the creek banks. The creek was still, stopped by the green logs bridging the banks. Somebody had started a stone dam here years ago and left it a third built. Stones still jutted from the banks into the green water and the mass of rotting logs. Water wept down the rough stone. She felt like the air she was breathing was so old it was leaking.

"It be the third decade of the twentieth century, girl." The voice was so low, so careful, Sadie wasn't even sure it was the preacher's voice, but she didn't turn around to see if his lips were moving. It was like hearing her own thoughts. She just kept walking, looking straight ahead, and letting the words creep up into her head. "It is half done with nineteen-thirty-four. Our family has been on this earth a long time. Getting ripe. Developing their feeling for each other and everything their eyes can reach. Just like you, Sadie. All of us are getting to our maturity. The blood's getting ripe, telling us what we gotta do."

He stopped talking as they started past the Baker place. The widow Baker wasn't a relation, but half-crazy just the same. Sadie knew the preacher didn't trust her. The woman was standing out in her front yard, one arm thrown over the head of her best milker.

"Mornin, ma'am." The preacher raised his broad-rimmed dark hat. The widow didn't pay them any attention; she was too busy babbling to her cow.

Saplings the Civilian Conservation Corps boys had planted dotted the hillside. A few of the boys were up there now in their blue outfits, just like soldiers. Supposed to be building a fire tower, she'd heard.

"Our family's got the best part of the Melungeon stock, Sadie. Our blood's got the most feeling in it. Now some has watered it down with other families, but we're still pure enough, at least so's we can do what's gotta be done."

A chimney stood by itself in a clearing on their left. A squirrel jumped out of the top and scrambled down the side. She used to know the family that lived there. There was a boy who tried and tried every year to catch a fish, but never could. Every time she'd see him dipping his pole she'd tried to explain to him that there hadn't been fish in that creek since before her daddy's time — the first families into the hollow had fished it all out. But the boy never would listen, acting like she wasn't even there. She remembered the old man one day in there screaming, trying to beat down the walls of his house. She tried hard to remember his name, but the preacher's voice was still at her, moving inside her like thunder trying to hold its breath.

"You're a Gibson. And the purest Gibson stock, not one of them pale Gibsons that live in the towns. You got the feeling and there's just no refusing it."

"What do you want from me?" she cried, still unable to look into his face. She stared at the truck coming down the road toward them, tried to concentrate on its bright new red paint job, tried to keep his voice outside.

He didn't say anything for a while. A caved-in barn surrounded two large trees on their left. The truck up ahead was slowing down. Sadie recognized Homer Goin's rendering truck. Somebody's horse or cow must've died. The truck was moving even more slowly now, practically creeping. The trees were so close here Sadie and the preacher couldn't get completely out of the road. She felt the preacher moving her to the side as he began to speak again.

"I don't want nothing much, Sadie. Some of your feeling, some of your blood."

She was sick from the stench. The truck hit a stone and a greasy piece of sour meat came flying out, slapping the dust beside them.

"Things are happening. I need that blood of yours. And I need you to marry. The family needs your blood-born, your child."

"Married!" Sadie was choking, her eyes filling with tears. She couldn't get rid of the smell.

"Yes, indeedy. I want you to marry Mickey-Gene for me."

"The fool! And a first cousin to boot! You're crazy you think I'm..."

She was too angry to hear the word the preacher said, but the way he said it made her go cold all over. She stopped speaking, stopped moving, stopped breathing. It was like she'd been shot. Her thoughts were frozen and useless in her brain.

"Legal in the state of Virginia, if that matters to you. This is going to happen, Sadie. It's your time."

Sadie thought of the gray eyes floating in Mickey-Gene's pasty face, his mouth opening with no sound. "But he's got no sense," she said softly.

"You got enough sense for the both of you. He's close to pure blood. He's just right for the baby you're gonna have. Now, that's gonna be a child with feeling."

"Wh... why, Uncle?" She didn't really want to know, but she wanted the preacher to do all the talking now. It seemed real important that she listen to everything he might say on the subject. And if she talked — it was just too dangerous to risk his anger.

"This world's changing. We're having bad times. Seems like us Gibsons always having bad times." The smoothness in his voice began to calm her. "But right now everybody's feeling it, I guess. Cept for CCC work, only jobs are a good fifty mile away, and that means mining those tiny holes in the ground, throwing a pick into rock over your head with water in the tunnel up to your knees. Cattle's selling at five cents on the pound, and the tobacco's coming in low as two. Costs more to sell it on the floor than it pays. People are out begging for a meal and anything a body'll spare from people just cant spare it. You think about some old-timer you aint seen in town a few months or so — likely as not some hunter'll find his body out in the woods where he was trying to dig out a root to chew on, the hounds drawn to the smell."

So what do you want from me? she thought, trying to hold back the tears. "How's my having Mickey-Gene's baby gonna help any of that?"

"Wont help us now but might help us later."

"How?"

"That's gonna take some time to work out. I've been dreaming about things, Honey. Somewhere in this world there be an army building places where they'll be killing thousands of people, maybe millions. I'd know more, but the smell of all those bodies just pulls me right out of my bed. Think about this hollow full up to the treetops with dead men, women, children. We're Melungeons, Honey. Why, state of Virginia still says we're coloreds. We aint supposed to vote, though some do. Personally I wouldn't care to. We're not part of that government — never will be.

"There's people'd like to kill us all out. Now you wouldn't want that to happen, would you?"

"No, I wouldn't, preacher, I…"

"You think about it. You imagine it. I bet you can smell them bodies too."

Sadie gasped, and her lungs filled with the decay.

"*Feel* it, Sadie!"

Her throat felt slimy with the stench, her lips rotting off her face.

"Oh, you got it, Sweetie. I *know!*"

Sadie could see her house just a little further up the road. She wanted to run, but the smell was choking her. She could barely see. She rubbed her throat, wanting badly to throw up, get some of the smell out of her.

"Go on. Dig it out. You dig out the stink and you'll just find there's always more stink right under it."

"Let me go. Please."

"It's not me, Sadie. You just have the feeling. You got to live with that. But I *can* make it a little easier for you."

The preacher grabbed both her arms and pulled her up toward his scarred face. Sadie glanced up at his eyes, but couldn't hold on to what was there. She dropped her gaze to the crooked scar that snaked his cheek. It writhed suddenly, as if to leap out of his skin. The preacher grinned, his teeth snagging on blistered, uneven lips. "You be at the church meeting tonight, girl. Or I'll tell your daddy about what happened down the store today. Then I'll tell your momma about what your daddy's been wanting to do with you. See if that makes her love you more!" Sadie knew she was showing herself to the preacher, but she couldn't hide from him. He seemed to suck it right out of her. "Yeah, I know all about that. Not much I dont know. And I'll find a way to make that happen with your daddy, if you dont do exactly what I say. Hear?" He dropped her. "Be there?"

"Yes. I swear, just don't..."

But he'd already turned and was striding away from her, enormous brown boots pounding the road. His body was a shadow the afternoon sun seemed unable to lighten. His clothing was crisp and rustled like dry leaves in the boiling air.

*   *   *

THEIR HOUSE WAS all lit up, and it still two hours before dark. Her daddy had even hung a couple of lanterns on the porch, and that meant company. Sadie pulled her skirt tighter in back and walked carefully to the back of the house. Her tiny room had a door that led on to the back porch — it had been used for firewood storage before she was born. If her daddy was drunk enough maybe he wouldn't hear her come in. Her momma was always off visiting and usually not home until late.

But tonight Momma had a visitor. When Sadie walked up to the house she heard the women trying to sing "Poor Orphan Child," that song by that family over in Poor Valley that got so famous, the Carters. The idea that anybody from those parts could get famous for singing was like something from a storybook, and when the record come out people from all over went down to Levitt's General to listen to it. Nobody she knew in the hollow had the electricity, so no record players or radios neither, but Levitt's had both. Least all the folks had mouths though, and they weren't too bashful about using them for singing, especially if they'd been drinking.

She opened the screen door and stepped up onto the porch. The first thing she saw was her momma sitting in the doorway to the kitchen, sharing a smoke and a little bottle of shine with Uncle Jesse's wife, Lilly. They stopped hurting that poor orphan child when she came in, and Lilly made a little laugh like she was embarrassed. She was a church goer, so shine and cigarettes were things she was supposed to be staying away from.

Lilly was among the darkest of the Gibsons, "almost a nigger," Daddy'd always say, but not to where Uncle Jesse could hear it. Uncle Jesse was quiet most of the time; when he was drunk people'd say he was almost a poet. But sometimes he'd go mean, like something went bust inside all of a sudden, and you never knew what he might do. Daddy said he saw Jesse bite off a man's ear one time, then try to wrestle out the tongue with his fingers. Daddy said they used to call Uncle Jesse "mad dog" when he was a boy.

Sadie kind of liked the way Lilly looked and acted. Her aunt was beautiful, about the only woman in Morrison she'd ever say that about. She thought her aunt looked oriental, like some kind of princess in a story book. And she was quiet, too, but in a special kind of way. Like she knew about better things, but she wasn't about to talk about them in front of the likes of Morrison folk. And she'd been smoking a long time, and got Sadie's momma to start smoking, too. Lilly was like that, a leader. The other Morrison women would never admit it, but they imitated her.

Aunt Lilly nodded at Sadie. She was all in white. Her eyes and teeth sparked against her dark skin.

"Hello, Aunt Lilly." Sadie felt foolishly like dipping her knee and bowing her head a little.

"So where you've been, girl?" It was her momma speaking. For a moment Sadie thought to lie, wondering if somebody had already told what had happened.

"I was just down to the town for a little. Stopped and talked to Granddaddy on the way."

"Yeah. He told me."

Granddaddy wouldn't have volunteered that. Her momma must have asked him direct. He never said nothing to his daughter or son-in-law about Sadie's doings, never could tell what might get her into trouble. Sadie appreciated that, but it must have been hard on her momma, her own daddy not trusting her like that.

Her momma could be pretty if she wanted to be. Even in the gray housedress she was wearing now – it had orange flowers on it but they were so faded they looked like grease spots. She had a fine shape to her face, high cheekbones and a nose Sadie envied. Hers always felt swollen up. If she'd just do something to her hair, and if she'd eat better. Since she took up smoking she hardly ate at all, and never with the family, just a little on a plate by the stove. She didn't even sit down to eat. No wonder she was always so nervous. Sadie was gazing through the kitchen door, past her mother's head.

"Your pa's got his fool buddies over. No offense, Lilly." Lilly just nodded and blew a line of smoke. Uncle Jesse was in there, then. "I swear if this house caught fire tonight there'd be more than one in this valley praising the Good Lord tommorry!"

Sadie used to laugh at the smart-mouth things her mother said. They were certainly almost always true. But it didn't make things any better for her mother, or for Sadie. So after a while it just made Sadie mad. That kind of talk just made you feel worse. Granddaddy said Sadie's momma had gone hateful since the marriage. Sometimes Sadie wondered if her mother would have been so bad if she hadn't had her.

Sadie looked down the porch and through the screen: the sun was dropping fast. She needed to get into her room, but couldn't figure how to leave her mother yet.

"By the way, the Grans want to see you tonight. Uncle Jesse brought the message — dont know where he got it from. He's been drinkin too much to get it outta him." Her mother said it careful, like it meant something. And it did.

It was too dark for Sadie to find her mother's eyes. "Why?" She tried to ask it firmly, but it came out a whisper.

"How the *hell* should I know? I aint *seen* them since the wedding, Missy!"

That was true. Sadie knew her mother thought it was because she'd come from outside the family, and a lot of the Gibsons resented that. *Dilution*, was the big word the preacher used for that. But the Grans hardly ever saw nobody. They never went into town, or to any of the socials, and nobody went to see them, either. Except the preacher. People said he went there most every week. But Sadie had never heard of anyone else visiting there in years; she didn't even know how they got their food. It seemed a shame — they didn't live that much further up the mountain.

But Sadie had never visited them, either. The kids at school said they were devils.

She felt herself trembling. "I have to go?"

Sadie wished she could take that back. She went stiff all over, waiting for her mother to scream at her, or maybe hit her. But her mother didn't say anything for a while. Then, finally, in a voice that made Sadie want to cry it sounded so gentle, "I guess you gotta, Baby. They're the Grans, and they never asked nobody before."

Sadie looked down at her yellow dress, still gathered in folds behind her. She wondered why her mother hadn't noticed, or why she wasn't saying anything. "I'd best be changing," she said, and started for her room.

"They're the Grans, but they're still just Gibsons, Sadie. I never knowed you to change your dress afore dark."

Sadie stopped, wondering if her mother knew about her period. Maybe older women sensed that kind of thing. "I gotta go to church meeting after. I promised the preacher."

Her mother's laughter was like a donkey braying. "You're gonna handle snakes!" The cigarette dropped out of her mouth and rolled on the floor. Aunt Lilly stamped the sparks out, looking a little mad. Momma must have forgotten that Aunt Lilly and Uncle Jesse were part of the preacher's congregation.

"You oughtn't to go, child," Lilly said. "That church is no place for a young girl like you. Best keep away."

"I'm just gonna *watch*. I promised I'd go."

"You're gonna *watch*, huh?" There was a last, brief explosion of laughter from her momma, but this time it didn't sound like laughter at all.

"Sadie, girl — let's talk about this," Aunt Lilly said.

"I probably wont even stay the whole time." Sadie tried to slide kind of sideways into her room without showing her backside.

*   *   *

SADIE WIPED HERSELF clean with the dress — she'd find some place out in the woods to dump it tomorrow. She didn't have so many dresses she could afford to dump one like this, but she just, just couldn't wear it no more. Momma would find out though, when some time passed and Sadie hadn't been wearing it. Sadie didn't know what she'd say, but it didn't matter. Momma would be so mad no matter what she told her.

She really didn't have a "good" dress — her momma made most of hers out of those fancy print feed bags — but she had a blue one that was pretty clean. It had some bad tears, but they were along the seams, so maybe she could just pin them up and nobody at the church service would notice, especially if they were consumed by the spirit like they all got at the preacher's sermons.

The walls of her back porch room were old gray planks, just like the regular outside walls, except those walls were two boards thick everywhere. In her room there were places where the planks that made her walls didn't come together just right, leaving narrow little spaces. Where her walls faced the outside her momma had pasted newspapers to help block the cold. She'd read the stories on those papers maybe a thousand times. But spaces between the boards on the inside wall were left open to let the heat through from the wood stove in the front room. She could put an eye up to the cracks and see what went on in that room. And the walls were so thin she could hear almost everything going on in the whole house.

She hid herself behind her dresser, just in case one of them drunk men had his eye up to one of them cracks, changed into a fresh pair of flour sack panties her mother made, then arranged the blue dress as best she could. She then put her face up to a wide crack to see what those nasty men were up to.

She knew her granddaddy was right — not everybody in the state was like the folks she had to put up with every day — and not every man was out to get every young thing he could, but how could she really know for sure when those were about the only men she knew anything about?

Her daddy was sitting on the floor with a bunch of men playing dominoes. This was a regular weekly thing, although Sadie was pretty sure they almost never finished a game. They either broke up with a fight or got too drunk to handle the tiles proper. This was the kind of ignorant stuff that gave the hollow people a bad name, but she didn't know nobody else behaving like her sorry daddy and his friends.

"I'll just take me one from the boneyard." She saw her daddy dip into the stock of unused dominoes. She knew everyone else there: Uncle Jesse Gibson; Luke Grogan, whose wife committed suicide last winter and everybody was saying he hadn't been home in a month; Speed Sexton, whose wife May was said to have visions; and Buck Willis, a dreamy sort of fella who nobody knew a whole lot about. He never said that much about himself and what he did say didn't make much sense.

"Your turn, Buck," her daddy said. All the men waited, watching Buck's face like it was the most interesting thing they ever seen.

"Shit or get off the pot," somebody finally said.

"I was just thinking…"

Her daddy groaned.

"No… I was just thinkin how I farm only the *flat* patches of my place. I figure it must be because I was Gyptian oncet, you see. I member it clear as a bell. I member livin a long, long time ago. And I member hot weather, so hot the eggs was fryin inside the chickens. And I member sand."

"Make your damn play, Buck," her daddy said.

"Maybe us Melungeons was Gyptian in the oh-riginal," Buck continued.

Her daddy slapped the boneyard, scattering the dominoes all over the room. "Hell, let's do some *bettin!*" he shouted.

"I'm too drunk to bet wit you," Luke said. "Hell, you'll do most anything for a bet, Bobby. Aint sportin to bet wit you."

"How bout you, Jesse?"

Uncle Jesse had been drinking a long time. Most days he started right after breakfast. He pinched a wrinkled picture carefully between two square-tipped fingers.

"Ah, Jesse." Speed, also quite drunk, sounded as if he was ready to cry. "Why you want to look at that thing for?"

The other men didn't say anything. Sadie had seen the picture before. A funeral picture of Jesse and Lilly's first child, a daughter who died when she was two; it was faded to a pee-yellow brown. The little girl wore a dainty silk gown and was leaning against a pillow held up by a man's rough-looking, stained hands. Uncle Jesse's hands, Sadie figured. Her eyes were closed. First time Sadie saw it she'd asked if the little girl in the picture was sleeping. Lots of folks kept funeral pictures — if the child died young and hadn't had a picture taken it was considered a last chance to get a record to remember them by. But she'd never known anyone else to carry one with them.

"One of these days I'm gonna find who killed my baby," Jesse said. "Lord'll help me, and Lord help me when I do."

No one said nothing. Everybody who knew Jesse was tired of arguing the point. His daughter died of the small pox.

"Come on, boys," her daddy said. "I need some bettin done here. Help keep me outta them mines."

"Help keep us all outta them mines," Luke said.

They were all scared of the mines. Most everybody had at least one relation broke his back from a rock fall. Sadie had seen her daddy do this before. Talking about the mines got some men into a betting mood. She thought it kind of funny that he should use that. Her daddy was scared half to death of them mines. He'd worked one week in that mine at Tempco and he wouldn't talk about it, but some nights he woke up screaming.

"Okay, Bobby," Luke said. "So what you want to bet over?"

Her daddy grinned, his lips stretched tight. Two year ago, when Sadie was first seeing her breasts, her daddy had come to her in her bed and kissed those breasts goodnight. "Ever see a man et a live mouse afore?"

"Seen a geek in Kingsport oncet," Buck said. "Damn fool bit the head clean off a squeaker!"

Her daddy grinned again, staring straight at the wall of Sadie's bedroom. "Well, that's what I'm aimin to do."

Her daddy brooded most of the time. At least he had ever since Sadie started growing.

"Give you a quarter, Geek Man!" Luke shouted.

"Hey, me too!"

"Well now." Her daddy gazed down at his long, dark-brown fingers as if admiring them. "Buck, you find us a mouse. Should be one in the woodpile out back." Buck leaped to his feet, stumbled, cackling, and then stomped out of the room.

Sometimes her daddy stared at her a long time. When her momma talked about her seeing boys soon her daddy just laughed. "Too ugly," he'd say.

One day she saw him looking through her boxes, holding her dresses up. She'd wondered if he was sniffing around for blood. Momma didn't give her daddy everything he needed, but Sadie was never clear on what it was she was supposed to do about that. She was just a girl, and Daddy wanted more than that.

Buck didn't come back for a long while. She'd always heard Buck was good at catching little critters, but catching a live mouse inside a woodpile with it almost dark outside — Sadie couldn't imagine nothing much harder than that. She waited nervously, her forehead getting sore from rubbing it against the wall when she shifted, trying to see as much in the front room as she could. She was going to miss it — she had to leave for the Grans soon. But just as she was about to give up Buck came back with a mouse, dangling it by its tail. It had some blood on the side of its head, which looked a little lop-sided. It struggled weakly. "Tweren't easy," Buck said, "had to mash it up against the house a little with my boot."

"That's no way to treat a critter," her daddy said in a scolding tone of voice. "And I bet that mashin you done dont help the taste none. Go on, give it here."

Her daddy held the mouse tight in his right fist, only its little furry head exposed, its eyes tiny coals, its whiskers trembling.

He held his fist up and shook it at Sadie's bedroom wall, a serious expression on his face, like he was going to toast somebody like in that movie she saw over in Wise County.

Sadie knew that in his way her daddy loved her and that in some way her momma was wrong for trying to keep love out of their house. Love ought to be in a house, somehow.

He stared right at the crack Sadie was peeking through. He stared right into Sadie's eyes. *He knows I'm here watching*, she thought, and started to go away, thinking for just a second her going might save the mouse's life. But she was held by her daddy's eyes, by the way he held his fist, the seriousness of the whole thing.

Suddenly her daddy's fist went up to his mouth and she almost thought he was going to gently kiss the little head, when blood splashed over his nose and down his hand. He took the fist away and the blood covered his chin. The other men were laughing, sputtering, cheering. And still he stared at her. Sadie's lower belly tightened.

The tension made her sick, but the wetness didn't come between her legs again. She held her daddy's eyes grimly, even watched while he chewed. *He knows, he knows*, she thought.

She had to spit out the blood taste, the bad mouse taste, for several minutes before she could leave the house. She continued to cough and spit on her way to meet the Grans.

SADIE GOT TO the place in the road where she was to turn and climb the rock-studded path to the Grans. It was more like a goat trail; the preacher went the back way on his visits, taking that old logging road — not more than two deep ruts in these times — to the top of the mountain, then there was this private little stretch that wound up to the house that somebody had built long ago. The preacher paid some boys every summer to clear that dirt stretch, just to the back of the house. They didn't touch the kudzu up around the cliff — everybody said there was no sense in cutting it, it would just come creeping back again, might even eat up more of the hillside on account of being disturbed like that. Some of the boys claimed to have seen the Grans while they were working back there, said they wandered the house without no clothes on and that they had long hair and swollen up heads and scabs all over their skin. Sadie didn't believe any of that.

Just around the bend was Granddaddy's house, then the town. For a few minutes Sadie stopped and thought about dropping in on her granddaddy. As long as nobody brought up her daddy the talk would go okay; her granddaddy was special fond of her. Right about now he'd be sitting in his front parlor, maybe reading *Treasure Island*, or *Twenty Thousand Leagues*, or *Huck Finn*, or Walt Whitman's *Leaves of Grass*. Granddaddy dearly loved his Whitman. The parlor had two overstuffed chairs; Sadie always sat in the green one while Granddaddy read to her from one of those books. They didn't have no books at home, not even a Bible. Sometimes Granddaddy would cook her a meal and it was always a lot better than her momma's cooking. "An old buck needs to know enough to fend for his self," he'd say, and wink.

But the thought of being in her granddaddy's house tonight — that *regular* home like she imagined homes were supposed to be, just like she'd always read about in the books and magazines he gave her — didn't seem right tonight, not after seeing what happened to Fred Shaney and talking to the preacher and seeing that blood all over her daddy's chin and then having to visit the Grans. And having her period. Maybe that most of all. Next time she visited Granddaddy she wasn't going to be the same, and he'd probably know that right off.

She still had mouse taste in her mouth. Salt and hair and old sour water and that little crunch like chestnut pieces caught between her teeth.

Granddaddy used to talk about the Gibsons. From the outside, but not like he was better than them or anything. "They aint all crazy, you know," he used to say. "Your other granddaddy Orson Gibson was one of the finest men this county has ever seen, a man generous with his time and with his hands, a reading man, and there's nothing wrong with you, either, Sadie. Remember that now." Sadie had sat still and listened hard. She never heard nobody else talk about these things. She only wished Granddaddy Orson had still been alive when she was born. "Your daddy and the preacher and some of those others that think themselves 'pure bloods,' — they aren't that way cause they're Gibsons. Nosir. I suspect it's something peculiar to that small group within the family, that one gnarly branch. But whatever it is, I couldn't say. It's like they're getting a little crazier every year. There's something inside them that they're all getting worked up about, like it's all building to something. What, I dont know. But you're okay, Sadie. Your momma isn't a Gibson. She's got my family's blood in her, my blood." But Sadie had never been much reassured. Anyway, she'd better hurry on up the mountain. She didn't know first-hand, but she figured it didn't pay to keep the Grans waiting.

The climb up to the Grans' house didn't take her as long as she'd expected, but it was still well into sunset. The sky had gotten some of that orange color into it. The path led up to the side of the small shack, a smaller place even than her house. It looked to be all one room, part of it up on piled stones.

The two withered forms on the front porch were sitting. They both looked bald, but then Sadie realized the woman's hair was just so thin, so white, you couldn't see it unless you were close up. They were just two very old people.

"Grans," she said softly. There was no answer, so she moved around to face the porch. She had never seen anyone so old before. Their necks looked as if someone had let some of the air out of them. The woman stared straight ahead with pale, seemingly lidless eyes. The man looked to be sleeping.

"Grans," she said again, a little louder this time. She didn't know what else to call them. She was unclear as to their exact relation to her, just that they were old Gibsons. None of the family recounting by uncles or aunts ever called them anything else. Sometimes she would ask, and would get a blank stare in return. Then the uncles and aunts would debate the thing — either they were distant cousins or brother and sister-in-law to Walt — which was surely impossible — or from some other branch entirely. Some in the family claimed they weren't real Gibsons at all, but that was a minority opinion. Uncle Jesse once said he'd heard they were Walt Gibson's mommy and daddy, who he brought into the holler after marrying that Indian woman and building the first house. But Uncle Jesse had been real drunk at the time, so most everybody laughed. Except the preacher. They say he just turned and walked away.

Nobody knew how old they were. If you believed Uncle Jesse's story they would have had to have been impossibly old. If you believed Uncle Jesse's latest elaboration on his theory, also shared by Speed Sexton's visionary wife — that the Grans were among the first Melungeons found on Newman's Ridge by the explorers back before 1700, and that they were old even then — then they'd entered the land of myth and fairy tale. It was all craziness. No wonder folks told spook stories about them to their kids. It was hard to think about the hollow without thinking about them. Sometimes Sadie dreamed about them, perched up there on the mountainside all by themselves, like angels.

"Grans..." she said again.

"Elijah, darlin," the old man said in a voice full of gravel and pain. "Call me that. And this here old lady..." He moved his eyes ever so slightly in the direction of the woman. "Addie."

The old woman barely nodded her head and licked her lips with a pale, lizard-like tongue. She appeared to be blind, her eyes white, clouded over. "Sadie..." she whispered harshly.

"Bobby's girl, out of Orson and Cleo Patty."

Sadie nodded, and then felt like a fool. "Yes," she said, quaking.

"Come up here on the porch," Elijah said, then sighed so deeply it was like all the air had suddenly leaked out of him.

Two fat hounds lay under the porch steps. They were almost as wrinkled as the Grans, and at first Sadie went a little sick with the notion that they were dead, but then one twitched an ear and a lid floated lazily up a wet eyeball.

"Nice to have company," Elijah said.

"Mail never comes," Addie said.

"No, that's a fact," Elijah said. "Mail never does come, does it, Addie?"

"No..."

The door in front of Sadie was wide open. She could see a small bed, a dresser, and the rest of the house full to the ceiling with boxes of metal, jars full of buttons, straightened nails and other small things, burlap sacks filled and bulging with cloth scraps, bottles, old calendars and newspapers and greeting cards, old clothing and oddly shaped handmade wooden items. It looked like they saved everything. Some of the items on the bottom layer appeared collapsed and rotting, the decay spreading upwards like a disease.

A wooden cross, maybe three feet high, hung over the bed. The wood was stained and warped. It looked even older than the Grans.

"It's all ass shit," Addie said suddenly.

Elijah coughed drily a few times, until Sadie recognized what he was doing as laughter. "Never thought to swap her," he said. It sounded like an old joke, repeated endlessly.

Sadie sat down between the two, like them staring straight ahead across the valley. "You wanted me for something, Grans?"

"Elijah," he said.

"Elijah."

"And Addie, honey."

"And Addie."

They sat that way for some time. When Sadie was younger, she might have thought the Grans had forgotten her. But she had learned that adults were like that sometimes. Talking took a while. You had to learn to use all the silences.

Across the valley she could see a ramshackle barn, a broken-down stone wall attached. She couldn't remember who it belonged to.

"Yessir, I like them mountains," Elijah said. "Gives you somethin to rest your eyes against."

Down below that barn was a small sleeping cabin, looking greasy in the dim light. Dogs ran back and forth the length of the porch, jumping into the trash pile at the end and tearing it apart. A sour smell was working at her nose, beginning to sting her eyes. She turned her head away.

"We sold the coal rights to that land on them long deeds. Fifty cents an acre. Signed our X's big and black as you please. Dumbest thing we ever did."

"*The* dumbest," Addie said.

"I put a lot into that holler. Now I cant, I cant…"

"Spit it out," Addie said.

"Get a thing out. We owned… we owned all you see."

Sadie looked out, trying to see as far as she thought the Grans might be seeing, and as far back. She didn't know, but somehow she was sure they could see a lot further. They'd owned it all.

"Worked in the mines… and I was already an old man. Hell… six or seven a day got kilt. Their kinfolk couldn't afford to bury them."

She remembered she used to walk up that old logging trail above the Grans by herself. It was something special in the fall: you could look down into the hollow and there would be gray, pale blue, and orange trees.

"Walt, he used to shoot his meat... out there in the woods. Afore all these others come. Raised his corn down in the bottom, just enough for his bread. Used a deer skin with holes for a sifter. Fires kept the bear and deer away."

Maybe she could stay with the Grans up into the night. That way she couldn't make it to the church meeting and the preacher wouldn't dare blame her because she had been with the Grans.

"Been here a *long* time, Honey. Way back afore, buried our kin above ground. Little houses... over the graves. Ever afternoon we bowed toward the bell. Dont rightly remember why."

Sadie wasn't sure if Elijah was talking about the Gibsons in general, or him and Addie personally.

"Oh, been here *years*. Cant recollect how long. Nobody knows where we come from, and I swear I dont remember. Seen lots of starvin times. This aint so bad. Folks used to eat the sparrows they was so hungry."

They were trying to give her information here, memories, history. Sadie wondered what it was they meant to prepare her for, and *why*.

"Chillen," Addie croaked.

"That's right!" Elijah's voice went higher. Sadie thought he sounded kind of happy. "Dont have a child you dont have nothin."

"Once the midwives done cotched them, they yours forever!" Addie almost shouted it.

Elijah made his dry, coughing sound. "Never thought to swap her," he said. His voice went lower. "You got *our* blood."

Addie cackled. "Gettin creatures born is important work!"

"I promised the preacher I'd go to church tonight," Sadie said softly. "See there, almost pitch dark already."

"Gettin old," Addie said. The whites of her blind eyes glowed in the dark. "Not much time. Dont need it. Dont want it."

"Need *new* blood. Me an Addie, we got so old, full of forgettin, we got sick of it all."

Addie began a paper-thin, brittle wailing.

"We got sick of the preacher, too," he said. "Even if he is one of our'n. Crap gets out of hand."

Addie rocked back and forth, her mouth open, wordless.

"You get tired of livin, keepin the feelin what it should be, stoppin it from goin bad. You get tired of ownin that. You just wanna lay it all down and rest."

Sadie had started down the steps, trying hard not to listen.

"Other people's got the feelin, too, Honey. Their turn now. Me an Addie, we done our part."

When Sadie got to the path she started to run, but the old man's words came too fast for her. "Body shouldn't have to live *forever!*" he shouted in a breaking voice. "Time for some of this *new* blood!"

Either Addie began to scream, a throat-rending screech followed by a rattle, or it was the tearing of Sadie's own thoughts as she stumbled down the steep path.

Chapter Five

GRANDMA HAD DECIDED it was time to take a break from the stories, whether because she was tired, or because she'd seen the deep lines of exhaustion in Michael's face and was taking pity on him. He made himself stop shaking. His hands felt weak, and as if they would surely float away if he didn't watch them.

He didn't understand what was happening to him. When she talked about her first period he'd felt a dampness, a rawness between his legs, and a stiffness in his lower gut. When her father, Michael's great grandfather, bit into the mouse, he'd tasted what she tasted and what her father had tasted: the sharp salt of blood and the dryness of hair fiber and the crunch and grit of bone stuff. There was danger in those stories, and it was beginning to touch him as well.

When Sadie talked about the men she knew as a child Michael felt disjointed. Each storied male brought a face, and the need to enter into another's feelings, to infiltrate his voice. Again and again he saw his own face in her memories, as if all the stories were about him. He asked if she had some photographs he could look at. She promised to come up with some by the afternoon.

Michael went out on the porch for some cool mountain air. It was the closest thing he had now to a tranquilizer. If he'd been back in his old neighborhood he would have gone to see Bill the Pill Guy by now, an old hippy who would sell you a pill to correct any pain or trouble or anxiety described to him. He couldn't tell you the names of any of these pills, just their benefits. Michael hadn't believed that the fellow knew what he was doing but he'd still gone to him because his pills always seemed to work. Of course he'd been foolish, risking his health that way, but listening to his grandmother's stories, preparing for god-knows-what, felt even riskier. He'd studied History in college — for a long time it seemed the most real, the most important discipline there was. Now he felt he had far too much of it. The past had overstepped its bounds; there was no more room for the present.

He needed someone like Allison in his life. But although he needed Allison, it would be unfair to call her now, to put her through more, to put her through any of the bad things that might come from being around him again. The last week they had been together he had been so tense, and consequently, cruel. He'd picked arguments over insignificant things — the cereal she'd bought, the clothes she wore, a damp towel left in the wrong place. Every afternoon he would make himself go outside so he wouldn't have the opportunity to say more mean things to her.

He remembered that one of those afternoons he'd been sitting in the alley watching as a skinny gray cat made its way down the narrow lane lined with cans, bins, and boxes. Most of the cat's fur had been shaved from the left side of its head so that its face looked almost human from that angle. An ugly scar ran from under its left eye down the side of its face almost to the mouth. Michael had assumed it was recovering from some sort of surgery. At one point it had put its paws together, looked up at the sky, and made a screeching noise.

Michael stood up suddenly and had to grab the post by the steps. *I called it Reverend*, he thought. *I called that cat Reverend.*

That afternoon Grandma gave him the photograph albums to study. These were full of pictures of the Gibsons and other inhabitants of the town for generations back. Pictures of Sadie herself, her hair yellow and eyes bright. He was amazed at how closely the images matched his imaginings. But there were differences. Her father, Bobby Gibson, was much better looking than he'd imagined, dark-skinned with high chiseled cheeks, and the one image of the preacher — taken in secret, Sadie said, made him look small relative to the people gathered around him.

"Think about what you see," Grandma said behind him. "Then feel what you see." It was uncomfortably like being in school again.

He flipped through page after page of pictures, the same people in different settings, in different poses, at varied occasions. Layer after layer of photographs, peeling back, and each new layer told him something new. He felt his shoulders stoop, his hands palsy. He grew old, then drew back to when things were newer, the sun on his face, warming his hair.

His grandmother looked so old; her skin was like cracked porcelain, glued and reglued but with all the fractures still showing. Something had drained her, cost her, and robbed her. He didn't have the words for it and it made him feel like a fool. There was nothing he could do for that little girl from the thirties; there seemed to be even less he could do for her now. Again, he questioned exactly what it was she was asking him to do here. Did she understand he wasn't good at much of anything, and never had been?

"Clarence Roberts and his son are here," his grandmother said to him from the parlor doorway. "I think you best take a minute to say hello to them."

Of the few dozen or so population left in the town of Morrison, Clarence was the only one he'd actually talked to. Miss Perkins and the others, everybody his grandmother had told him about, they were long gone.Clarence and Benny were waiting politely at the bottom of the porch steps. Clarence made a living doing routine maintenance for various real estate companies that still owned parts of Morrison, and for private citizens like Grandma Sadie. He dressed the part, and acted it. In the city, Michael had never met anyone so deferential. Benny hid behind his daddy's leg; Clarence held on to the boy's collar. Here in the mountains the children were trained to stay close when strangers were around.

"Hello, Clarence, Benny," Michael said awkwardly. "You're here to clean out the weeds in that ditch line across the road."

"Just takin what the Good Lord sends us," Clarence said easily. Michael didn't know what to say. Benny looked up at him with wide, frightened eyes.

"This will be done today, wont it, Clarence?" Grandma had stepped up behind him.

"Cant promise you nothin, but I spect so."

Benny had squirmed away from his father and was looking at a butterfly on a bush. Clarence reached over and pulled him back. "I'll give you away to that man if'n you dont behave, Benny." The boy looked stricken. Clarence looked back at Michael. "Best be gettin on with it, I guess."

"Sure, thank you, Clarence."

"That man's never been outside this valley," she told him later. "His son probably wont leave, either. Granddaddy once told me Appalachia was a reservation and probably always would be. One of the truest things the man ever said."

Clarence and his son crossed the gravel road and approached the weed-choked ditch. Above their heads, a new shoot of kudzu drifted down from the upper branches of the thick wall of trees. Michael stared as it wiggled slightly in the breeze, making a lazy S.

"Your daddy always held you back. I'm afraid I cant explain that." Grandma rocked furiously, as if gearing herself up to continue the story. "I heard him one time tell you 'You cant do nothing,' but that was always something he'd believed about himself. You looked like him and talked like him — he felt you in his bones. He couldn't handle all that, I dont reckon."

"It's okay, Grandma. I think I'm beginning to pull some of the pieces together."

"Just remember that the way you feel their voices is just like real good guesses — you'll never get them xactly right so dont start gettin too cocky."

"I'm trying, Grandma."

"Gettin stronger every day."

"That I am."

"When you feel somebody you have to *give* yourself away to them, and that's a real hard thing to do, Michael."

"A real hard thing, Grandma."

"Dreamin makes it better."

"Yes, ma'am, dreaming makes it better."

"You're a survivor, Michael. Just like me."

"Just like you."

"So now you're ready to handle some snakes?"

He hesitated a second or two. Then he lied. "That I am, Grandma. Set them loose."

Michael looked out the window. Clarence Roberts was beating a stick against the weeds, calling out Benny's name. It was the second time today the boy had gotten lost out there. Michael knew there probably wasn't any danger, but he didn't want to watch.

Numerous long streamers of kudzu now hung from the branches of the trees on the other side of the ditch. It seemed highly unlikely that any plant could grow that much in an afternoon. Michael's best guess was that bunches of it had gotten caught up inside the boughs, and then a little wind must have unsnagged it all to make it drop down out of the trees like that.

The kudzu was green and deep, and he was remembering voices in the valley he had heard only once, from a twelve-year-old farm girl, and some voices he had never heard before at all.

Chapter Six

SADIE DECIDED THERE was one thing she needed to do before church that night, and that was to go apologize to her granddaddy. It didn't matter if he saw the change in her, she reckoned. After tonight she was likely to be changed even more. It was a peculiar thing. She was just going to church, which was supposed to be something good folk did, but she felt like one of them condemned prisoners fixing to walk to their final judgment. And what if she got bit and died? The preacher was always saying that some did get bit, but the ones that had the right kind of faith survived. Sadie doubted she had that kind of faith. She didn't trust nobody. And if she was going to die, she wanted things right with her granddad first.

She knocked on his screen door but he didn't answer. Of course when he wasn't sitting there reading one of his books he was out working somewhere, so she went around the side of the house to the barn. Granddaddy's barn was something special — he built it pretty much all by hisself and he took pride in it. It was the *straightest* barn she knew of in the whole county. Most of them leaned this way and that like a lame fellow or a drunkard. But Granddaddy's barn had all kinds of bracing inside, and to show it off even more he painted it bright red like they did in the nicer parts of the county, and he repainted it every other year so that it was as red as red can be. Whenever Sadie saw that red barn behind his bright white house she thought of a candy cane.

He was just inside the barn, sitting on a bale of hay, bent over with his head bowed like he was praying, both arms stiff on his knees. He had his hat off, so that the bottom part of his face looked red as a tomato, and his forehead that had been covered by the hat was white as flour. She almost never saw him with his hat off, not even inside the house.

"Granddaddy? You okay?"

His head went up a little but not all the way. "That you, Sadie?"

She came closer. "You see me now okay?"

His eyes squinted a little, and the lines in his face got deeper like he was in pain. "I reckon."

But Sadie suspected he was covering up. "You want me to go get somebody?"

Granddaddy made a little tired laugh. "Who would you go get?" And that made her feel bad — her granddad didn't have many friends in these parts.

"I dont know. Momma maybe."

"Now dont go bothering her any. I'll be alright. Just tried to do a little too much today I reckon." He moved his head forward like he was trying to see better. "That your good dress you wearing? You fixing to get *married* or something?" He made that tired little laugh again.

"Oh, Grandpa, I aint even dating! No, I… well I just thought I'd go up to the church tonight."

"What, that Signs church? Those snake handlers? Your folks know about that?"

"Oh, they know. It'll be alright."

"Awww, well. You just be careful. I'm not going to say nothing about them — people believe what they believe and I know some fine people who've taken to picking up snakes. Long as folks are sincere, who cares what they believe? It's not what I believe but I dont believe a lot of things. Just be careful who you put your trust in, and the preacher, well, can you say you really trust that man?"

"Well —" Of course she didn't. "He *is* family," she said.

Granddaddy raised his hand. "I know, I know. Never you mind, sweetheart."

"Granddaddy, I'm sorry about how I was, earlier."

"Never mind that. Older folks shouldn't be parading their quarrels around children. It isn't right that I said something like that."

"That's okay." She looked down, scraped her shoes against the ground. She realized then she should have probably put on her better shoes for church — they didn't have as many scratches and tears in them. "There's just lots of things about — I dont know — my family, this town — I dont understand."

"Lots of things I dont understand, neither," he said, "and at my age it's pretty near too late to try. There's just one thing I want you to think on some. You spend your whole life down here between two mountains and you think the whole world's like this. But Honey, the rest of the South isn't even like this. And lots of folks cant seem to figure that out — they judge us by our lowest. That's the thing what bothers me."

"Maybe, but how does that matter to me? I have to deal with what I see with my own two eyes, and what I can feel, and what I can smell, and what I can taste. And right here and now, things taste pretty bad."

She felt a pain in her left side then, numbness in her arm, and she saw the way his face wrinkled up. "Granddaddy —"

"Sadie, no more stealing from Miss Perkins' shop, okay? You don't need to do that — you're better than that."

She felt her face go hot. She thought she would just about die. "Grandpa, I'm sorry. I don't know why —"

"It's alright. There's lots of reasons we do the things we do, but that has to stop. I found out and I paid her. She's not going to tell your folks, but you've got to promise me, no more."

"I promise." She felt that pain again. "Grandpa —"

"Best be getting on to that church, sweetheart. I've got lots to do here."

"Okay, you take care," she said tenderly. She swung around and started walking away then, the pain burning brighter for a second, then gradually softening the farther away she got. "Love you!" she shouted back over her shoulder.

"Love you, too!" he cried out, so fiercely the pain came into her side again, spreading into her ribs, and then into nothing. She would always wonder if she'd hurried away thinking the preacher would be mad if she was late, or because she'd wanted to outrun her granddaddy's pain.

Sadie's hands went sweaty as soon as she saw those words, "The First Church of Signs of His Return" printed in thick black paint on three gray barn boards nailed to a maple downhill from the church building. She figured the tree didn't much like being nailed into because it had bubbled up dark brown sap that dripped across the middle of all three boards. Course somebody like the preacher probably thought that a good thing — it looked like dried blood.

The preacher's house was past the church, further up the hill, where the land started flattening out into woods and cornfields and the like. It looked dark and dreamy now with the sun down and a lantern hanging on the front porch. Folks said the preacher mostly walked around the house in the dark, only using the lantern if he had somebody with him. Sadie wondered how he read his Bible with it dark like that, and that made her picture him with his eyes glowing like some critter back in the woods. She shook that off though because it scared her.

The church didn't look too much like a church except it'd been whitewashed until it was as white as white can be. It didn't have any kind of proper steeple or a little room on top for a bell like the Baptist Fellowship over in Clinch had. Sadie hardly ever went to church but when she did she went there to the Clinch church with her momma. She'd liked it — they had real pews to sit on and the people were all pretty quiet and dressed up nice for the service and smiled a lot and talked real polite. None of the mountain churches were anything like that and this one was supposed to be the worst.

What this church did have was a big ugly drippy cross painted on the side of the building with that same rough black paint that had been used on the sign. There were torches stuck in the ground for the people to see their way in and they made that paint shiny like it was still wet. The church also had a passage from the Bible painted on it in crooked lines and letters all different sizes like a crazy man did it (which he *was*). She could just imagine the preacher climbing up and down ladders with a messy brush and paint can in his hands, and skittering around hanging from a rope making all those letters.

> *And these signs shall follow them that believe; In my name shall they cast out devils; they shall speak with new tongues; They shall take up serpeants; and if they drink any deadly thing, it shall not hurt them; they shall lay hands on the sick, and they shall recover. MARK 16 17-18*

Those two Bible verses filled up most of that side of the building, even a little bit of window glass where he'd made one of the l's too tall. She noticed right off that "serpents" was misspelled. She didn't know if that made it a big mistake because it was in *big* letters, or if maybe that was the church way of spelling serpents. She had to give the preacher a little credit. There wasn't nobody going to walk into that church without having some idea what went on there.

People were trailing in from the cow paths that ran up the slopes and through the woods, mostly farm people she didn't know — there were lots of folks in the back hollows that almost never came into town and just had their store orders sent up on a wagon. Off on the left side of the church somebody had tied a few horses to the fence. There were only two or three cars she knew of in the area, and she had no acquaintance with their owners, and it was looking like none of them went in for snake handling.

She heard some familiar voices coming up from behind her so she hurried on inside. She wanted a seat out of the way so she wouldn't have to talk to nobody. This was a punishment, not a social visit.

Inside the building everything looked all smoky yellow and brownish because of the oil lamps hanging on hooks along the sides and up by where the preacher was supposed to do his business. She looked around and there wasn't a lot to see. Somebody had made a cross out of two thick, more-or-less straight branches and nailed it to the front wall. They hadn't even bothered to paint it — so it looked like this was some kind of outdoor church in the deep woods — the preacher should be doing his preaching outside with a cross like that, and maybe there should be a big campfire.

The pew benches were home-made like that, too, made out of split logs with legs attached. Except toward the back and on the sides there were a few extra seats somebody had rigged up out of old boards. They'd made the benches kind of low, though. When she sat down on the last bench back in the far left corner it made her knees rise up. She couldn't imagine some of those old folks getting up off a bench as low as that. Then she noticed that they'd put regular kitchen ladder-back chairs at the end of some of the rows and against the side walls.

The walls were pretty bare — except for the lamps there were a bunch of long nails to hang coats, and this faded cardboard picture of Jesus they'd put up near the cross. There was melted candle wax on the wall near the cross, but whatever had been there to hold the candles was gone, and no candles had been replaced.

The room was big enough — she reckoned a good thirty-five foot by forty or so — that the light from the oil lamps couldn't fill it, which turned the yellow air all gray down the middle and in the corners like where she sat, and high up under the roof, where it was smoky looking and just plain spooky. If she looked close enough she could see clouds of dust drifting by, smoke from the outside and dust from the floor and people's boots. Sometimes the clouds would move in funny ways, and make shapes a bit like whatever she was thinking about.

There wasn't a proper pulpit, or anything for the preacher to stand on while he was preaching, but Sadie couldn't think of any holy man that needed one less, excepting maybe Jesus himself.

She could see signs of the preacher's pacing in the worn boards and bruised varnish that made a rough circle in the floor below that picture of Jesus.

The elderly Collins sisters came in, but they didn't sit together. One of them nodded at Sadie, but she couldn't tell them apart so she didn't know which one. She'd always thought of them as kind of proper and prissy — the last people she'd expect at a snake-handling meeting.

Then a whole crowd of farmers she didn't know came in, and in the middle of them that awful Mr. George Mackey, his head bobbing above them all like one of those balloons she'd seen at the fair. She bowed her head and turned her face away, her hand on her forehead like she was crazy praying. And she *was* praying — that Mr. George Mackey wouldn't see her.

Then a little old man shuffled in, his face all pale and rubbed-out looking, his eyes like they were peeking up out of the bottom of some well. He was looking straight ahead like if he got distracted by just about anything he'd lose his way. He looked awfully familiar, except she was sure she'd never seen that face before. Then she knew with a shock it was Will Shaney, whose boy Fred had bled his life out down by the livery.

Some others trailed in after it was time to start, Uncle Jesse and Aunt Lilly being the last. They must have hurried up from her house after that little party they had with her parents — Uncle Jesse's shirt wasn't even tucked in and he weaved when he walked like he was dancing a waltz or something. Lilly turned her head and looked straight at Sadie as if she'd known exactly where she'd be sitting. She did something with her mouth that wasn't quite a smile. *I see you girl*, was the way it felt.

Sadie always thought these snake services were supposed to be loud, lively affairs, but so far everybody was quiet and hardly looked at each other. It was like they were all waiting for something. Then two men got up and opened the double church doors wide, and everybody turned their heads in that direction.

His face came like a ghostly oval out of the blackest part of the night, rushing towards them like he had wings, the rest of him so dark that pale face was all she could see, like he was the moon or something, set loose from its heavenly tether and flying through the night sky. Then as he got closer to the opening she saw that the preacher was running, hell-bent down the path from his house, his black coat flapping like he was a huge bat, his big black hat pushed down hard over his eyes. "Holyyy!" he cried. "Holyyy!" he screamed, sounding like his throat was on fire.

"Holyyy!" most of the members cried back. "Holyyy!"

"Holy, holy ghost!" the preacher cried, running up the aisle to the front of the church. "Holy ghost, amen!"

"Holy ghost, amen!" the congregation echoed back. They were all standing now, and not wanting to be noticed, Sadie was standing too.

The preacher walked around the room then, moving fast, charged with feeling, going row to row greeting, embracing, scolding. Now and then he looked directly at Sadie and she withered. Then he ran up to the front and shouted something at the ceiling impossible to understand. It was like he had three tongues all trying to say something different at the same time.

The preacher turned around and took his hat off, tossed it to a young girl at the end of the front row. She squealed when she caught it. "Oh, I feel good tonight!" he shouted. "Going to save me some sinners tonight! I can feel it in my hands!" He held them up for all to see. Sadie stared at that dark patch on the palm of his left hand. People still talked about how he'd almost died the first time he got bit — two weeks in bed out of his head, screaming at the Lord and trying to make a bargain. He'd lived, but part of his hand had rotted away.

Sadie kept staring at his face. He looked different, handsomer, standing up there. Still scary, but it was that kind of scary preachers always had, because they talked to the Lord and knew you were sinning. Not the dark and evil kind of scary she knew from the preacher first hand. And try as she might, she couldn't see the scar she knew was on the left side of his face.

"And I can feel it in my feet!" He did a little dance except you couldn't call it a dance because these people didn't believe in dancing. So maybe it had some kind of church name — like "celebrating" or "praising" — that made it okay.

Whatever you called it, the people liked it, because they clapped and cheered.

The preacher stood up straight then, like he could stretch every bone in his body to make himself taller, and he was already a tall man. His lips spread out like they were reaching for his ears. He made probably the widest smile she'd ever seen, but it was the way she imagined one of them African crocodiles in her geography book smiled, because his eyes weren't smiling at all. They were like two black stones down at the bottom of the creek.

The dim light of the church appeared to gather in the whiteness of his face, and it wasn't like he had skin at all. She'd seen limestone cliffs like that, pale and cracked and flaked off from the rain, the lines black as coal seams, so that his mouth was like a wound in the side of the mountain, the tight lips hiding secrets that went back before Melungeons, went back before folks even walked on two legs.

Then he opened his arms out like he was going to embrace the entire congregation and he said, "If this be your first time in our little church, well, welcome. Welcome. But let me be clear bout this. The First Church of Signs of His Return is a Jesus Only church! In this church we believe in one God, one Spirit, and all of them the one Jesus! Jesus only!"

"Jesus Only!" most of the congregation roared back.

"Jesus only, Holy Ghost amen, bless His name, Jesus only!" he shouted, stomping his feet.

"Jesus only!" they roared again.

"Jesus only Jesus only Jesus only Jesus only…" the preacher hollered, tossing his head back and forth, his voice becoming more and more tortured, hoarse, and torn.

"Amen, Brother, Amen!" the congregation shouted, but not together this time. People kept repeating it, their voices overlapping as they stood up, waved their hands in the air, sat down, stood up again and shouted it some more. It was like they wanted the whole world to know and they didn't care what nobody felt about it.

The preacher waited until the shouting died down and then he said, "At this here church we aint got no preacher been to no school to learnt how to preach! At this here church you're stuck with *me!*"

A couple of the men laughed. The others shouted, "Praise be!"

"This here preacher never were *told* how to preach! This here preacher been *called!* And you know who called him dont you?"

Old lady Woodard jumped up and down. "Jesus called you! Jesus called you!"

The preacher pointed at her like she'd just won the big prize. "You got that right, good lady! Jesus called this preacher! But Lordy, I give him one sorry mess to work with!"

"No!" several folks said, like they were surprised. But Sadie figured they must all have heard this before.

"Oh, yes. I confess I was a *terrible* sinner! I used to drink! I used to carouse!" He said that last word like he was growling. "I used to stay out all night in the arms of sluts and whores!" Old lady Woodard shook her head, weeping and howling. "But then the Holy Ghost came! And the Holy Ghost moved on me!"

The congregation was shouting again, saying "Amen!" and "Praise his name!" and "Holy Ghost!"

"I was rescued from the lion's mouth!" Sadie was watching his lips now, moving like worms fat with venom, jumping and dancing on his face. It was like they wanted to kiss everybody in the congregation. "He's there to help the good ones, but he's there to help the sinners too, the back-sliders and even the blasphemers. 'For because he himself has suffered when tempted,' they tell us in Hebrews, 'he is able to help those who are being tempted.'"

"Praise Jesus!" someone shouted.

"Tempt us, oh, do tempt us, Lord Jesus have mercy!" a drunken voice shouted from her right. Sadie looked over there and saw her aunt trying to hush her uncle Jesse. Terrified that she might laugh, Sadie pinched herself hard under her left knee.

"I say I was a sinner, I was a carouser, a drunkard. I lay with all *kinds* of women!" And the congregation kept shouting "No!"

"But I was *saved!*" The cheers erupted again. And although that crowd couldn't have been dancing, they certainly looked like it.

"You tell them, Preacher! You tell them!" Uncle Jesse shouted again. Aunt Lilly was jerking on his arm.

"I aint like some preachers — I *know* what it's like to be a *sinner!* I tell you I can feel their trouble! And I'll tell you this." He held up a little Bible, waving it in one hand. "I believe every word in this book is true!"

This was greeted with a chorus of "Amens," "Yeses," and "Holiest of Holys."

"Oh I used to *love* me a fight! I used to live ever day in sore *need* of a fight! But now I fight for Jesus!"

Sadie had heard her mother say that when the preacher was a boy pretty much everybody was scared of him, even the Grans. "That boy was one dirty fighter," Momma said, and then Daddy told her to shut up, because if it ever got back to the preacher that she'd said that, well, there'd be hell to pay.

"I'm getting ready for Jesus!" the preacher cried out, striding back and forth in front of the cross like he was some kind of proud rooster. "I'm walking his way! I'm talking his way!"

"Walkin for Jesus, Amen!" said an old woman Sadie didn't know, who made walking movements with her legs without going anywhere, like she was a soldier marching in place.

"I'm gettin ready! Dont stop me! I'm gettin ready to leave this world!"

Some of the church folk laughed, but Sadie couldn't find the joke in it. It made her go cold all over.

Suddenly the preacher stopped his stepping and ran up to a man sitting at the end of the third row. "Are you wearing short sleeves in *my* church? Lord, dont tell me you're wearing short sleeves in *my* church!" It was a hot day, but as Sadie looked around she saw that all the men were wearing long sleeves. "We dont dress immodest in my church, Mister!" the preacher shouted into the poor man's frightened face.

The man got up and ran out the doors, the preacher after him. The congregation was still; no one said a word. The preacher stopped at the double doors, gazing outside as if listening. Then he slammed the doors shut so hard they made an awful cracking noise. Still no one said a word. The preacher walked back up to the cross slowly shaking his head.

"This country — it aint what it used to be," he said, his voice low and sounding troubled. "Down here in these hollers we're a long ways off from Washington and DC. They tell us there's this *great* big depression going on. They tell us folks are out of jobs and out of money. But I tell you this, when did folks like us down in these hills ever have good jobs and good money?"

Everybody cheered, men got up and stamped their feet and shouted "Never!"

"I tell you there aint no way we can know all what goes on up North. I tell you I dont know but I spect there's stuff going on up there'd turn a baby's hair white! And for sure they'd love to deny us the right to worship this way. But we will not be denied! I love this country, but first in my heart is Jesus!"

"Amen! Jesus first! Praise Jesus!"

"This may be a small town up here in the mountains, hardly more than a few buildings at a crossroads, but it's got more than its fair share of whores! I say it's got whores crawling all over these hills! Down in the dirt spitting and writhing no better than animals! Sorely tempting to a man feeling low."

"Yes, Jesus!" she heard her Uncle Jesse say.

"But I tell you we're *better* than a bunch of hogs wallowing in the mud. We're *better* than the beasts of the field. Jesus, he's got a *plan* for us! And he aint gonna be *satisfied* till we're *sanctified* and *biblicized!*

"So we got rules in this here Jesus church. In His name we got *rules* to keep this a holy place! First rule being no sluts!"

There was a scattering of *amens*.

"Second rule being no blasphemers, no drunkards, no adulterers!" This time the amens were more numerous and spirited.

"In this here church there'll be no dancing, smoking, chewing, or drinking."

"Praise God!"

"We dont need no beer, tobacca, or swearing."

"Praise Jesus!"

"We're the lucky ones — we're *inside* the sanctuary of our Lord Jesus's loving arms! They tell us in the *Book of Revelation*, they tell us outside are the dogs and the sorcerers and the sexually immoral and murderers and idolaters, and everyone who loves and practices falsehood. But once you're inside the church you're safe from all that. In fact you can take the church wherever you go, because this church, it aint just a building, it aint no single place, this here church is a state of mind!"

"Oh yes, Jesus! Praise be his name!"

"And I'll tell you something else. We dont need no *store bought* medicine — that's for fools!"

A man stood up in the back and shouted, "Took some of that last winter when I was sick and didn't do me a *bit* of good!"

"If you take medicine for your ills it's a sure sign you aint got no faith!" the preacher shouted. The man, looking embarrassed, sat down. The preacher started walking back and forth at the front of the church like he was nervous, like he could hardly contain himself. "If you're sick, take it to Doctor Jesus! If you're troubled, take it to Doctor Jesus!

"There are some things we weren't *meant* to understand! That's why we've got *faith!* If you got *faith* you dont *need* to understand!"

An old woman stood up and raised her arms, walking in circles and shaking her hips, shouting, "Looky here, I got faith. I got faith!"

"Thank you, Sister, I know you do! I know you do. And I know some of you come a long way to be here tonight. But I think some of you came expecting salvation to come *easy*."

"Not us, preacher!" someone shouted from the back. "Aint nothing good come easy!"

"Amen, Brother, amen. Aint that the *truth?* It aint like it weren't no hardship for Our Lord Jesus Christ! It weren't no easy ride for him! No sir! You ever get the spikes nailed through your hands you tell *me* how easy it was!"

The preacher was walking up and down the center aisle, crouched low, prowling like a thief sneaking up on a chicken coop, and laying his feet down so that his shoes just slapped against the floor, and with each shoe slap he made a *Huh* sound, like he'd just been punched in the gut. "Sometimes we fail. Huh. Sometimes we sin. Huh." It seemed the silliest thing, but the folks in the congregation couldn't keep their eyes off him.

"I tell you there aint no rewards on this earth. Huh. I dont care how much you own. Huh. There aint no rewards. Huh. No sir!

Huh." Then he got down even lower and darker looking if that was possible. He was walking so low it was like an animal in a dark coat prowling up and down the aisle. "Every step we take is a step toward death! Huh! Ever crawl of a tiny little baby is a crawling toward death! Huh!"

"Oh, Jesus, it's true!" a lady in the front row wailed. "Every step we take!"

"But Jesus, he gives us his con-so-la-tion!" The preacher had stood up and was half-shouting, half-singing. "He takes us in his-o-so-loving arms! Sing with me now, would you? A little bit of 'Bright Morning Stars.'"

The preacher started singing then, and Sadie had to admit he had a pretty fine singing voice, cept maybe a little low and growly for her taste. But he sang like that's what he lived for, and everybody else, including Sadie, stood up then and joined him, repeating the lines he sang after he sang them.

> Bright morning stars are rising
> Bright morning stars are rising
> Day is a breaking in my soul
>
> Where are our dear mothers
> Where are our dear mothers
> Day is a breaking in my soul
>
> They have gone to heaven a shouting
> They have gone to heaven a shouting
> Day is a breaking in my soul

And that last part, he shouted it more than he sang it, his head thrown back like he was shouting straight up at Jesus or God or whoever it was might be living up there, letting them know he was coming. Or *warning* them he was coming because Sadie figured that whenever he got up there there'd be Hell to pay.

He shouted those lines with all his voice would give him. He shouted like he was trying to make the deaf angels hear him, until his voice cracked and he had to preach hoarse for a while. His voice got rough and raw, and then it got all mournful sounding, like he was being tortured by demons.

And all the folk in the church were clapping and shouting and stomping like they'd all gone crazy, like they'd shouted out their minds, their eyes closed and their mouths open so wide it was like their jaws were broken.

This went on for a long time until the preacher just stopped it all of a sudden. Grinning, and mopping his forehead with an old gray hanky, he raised his hand and said, "Enough! That's enough now!" And the rest of them, they just stopped like they'd just been turned off. "Lordy, dont it feel good," he said.

"Amen, amen," they all said.

"But it takes a lot out of you, man my age." There was scattered, soft laughter. "Well, then, anybody here needing healing? I *know* I do!" He laughed. "But anybody else?"

He said that last part so softly she wasn't sure she'd heard him right, but the people responded, several walking up the center aisle slowly, mostly women, making a line. One by one he took them in hand, pulling them into a firm embrace, and then laying his hands on their shoulders, then their faces, then other parts of their bodies.

None of them announced what was wrong with them, and the preacher didn't tell. But almost everybody in the hollow over the age of twelve had some kind of ailment, some injury — rheumatism and arthritis in the older folks, crippled limbs or wounds or at least a couple of unpopped Bible cysts in the ones younger. Pain was living up here in the mountains.

All during this he spoke softly to them, occasionally raising his face to the ceiling to croon aloud "Glory be to God!" and "Praise be!" then tilting his head back towards them, sometimes touching forehead to forehead, whispering to them like he was their boyfriend or something, rubbing their backs, then looking up to the ceiling again and shouting "By the power of signs and wonders, by the power of the Spirit of God — !" And their bodies would jump and wiggle like they were throwing some kind of fit.

Now and then somebody'd fall to the floor after he said something to them, like they'd been overcome, couldn't control themselves. All of them women, the ones falling. And when they fell, it was like it was catching, because other women out in the congregation started falling too, so pretty soon there were so many women lying on the floor of that church Sadie was afraid they were going to get stepped on, because the other people still standing up were all dancing around and shouting, she guessed celebrating that these folks were going to get healed.

"Behold the words of Micah!" the preacher shouted. "'They shall lick the dust like a serpent, like the crawling things of the earth.'"

She didn't understand — were all these women like the preacher's girlfriends or something, or like Jesus's girlfriends? Because they acted that way. They acted like they loved the very dust he stepped on.

The preacher was bent over one young woman now, praying loudly and speaking so fast Sadie couldn't quite understand what he was saying. He put one hand on the woman's head and the other practically between her legs. She snapped and moaned. "Jesus, let me not help her as a man helps a woman, but as your instrument, oh Lord Sweet Jesus!" Then he turned his head and Sadie swore he was looking straight back into her eyes.

No one else seemed to be watching the preacher. The women were hopping up and down in their plain seed sack dresses. The men in their dull white shirts and overalls were hollering and waving their heads around with their eyes closed. All of them were stamping their feet and clapping their hands. Somebody brought out a tambourine, and then another, and another still. Like it was a miracle like that story about Jesus and the loaves and the fishes, the miracle of the multiplying tambourines! Somebody was banging on a beat-up guitar. A bunch of people were beating on their pews, slapping their chests and their thighs and making nonsense sounds come out of their wide open mouths.

They were like a bunch of wild people with their lips loose, tongues flapping, eyes rolling. Sadie's ears were splitting from the shrieks that surrounded her like she was in the middle of some kind of whirlwind.

"Oh how I love Jesus!" The preacher was standing again and shouting, waving the little Bible around in the air. "Oh I dearly love him so!"

A couple of tall, skinny men were dancing wildly. *No*, Sadie reminded herself, *these people dont dance*. So those were two skinny men wildly worshipping, their four feet moving as if they were on fire, faster than what she thought feet could move, like four independent animals in their hard leather shells moving like their little animal brains had exploded.

One of the men bent backwards so that his back was practically floating above the floor, his shoulders pumping like he had motors in them.

The preacher ran over to the man and all around him, pointing. "See how the power of the Holy Ghost gets on him! See how this man can move when it's the Lord holding onto them legs!"

The man straightened up as if the preacher's voice had electrocuted him. Eyes shut, hands waving, the man started walking slowly backwards in circles. He did it so deliberately, so rhythmically; it was like a dance, but in reverse. *It was a Jesus dance!* Sadie thought, and made herself laugh.

Then the fellow's spine jerked suddenly, snapping like a whip and he fell to the floor. She stopped laughing. Was the preacher making this happen?

"See! See what Jesus can do?" the preacher shouted. He ran to the poor man on the floor and started dancing around him.

Other men joined him in the circle, bodies jerking wildly as if an electrical jolt was passing from one dancer to the next.

Other members of the congregation, both men and women, moved around the group, making circles around circles, gyrating, jerking, and praising the Lord. They turned into a mass of straining faces, their hands raised and shaking.

She stood up, not wanting to be the only one still sitting, not wanting to be singled out, but she couldn't see any way she could ever make herself move like they did.

Sadie froze watching as the congregation slowed down and member after member dropped to the floor or onto the benches — pale, worn-out, quivering — the preacher started pacing with his head thrown back, staring at the ceiling. "What's that Lord? Oh, I know we can do better. If we cant do better I'm not doing my job, and Lord if I cant do better you should take me now. I am in your hands, Lord, in your hands! I have no will except whatever will you would give me. I have no life except whatever life you care to bless me with!"

One old woman who'd never sat down, who'd just kept going and going even when much younger folk had collapsed — began to scream and bark and lurch. She suddenly went stiff, grabbed her chest and fell to the floor. Sadie leaned forward, sure the woman had had a heart attack, but no one else seemed at all concerned.

The preacher pranced over her body a few times shouting "Take these, our pitiful garments of flesh! God is good! God is great!" He ran up and down beside her. Sadie was sure he was going to step on her. But the old woman didn't move at all. Maybe she was already dead, and it didn't matter what terrible things folks did to her body now. "Hallelujah! Hallelujah! John 5:25! 'Truly, truly, I say to you, an hour is coming, and is now here, when the dead will hear the voice of the Son of God, and those who hear will live.'" The preacher held out his hand and one of the men handed him a bottle with some oil in it. The preacher crouched over the old woman and took an oily finger and drew a cross on her forehead. Still she didn't move. Somebody had to do something! And then mercifully two big men went up to the front and carried the old woman outside.

Then all the folks looked like they'd been poured out on the floor, their faces all white but for the shadow around the pits of their eyes. Some of them had a hard time figuring out where they'd been sitting, wandering up and down the aisle and whispering, the preacher glaring at them the whole time until somebody took pity and made a space for them. Several men were still standing, weeping on each other's shoulders.

Several of the members sitting in the front pews still wiggled around as if they were in the grips of a great emotion or simply out of their minds in pain. They folded up their bodies, mouths stretched out like their faces had frozen at the extremes of some scream, flesh sweating so badly Sadie wouldn't have been surprised if they'd actually started sweating blood.

The preacher didn't say anything for a while, just walked around as if he was taking the measure of his flock, deciding who was wanting and who had even a little chance of pleasing him in this life. He had a sour expression, like he'd just eaten a bad piece of fruit but wasn't about to give anybody the satisfaction of throwing it up. Sadie slunk in her pew, sure that if he even looked at her she'd start bawling and not be able to stop.

"As much as I love these hills I cant deny it's a hard life, harder than most I reckon. You pay for living here with your blood and your kin's blood. And if you got a last name of Gibson, or Collins, or half a dozen other'n well I dont need to tell you folks life can be harder still. There's people in this here county would as soon spit as smile on you and your kind. Same as the rest of the country I reckon. They dont know us. They dont care what happens to us."

"That's right! They dont care!" someone shouted. "Nary a one!"

"Bout the only comfort for folks like us is in our Lord Jesus Christ. Cause Jesus, he *loves* the poor people. He loves the forsaken, the mistaken, and the denied! Read your Bible! 'It is easier for a camel to go through the eye of a needle than for a rich man to enter into the kingdom of God.' Matthew 19:24. I reckon that gives folks like us a leg up as far as Heaven is concerned." Some of the people laughed, but the preacher's hard expression didn't encourage much laughter. "Remember the Israelites? Even the lowliest of the low have power on God's green earth! And I tell you sweet brothers and sisters, each and every one of you need to recognize the powers that Almighty God has bestowed upon you. You know what I'm talking about! Some of you more than others!" Sadie knew he was talking about her, and when she made herself look up into his face, there was his scar, big and bold and red as could be. "You learn to *seize* that power, you learn to love that power, and I swear nobody will be spitting your way again."

The preacher started pacing back and forth then, swinging his arms, rocking his shoulders, shaking his head like he couldn't stop himself, like he could hardly hold himself back from something, something awful, but Sadie couldn't imagine what.

"Mountain folk like us, we're on the shy side. We'd rather do than talk, and we dont always speak up, even when we're in a world of pain. But people, you got to open your mouths and let the words come out! Not the words that men have taught you, not those words you learnt in school, but the ones Jesus put into your mouth. Let Jesus be the one to train your tongue!

"Member that place in Acts 2 where our Bible tells us 'and suddenly there came from heaven a sound like a mighty rushing wind, and it filled the entire house where they were sitting. And divided tongues as of fire appeared to them and rested on each one of them. And they were all filled with the Holy Spirit and began to speak in other tongues as the Spirit gave them utterance.'

"And right there in Mark 16:17 it says 'they will speak in new tongues!' So let's hear some of these new tongues! Let's hear what the Lord gives us to say!"

The preacher kept walking around, swinging his arms, twitching like he had hundreds of insects stinging him. The rest of the church was the quietest they'd been since the services began. A couple of people stood up, looked like they were about to say something, but it was like they suddenly lost the words, or were too shy to say them. They sat back down looking embarrassed.

Then this sound started, this low sound like from deep inside a cave, and at first she couldn't tell where it was coming from. Then it got louder, and she watched the preacher, who was back up near the cross now, and he was all tense, then swaying, his bones loose like all that connected them together was a little bit of string. And the sound was coming from him — she just wasn't exactly sure how.

Then the preacher opened his mouth more, and he started saying things, and the people sat up, most of them, like they'd been slapped.

"Glory be to God hallelujah!" the preacher said. "Ah sa lelogo shelagalah!" he shouted, or something liked that. What was he saying? Had he gone crazy? He sounded just like that auctioneer down the county fair last year.

The preacher was strutting like a rooster. His head moved back and forth. "Shi rilly yaya shang be to goddah holly lujah! Glor holly to goddah lujah!"

The preacher walked around the inside of the church, marching with his elbow brushing the walls, circling every member of his flock like he was herding the bunch of them in. It made Sadie awfully nervous to see that, to see him up front, then behind, then right beside her. He kept running faster and faster, saying all that nonsense, then raising his arms out to his sides like a little kid playing airplane, then screaming "Where are my saints! Where are my saints?" Certain people stood up and delivered their own version of whatever it was he'd been shouting, each in their way praising the Lord with their "Muss alowa goddah! Shah ally lawja!" The spirit took them one at a time, and then the spirit took them in waves, standing and shouting, turning in circles, laid back in the pews with their heads roiling around, lying on their backs on the floor with their hips jumping. The people in front were shaking and twitching, the people in back still standing in their rows but waving and shouting, some with eyes big as eggs, or rolling into the backs of their heads, the whites glowing in the light from the lanterns hanging along the walls.

At last the preacher came to the center of the church, his body stiff and his legs locked like a statue in the middle of the aisle, only his knees twitching, and his hands making grabbing motions with his fingers dancing as if they expected money to be dropping out of the rafters at any second and they were anxious to grab some. The people started pushing around him, climbing out of their seats and making a tight but writhing circle, like the muscles spasming around the mouth of someone trying to swallow their own tongue, but the preacher was the tongue, the preacher was the muscle making the words that were going to draw the Lord's grace down upon them all. And he threw his head back, his neck swelling like a serpent in the act of devouring the sacrificial lamb, and then there was this gorgeous flood of *ahs* and *esses* and *m's* from so deep inside him it was as if he was dredging it from the floor beneath, from the ground beneath, from somewhere deep within the mountain that fed and sheltered and buried them all. The sound started low enough to stir the belly but kept climbing higher and higher until it broke apart into this high speed chatter that was like a thousand tiny mouths eating the thoughts right out of Sadie's brain.

SHE MUST HAVE fainted because after another slow blink she saw the preacher floating over her, the sweat pouring off his face and gathering in her eyes. "Will my saints come help me with this poor lamb?" She almost expected angels to descend. Instead it was several men who came around and lifted her, so that she rose up out of the midst of that congregation and was brought forward to a seat in the front row with the older women who stroked her arms and fanned her face murmuring "praise you child, sweet Jesus praise this innocent lamb."

The preacher stood before them with his arms outstretched like he was Jesus himself crucified and his sleeves rolled part way up to show off his terrible scars. A long scar on his left arm curved through the crook of the elbow and wandered down almost to the wrist. She'd heard tell that once in his early times he'd got snake bit in his arm so bad they had to cut it down its entire length because it swelled up dark and evil. And then there was that terrible place on his palm. The preacher was close enough that hand hung down right by her face. The veins looked gathered and tied in that dark place and there was a gob of skin and muscle missing. Some said it was actually because he'd paid a man to take some ten penny nails and nail him to that big tree on the side of his house, but most agreed to that bad snake bite story, how the poison had made a portion of his hand rot away.

The preacher didn't always handle snakes in his sermons. She'd heard that in one service he drank poison. In another he held the flame of a torch to his bare hand. But there was something about the way he stood there that made her think there'd be snake handling tonight. Somebody opened the doors. She could see some of the people twisting around but she couldn't take her eyes off the preacher. Then she heard the heavy feet coming up the aisle, and four men carrying a wooden box wide as a big man's chest and long as a coffin coming around the preacher and setting it down behind him. It had black iron hinges and straps and a scattering of holes about as wide as your finger along its sides and every now and then something glistened and moved behind those holes. Afterwards the men passed in front of the preacher and he gave each of them a holy kiss mouth to mouth and they went back to their seats and everybody was still, watching him.

Then an old woman came up beside him and handed him a bundle wrapped in a ragged bit of bed sheet stained with dark rusty blotches and yellow streaks and green marks and Sadie couldn't imagine what might have made all those different stains. He unwrapped the bundle and there was a big old worn Bible inside — its cover scarred and broken and bits of paper and ribbon and string hanging out in all directions from within its pages and the whole of it out of true. The old woman took the torn bit of sheet and held it to her cheek and returned to her seat.

The preacher stood there thumbing through the giant Bible at his leisure as if he was the only one in the room, his lips moving, and sometimes his gaze floating toward the ceiling. He kept pulling out ragged pieces of paper that had things written on them, scrawled pictures and doodles and the handwriting so thick on some of them she couldn't see how a body could make out enough to read. He kept mumbling things nobody must have been meant to hear except maybe God and His angels, and the congregation must have been used to it because nobody said a word. They didn't even seem restless. He'd read a passage to himself and then he'd pull out a slip of paper and read whatever he'd written on that. Finally he opened to a page and laid his hand there, gazing out over his flock. "Folks ask me why I do this. I tell them it's because it's writ down here in my Bible, plain as day. They ask me do I do everything that's writ down in this here book and I tell them no, no I dont. I aint Jesus. I dont exactly perform miracles, but I've seen my share of miracles happen. I dont feed the multitudes with a couple of fish and a little scrap of bread. And I aint been crucified and Lord knows that I aint come back from the dead. I'm just a mortal man and try as I might that's all I'm ever likely to be.

"But I believe even a poor man, an ordinary man can do wonders. I believe the people we come from could do wonders. I believe some of them we come from could trace our line all the way back to the olden times, the biblical times of the old disciples, the times of Jesus hisself. I aint saying they was as great as Jesus, but I believe they was great enough for poor folk like us.

"I say we got some today with this wonder in them. I say maybe some here right in this room got this wonder in them. I say maybe we got a saint or two here today greater than all the old saints what ever lived."

He held up his Bible and started shaking it like he was angry. The ribbons and the strings and different pieces of paper fell out all over the place but he didn't seem to care. He kept shaking it and shaking it and he seemed to get angrier and angrier. Some of the congregation looked nervous and afraid. Even his small group of saints up close kept their mouths shut.

"In Genesis the Lord tells us that the serpent was more crafty than any other beast of the field. And in Matthew he advises us to be wise as serpents and innocent as doves. Then in Mark he reckons that maybe we ought to pick up them serpents because they give us power; so that even if we drink poison, it wont kill us, and he even gives us the power to heal as a reward for our faith.

"Now you all remember that story in Acts when a viper come out and fastened on Paul's hand. I know you do because I told it to you just last week! Remember how he shook off that serpent into the fire and suffered no harm?

"Well, it's writ large on the walls outside this here church. We handle snakes to declare our faith. That's just what we do! Any folks in here too scairt to watch us then you best leave now!"

Nobody left, but Sadie reckoned that even if they wanted to leave they'd be too afraid to, not with the preacher up there staring them all down and shaking his Bible with that terrible, vengeful hand.

"Okay then." He nodded and smiled hugely showing all his teeth. "Let's get her going. Let's have some of my saints up here to witness!"

Sadie didn't really understand who these saints were. Some looked to be people who'd been going to this church a long time. Others, the bigger ones, the taller ones, all of them men, reminded her of soldiers, the preacher's soldiers.

A few of the men in the crowd got up, a couple of those who had carried the box in and some others she had seen being active earlier in the services, and a couple she was sure she hadn't seen before — two skinny male twins who were probably in their seventies, and had identical sunk eyes and no expressions on their faces. There were also some women, older ones mostly, and a couple of ancient ladies who looked like they might die if they got a whiff of bad breath, much less a snake biting them. She saw a teenage girl rise up on the other side of the church, then get jerked back down by her mother.

The thing that struck her about all these volunteers, these saints, was that she didn't know any of them, which seemed strange in a community this small. So they must have all been folks from out on the farms who didn't get into town much, or maybe they lived somewhere a long way away, and had these hard journeys every week to get into the services. All the people she knew, including the ones she was related to, were content to just watch. Oh, they might get up and praise Jesus and dance around celebrating their love for Him, but they knew the preacher too good to be standing up there next to him when he had snakes all around. They might accept him as their leader, they might respect him as a preacher of the gospel, but that didn't mean they were going to trust him with their lives.

Even the loyal ones that did get up, they were walking up to him so slow, not excited like they were before. The preacher spread his arms to them, his black coat bunching up on either side of his neck like a buzzard's shoulders. "Come on now, come on," he said, like he was speaking to a child, or some critter he wanted to catch. "Dont be shy. None of us got nothin to be bashful about in front of the Lord." He stretched his arms out even wider, letting his head fall back in some kind of secret pleasure, wiggling his fingers, welcoming, directing. "Now boys," he said to a couple of the men, "I'd like you to stand at both ends, and you women, you line up behind, watching. I want you to watch me handling them snakes. Then it's your turn." He winked, and it made Sadie go cold.

The saints did as he said. Then he made a couple of the women slide over a few inches one way or the other. Finally he smiled and ran up to the box, unlatched and flipped open a little door set in the top, smiled at Sadie, and reached inside the box without looking.

She gasped when he pulled out a big copperhead and slapped the little door back shut. She heard a little squeal from someone, and a whole lot of nervous laughter, and a whole lot of *Praise Bes* and *Hallelujahs*.

Sadie knew her snakes. She had to, living in the hollow. When she was little her ma or her daddy would kill one and bring it up on the porch for her to look at so she'd know the different kinds, and be able to tell the poisonous ones from the safe ones. This copperhead was a good four foot long, about as long as they ever got in those hills, with those dark brown hourglasses all up and down. She only knew they were called hourglasses because her granddaddy had one — it had been in his family a long time and sat up on the mantel.

The preacher handled that snake like it was no more than a cut off piece of rope, waving it around and teasing it, moving his own head side to side like he was the snake and the copperhead was the one in danger of getting bit. Sadie thought the snake looked a bit confused, but she was probably just thinking silly.

The preacher started stamping his feet and hollering, waving the snake overhead like it was some kind of skinny flag. "I can feel its power!" he shouted. "Oh Lord, it's a powerful thing! Lord I beseech you to bless me by taking this old snake's will and giving it to me so I can be powerful too!"

People in the congregation started getting up and edging closer to where the preacher was with his box full of snakes. "Praise the Lord! Thank God for Jesus! Hallelujah to Glory!" they shouted, both separately and at the same time, their words folding one upon the other until they made a kind of music, a kind of thunder that shook the very blood in Sadie's veins.

The preacher brought the snake down in front of him and started speaking right at it, like he was preaching to the snake every bit as much as he was preaching to the congregation. "In Acts the Lord God told us we will receive *power* when the Holy Spirit has come upon us!"

Then the preacher handed off the snake to one of them old twins and that man started dancing and whooping with it and waving it around. Then the preacher opened up the box again and took a bunch of snakes at once and handed them to the other saints and they started acting much the same. Sadie gritted her teeth against the noise and she felt herself rocking, praying the preacher would *Please Lord Jesus* stop and let her go home.

But he looked like he had no plans for slowing down. He looked at the congregation and he raised his arms shouting, "Come up now and have victory over these serpents!"

And the congregation did exactly like he said. A few held back but they were like peaceful trees in the middle of a wind storm, the rest of them waving around and uprooting and dancing around.

The preacher was pouring sweat. He was still wearing his heavy black wool coat, now drenched shoulder to shoulder with his sweat. He took one of the snakes and slowly wiped his brow off with it. Then he tossed that snake up and someone reached out and caught it and the preacher slipped out of his coat and threw it in a corner where it lay like a buzzard all broken up after falling out of the sky.

The excited crowd was passing around copperheads and diamondback rattlers with them awful black heads and the last bits of them mostly black, and those V-shaped marks all in between. And some of them rattlers were kind of yellowish and some of them blacker than the rest.

Sadie stayed back as far as she could, moving when she had to. Once some fellow tried to kiss her and she pushed him away.

"Member Isaiah forty, 'He gives *power* to the faint, and to him who has *no might* he *increases* strength. They shall mount up with wings like *eagles*; they shall run and not be *weary*; they shall walk and *not faint!*" With each word it seemed he stamped his feet ever louder. The crowd, too, screamed harder with every word and passed holy kisses mouth to mouth.

The preacher twisted a snake around his neck and held the head in front of him so he could kiss it. He pulled up a copperhead that was just then coming out of its skin and he rubbed some of that skin off and held it up for all to see. "This is life everlasting!" he declared.

He brought out a couple of ugly, dull brown snakes that looked all ghostly white inside their mouths. She'd never seen a snake like that before. Then she overheard someone say cottonmouth, and another said no, it was a water moccasin. They had to be close to five feet long. Somebody else said they didn't have them around here, they lived over on the coast, and wasn't it a miracle that he had one here to handle?

Sadie'd always been told that if you looked into the center of a snake's eyes the black part was all round and friendly in the safe ones but in the poisonous ones it was narrow and up and down and wicked looking. What kind of fool waited around to take a good long look at a serpent's eyes when there were dangerous ones around?

She didn't see the preacher for a few minutes and she was wondering what happened to him when she saw him coming out of the crowd prancing around like one of those ballerinas wearing a crown made out of snakes he'd piled on his head. He started spinning himself in circles and those snake heads all came out on the end of curved bodies like he had long hair flying.

One of the snakes writhed and snapped, and she was sure the preacher got bit but he just kept moving and shouting like nothing had happened. If anything it just made him crazier. He got two snakes and thrust them through his hair then right into his chest like he was daring them to bite. When they didn't bite he tossed them into the air and then caught them again.

After a few more minutes the preacher was carrying three and four snakes at a time, kissing their heads and tongues, sliding them down his body, wrapping them around his arms, laying one across his forehead so that he was wearing it like a living bandana.

The front of the church was a mass of bodies moving up and down swaying, singing, shouting, trembling hands passing snakes back and forth like they were sharing food or cigarettes. Sadie couldn't follow it all, and she wondered what would happen if she got up and walked out the door. Would anybody even notice?

But then the preacher was standing right in front of her with those two old twin saints and he was saying, "Come on up! Come on up! Folks, we got us a *shy* one here!" And before she could say anything the twins had hold of her on either side and they were helping her up like she was some kind of cripple and leading her into that crowd of snakes and saints and unfortunates like her who didn't want to be there but didn't know how to get out of it.

The preacher had a big thick rattler in both hands and he was passing that snake back and forth in front of her eyes like it was the grandest prize that ever was and he was teasing her knowing she couldn't wait to get her hands on it. The snake arched its back and swayed back and forth, rotated its head, and stared at her. She couldn't move. She couldn't breathe. Each of the twins had one of her arms and they were pulling them toward the snake, turning them so that her palms faced upwards ready to receive His bounty.

They laid the snake into her hands and it was like holding a length of pure muscle. It bent and it stretched and it made curls through the air and she so wanted to drop it but couldn't. Sadie's body shook so badly she was forced to close her eyes to keep from throwing up. She jerked as if something was being yanked out of her and even with her eyes closed she could see the shape of the snake like a smooth and heavy bolt of lightning glowing in the darkness.

She opened her eyes again or at least she thought she was opening her eyes but she didn't see the church, instead she saw the endless folds of mountains like a mass of giant snakes that had been cornered and piled into this part of the world. She screamed and opened her eyes again and there was the preacher hisself rising like a snake off the floor until he towered over her. Something appeared to rise out of the preacher's body, smoke or fire or just anger and bitterness and all the hatred she could imagine stored in one place. He howled like a wolf in pain. Sadie disappeared inside herself and everything went white and she was just this tiny speck of no-account nothing trying to hide herself in that endless sea of white.

When she opened her eyes again she was lying back in the pew, an old woman on each side of her rubbing her hands and wiping her cheeks and telling her what a wonderful thing, what an inspiration it was to see her touched so by Jesus Christ Amen!

She sat up a little and looked around and people appeared to be standing still and not making a sound. They'd all given up their snakes and they were just standing around watching the preacher as he pulled the biggest, longest rattler she'd ever seen out of that box. That snake kept coming and coming and with each new stretch the church lost just a little more air, just a little more sound, so that by the time it came to the rattlers at the end Sadie couldn't breathe no more and she'd gone completely deaf. The snake was as long as a tall man was tall and fat enough it could have swallowed most of the other snakes if it had a mind to. She kept thinking of how in the book of Exodus Pharaoh's astrologers threw down their staffs and those staffs became serpents, but then Aaron threw his down and that became the snake what swallowed them other snakes. So maybe the preacher was like Aaron with that big old snake of his, a snake that could eat half that congregation if it ever had a mind to!

The preacher was a strong man, but he had a time picking up the weight of that snake so that he could handle it. He had half of it down his back and another bit riding his shoulders, and some of it sitting on one arm as he tried to move the head end around with his other hand. "I dont care how big you be!" he shouted at it, "I dont care how ornery or full of the devil! I'm going to beat you serpent and that's a fact praise Jesus Hallelujah oh Lord Lord Lord!" The preacher twisted his head around then and stared at Sadie. "Come up here, Child! Bring your God-given power up here so we can whup this snake together!"

The old women tried to push Sadie out of her seat, murmuring encouragement and pleading that her uncle needed her help and not to let him down but she pushed their hands away, terrified, trying to climb back over the pew into the row behind and the people there were pushing against her telling her the Lord was calling and she knew what she needed to do.

The preacher managed to stand perfectly straight with that huge snake all up on him and he was waving his hand to Sadie, "come on, come on now" like she was just some shy lamb scared of being shorn.

Suddenly the rattler came back around and bit down on the preacher's hand. The blood spurted out and sprayed on the floor but the preacher didn't make a sound. The snake's body slipped off the preacher and hung there as the snake appeared to be using everything it had to attack that powerful and vengeful hand. The congregation sighed as one big creature as the preacher angrily held his arm up, the big rattler hanging from where he'd bitten him through the webbing between his thumb and forefinger. It dangled past the preacher's knees, and the tail snapped back and forth and slapped the floor around the preacher's feet. The preacher tilted his head back and howled like he was trying to swallow a tornado. He grabbed the snake about halfway down and jerked it out of his hand. He flung the body clear across the church where it hit the wall and lay there motionless on the floor. The fangs were still in his hand piercing the webbing and he held them up for all to see.

Nobody, not even all the saints and all the angels could hold Sadie back as she ran from the church and into the woods.

Chapter Seven

HER DADDY'S HOUND Bucket was poking her in the side with his damp nose. He did that when he was hungry, or when he wanted to go out, or when he had nothing else to do. Her daddy pretty much hated the dog, who he'd named "Bucket o' guts," but for some reason he still wanted to keep the animal around, maybe just so he'd have the pleasure of cussing at him. Sadie kept swatting at the hound, trying to say "Go away!" but she heard nothing like that pass her lips. Then she tried to say his name but her mouth just wouldn't behave. Her mouth said "Buh" and "Buh" and that was about as far as it would go. Then she remembered that Daddy shot Bucket dead three year ago when that stupid dog raided the hen house.

Her eyes were stuck tight but she managed to get them open. A dark face hung over her, a big mouth with not many teeth. "Child, you done hurt yourself. Dont move while I rub some Jimson Weed onto these here cuts. You know not to *eat* the Jimson Weed dont ya? Poison. But it takes the fire out these cuts purdy good I reckon."

"Granny Grace?" Sadie tried to raise herself up but a dark brown arm pushed her back down. "What happened to me?"

Granny Grace didn't answer at first, busy rubbing the leaves all over Sadie's arms and legs, and the side of her left cheek. Then she laid a hand on Sadie's right cheek, gentle like her momma used to when her momma still liked her. "Dont fret none, child. Found you out in the woods this mornin outside my place. Looks like you run smack dab into them trees last night. Woulda heard you, but..." She blinked her squinty brown eyes, and the clean part of her face colored some like she was embarrassed. "Well, I drinks a bit most nights. Heps me sleep when my mind goes runnin off somewheres I dont want it to go. Rolled you onto an old sack and drug you in here."

Everybody knew Granny Grace in those hills. There were three Granny women Sadie knew about around Morrison — Granny Collins who lived in town, Granny Willis over near the poor farm in the bottom land before you started up the hollow, and Granny Grace. Everybody said Granny Grace knew more than the other two, that she was the last of her old family come off that ridge down in Tennessee, but she was darker than most anybody else around here — even darker than Aunt Lilly — so some folks wouldn't use her, not even for catching babies which by reputation she was best at — some said she could turn a baby most every time before it come out wrong with no harm to the child or the mother. And when she couldn't turn it, and it died in there, well, supposedly she knew how to fix things so the momma didn't die.

Once Aunt Lilly told her all about how it was done. "Dont you get pregnant, Sadie. Girl your age that baby's goin to turn wrong most every time, specially if the daddy's the wrong kind. Dont let that daddy be the wrong kind, you hear?" And Aunt Lilly looked at her like she knew something, or at least wanted Sadie to tell her something, but there were some truths it did nobody no good to know. "That baby dies, they got to break it to get it out of you. They poke a hole in its head and they break its skull and then they pull and scrape it out of you in pieces!"

Some folks used Granny Grace, but some of them wouldn't let her in their houses, so everything she could do she had to do behind the house with everybody looking.

As far as Sadie knew, nobody ever knew where Granny Grace lived; it was always "back in them woods somewheres." So if she could figure out where she was she'd be the first. Sadie moved her head around. She was down inside a big

scooped out place under some kind of lean-to. The back wall
was rock, and in between the grass sacks and canvas hanging
down the sides she could see dirt walls built up. A bunch of old
house windows had been propped up in the front and made
steady with stakes and mud. All around there were rough gray
planks put up on flat stones to make shelves, holding jars and
crocks and bags full of stuff, some of which smelled awful sweet
and some that were nasty, about evenly matched so she couldn't
decide which was worse. She shifted her weight and heard the
crackling underneath her — a bed tick stuffed with corn husks
most likely. "I hate to ask, but do you have something I can
eat?"

Granny Grace leaned back and picked up something, handed
it over. "Here's a little cold tater. I knows it aint much, but times
is hard. Where was you runnin from anyhow? Child your age —
your folks be worried."

Sadie stuffed the potato into her mouth. She couldn't remember
the last time she ate something. "I left that snake-handling
meeting. My uncle, he scared me a mite."

"You a Gibson? Oh hell, girl, you goin to buy me some trouble!
Me and the preacher, we dont mix!"

"I'm sorry; I dont want nobody hurt cause of me." She sat up
and gasped from the pain.

"No no, Granny Grace, she dont mean for you to leave. I sorry.
That preacher, he may be yer kin, but that's one evil man — I
dont care if he do say he's a preacher of the gospel. Here now."
She put a warm jar of liquid into Sadie's hand. "You drink this
here sweet tea. Dont taste too good, but makes you feel better."

Sadie couldn't see through the dark, turning liquid. Things
floated around in it — she couldn't tell whether they were living
or not. "What's in this, Granny?"

"Oh, bit of this and that. Onions and ivy, snip of catnip,
cocklebur, wild clover, flax, red cedar, sassafras. Might have put
some marigold and wild cherry bark in there too, but I dont rightly

remember. Some sage, probly, and honey — I always put some honey into most things. A little sweetness make everything better."

Just a sip made her face wrinkle up. The onions especially were strong, and something so bitter she figured it had to be good for you. She couldn't taste the honey at all. She closed her eyes and tried to drink it straight down. She got almost to the bottom before a coughing fit made her drop the jar.

"You musta liked it!" Granny Grace said. "Most folks dont get past that first sip."

Sadie's legs were badly scratched, and in some places she must have run the branches right into her skin. The worst places had some kind of foul-smelling poultice packed into the wounds, with tobacco leaves spread over the top. She didn't remember getting hurt; she barely remembered running. It had been like her thoughts were on fire and she had to put them out.

"Can I go?" she asked. "I need to go. Ma and Pa, they'll kill me most likely for not coming home."

"Oh you can go. Granny Grace, she unnerstand. Just be keerful with them wrappins, best let them stay awhile."

"I should pay you. This is your business, healing."

The little old woman cackled like a hen getting its neck broke. "Granny Grace only charges the ones what can pay. Child like you, I just ask a favor. Go with me to the General Store to gets what needs gettin. Cant get everthin I needs out these woods no more."

"Well, I dont have no money…"

"No, child. Granny Grace has the money. She just got a face too black to buy anythin in that store. But if I come in with you, they think I been hired by the family. I give you the money and you do the payin."

"But if I come in with you, Granny, everybody in there will think I'm *pregnant* or something."

"Dont worry, child." Granny handed her a crooked walking stick with a swollen, gnarled head. "Granny'll set them straight. Let's get crackin."

Sadie herself was on the short side, but she had to bend over when she stood up under the lean-to, and hunch over even more as she started to go through the lopsided door (painted "haint blue," Granny said, to keep out any nasty spirits roaming the woods).

"Stop! Dont step over that there broom!" Sadie looked down at the stick she was about to step across. Granny scrambled over and pulled it out of the way. It ended in a ragged head of straw. "You'd be an old maid for sure!"

Sadie thought that would pretty much be a blessing, but she didn't say nothing, not wanting to be disrespectful. Her momma always told her you lost a tooth for every child you had. By that reckoning Granny Grace had had a bunch, or did a body lose teeth for mid-wifing them too?

Granny looked up at her and grinned. "In case you were lookin, I'm wearin my dress inside out. Fraid it cant be helped. I accidental put my clothes on inside out this morning — now I gots to wear them that way all day."

Right outside the lean-to there was a pen with an ugly goat and a big coop woven out of green branches for some skinny chickens. A few feet on the other side was a small oven made out of rock and clay. A little bit of cornbread, still steaming, lay on the flat stone out front of the oven.

The little area was pretty well hidden under low branches that had been tied and pulled to make a wall of green around and over Granny's place. Sadie never could have found it if she hadn't already been there.

Granny led the way in her stained inside-out burlap dress dragging the ground and the hem wearing down to string. The patch quilt shawl around her shoulders was big enough to swallow her twice over, and once in a while Sadie got a peek at things Granny had hid there: a glass jug from a cord around her neck and a basket with some eggs for trade and close to her chest the handle of a gun. They climbed the rise a spell until they came to a path Sadie kind of recognized. From there they had a pretty good view through the trunks of the open valley and the hills spread out below. It was early morning, the trees more gray than green, that part of the hollow below them smudged with dabs of yellowed fog.

"Goin to rain soon. Last night they was a ring round the moon and this mornin the rocks are sweatin."

Sadie had heard of that way of telling rain before, so maybe it was true. Granny Grace chattered on all the way down the mountain toward town, with nary a break to draw breath. Sadie didn't know if half of it was right — a lot of it just sounded crazy. But she listened politely, thinking that maybe Granny didn't get much opportunity for having her say.

"So's I told him if he soaked them seeds in milk first the melons that come would be lots sweeter and sure enough they was — now he gives me a bunch ever season free. I tell you, you gots to know *how* to plant and *when* if you want to farm this here hard mountain land — mostly rocks and clays and nary a square inch of that good soil they gots in the bottoms. You plant yer taters, turnips, beets in the dark of the moon. Then leave a bowl of cream and some cornbread out for the little people and maybe they'll help you out some!

"... I use a green fork from a peach tree to find water. Some folks use a bit a wire but that aint ever goin to be no good!

"... for aches and pains I use the chicory mostly, vinegar and mud packs if it be stubborn, garlic, black birch sap in a salve, and on the sore joints crushed boiled white walnut bark, wit some oil o'cedar.

"... I done wadded up some cob webs and packed them into your wounds to stop the bleedin, and then some of that witch hazel.

"... girl your age best sharpen themselves a ten penny nail. Keep filin it and filin it till it be *real* sharp, then hide it somewheres you can get to it quick. Then one of these old men be messin with you, you can protect yourself, stick him where it dont feel so good."

When Granny said that last bit of advice she laid her hand on Sadie's arm and gave it a little squeeze. That was all. Sadie knew it meant something but it was something she couldn't talk about, at least not yet.

Granny Grace stopped in front of Levitt's General and looked Sadie up and down. She bent down and peeled the tobacco leaves off Sadie's legs. Sadie scrunched up her face, but the pain wasn't too bad after a minute. "You look public enough I reckon," Granny said. "They just opened, wont be many folks inside. You'll have to go in first. I'll be on your heels — that ways they'll know we come in together."

Mr. Levitt nodded at her from behind the counter when she came in. Three old men sat on bulging feed sacks by the stove, but it didn't look like there were any other customers yet. One of the old fellows stared at her sleepily, like he might know her, but she didn't recognize him. Their small town was full of adults who knew everybody, and children who knew almost no one outside their own family. The store looked half dark. Mr. Levitt jerked his head a little when Granny Grace joined her, then he appeared to decide something, and nodded again. "If you ladies are here to shop, I'd best go turn on the lights in them other two rooms." He came around the counter and was passing Sadie when he paused and spoke softly to her. "Miss, I dont mean to embarrass you, but I cant sell your family nothing on credit right now. Your daddy... he's way behind."

Granny spoke up then. "No problem, Boss. She's got the cash." Levitt frowned at Granny. She pulled a hand out of one wide pocket, showing the dirty, wadded up bills in her palm. "And dont you go thinking the girl's pregnant. She aint!"

Mr. Levitt turned red and walked quickly away toward the dark rooms at the back of the building. Sadie's face burned so hot she thought she would faint.

"I got me a good salve for heat stroke iffen you need it child," Granny said. She went into her other pocket and pulled out her list. It was a ragged scrap of paper filled with writing, and drawing, and marks like what a bird's feet might make in the dirt. If it was English writing it wasn't like any kind Sadie had ever studied in school.

At that moment Missy Bacon came in with her little baby. Missy was only a few years older than Sadie and had gone to the same one room school, so they'd studied on different things, but Sadie could always hear what the teacher was teaching them older kids, and it wasn't much different, except the words got longer, and sometimes they wrapped around each other until they meant something else.

Missy was busy with the baby so she didn't even look up or say hello, wiggling her finger on it and making it laugh. "Dont tickle that baby under the chin if you dont want him a stammerer when he grows up," Granny Grace said. Missy looked down at the frayed little dark woman, turned around and left without saying anything.

Granny went to the counter and put her bark basket up there, shouting "I gots eleven cackleberries after the one what broke!" Sadie laughed out loud; her grandpa used that same name for chicken eggs.

Coming out of the back Levitt said, "Appreciate your honesty."

"Hell, body be a fool to try to cheat a store keep with countin." Granny glanced back. "You comin girl?" Sadie scooted up to her side. Granny was treating her like *her* granny but Sadie didn't mind, even if old Levitt did. Granny tore off part of the list and handed it to her, along with an empty feed sack from under her shawl. "You can read this part good enough," she said. "It's just the regular goods." She scurried to the back of the store without another word.

Sadie stood there shyly, not sure what to do. She often went into Levitt's to pick up something for her momma, but never for more than a couple of things, and never with this much money involved. The big Moon Pie display on the counter made her think about how hungry she was, and how sometimes when her momma sent her here she got an extra ten cents for a coal miner's lunch — a Moon Pie big as her hand and an RC Cola to wash it down. But she reckoned she couldn't ask Granny Grace for such a thing, it wouldn't be being grateful.

She heard Granny back in the back singing to herself, the Carter's "Winding Stream," her voice switching back and forth from harsh to sweet. It was enough to stir Sadie to move, and she went down the shelves then, picking out Lemon Junket, Fleishmann's Yeast, Baker's Cocoa, Ovaltine, and Knox Gelatine. The store was out of the Campbell's Oxtail and Mock Turtle soups. And she had to get Mr. Levitt to get the Del Monte prunes and Liebig's Extract of Beef down from the high shelves with that long-handled grabber of his. Every time she saw him do that she imagined he had a skinny, extra-long arm and it always made her laugh.

Her favorite thing about Levitt's Store was the light bulbs. It was one of the only places in town with the electricity, and it had a big beautiful glass bulb in each room hanging overhead, and when they were on they looked like little suns. Sometimes she spent too much time looking at them and they left her dizzy with spots popping in front of her eyes.

She filled her sack so heavy it made her stagger around like a drunkard, and still she had to get the corn meal, the flour, lard, salt, baking powder, coffee, salt pork, and sugar. How was Granny Grace going to get all this stuff back to her place by herself?

Sadie heard her in the back, still singing. The Carter's "Clinch Mountain" now. Most folks around there sang hymns to themselves, but she reckoned the chances of Granny Grace singing a hymn was kin to the chances of a hen laying duck eggs. Sadie almost never went back there. Mostly because that's where they kept the things her momma and daddy had to buy in person and never sent her to the store for — the shoes and the clothes and the bolts of chambray cloth and denim and the hunting and fishing supplies and the hardware and the tools. But also because on the back wall on top the highest shelf they had these six identical baby coffins, all of them stained dark and polished until they were like the most beautiful pieces of furniture in anybody's house.

There were always six of them, so for a long time she thought maybe they just never sold them, or maybe almost no babies ever died in the hollow. Then one day she saw Mr. Levitt bring one of them up to a sorrowful-looking couple sitting on chairs by the front window. She'd watched them a few minutes. They sat like they'd been nailed there and couldn't move, not even their hands, not even their eyes. And then Mr. Levitt brought them a polished box that was wider at one end than the other, and it had a metal plaque on it that said *Our Darling*, because she guessed it had come from the factory that way, so you didn't even have to put a name on it, which was a good thing, since she'd heard that some dead babies weren't even given names.

The couple had stared at that coffin like they were looking at their dead baby itself, and the woman had laid her hand on it, then took it off so quick like it burned. And Sadie reckoned that's the kind of baby she would have if her own daddy got her pregnant. It would be a dead baby and they all would burn.

After that poor couple left with their baby coffin she heard Mr. Levitt tell a customer he had to order another one right away, cause he always liked to have six on hand just in case. "Back during that Spanish Flu epidemic after the war I run out quick and couldn't get no more," he'd said. "Folks was having to make their own boxes for their babies. Round here we're accustomed to that for the grownups, but you like to do something a little special for the little ones."

Granny Grace seemed to be spending a lot of time at the back of the store and Sadie was getting antsy. More and more folks were coming in for supplies and trading. One farmer had carried in a passel of chickens with their feet tied together and their flapping and scratching and tortured cackles were playing all kinds of mischief on her nerves. She'd been out all night and looked it, her Momma and Daddy didn't know where she was, and being seen with old black Granny Grace was going to make folks talk for sure.

When Granny finally came out of the back she'd filled the jug she'd brought with lamp oil and she had a sack full of all kinds of spices she'd picked out which Sadie reckoned she must use in her cures. But Granny had them all mixed up so Sadie couldn't imagine how Mr. Levitt was going to figure out how much to charge. They went up to the front counter and Granny handed her pocket full of greasy bills and coins to Sadie and Sadie quickly gave them to Mr. Levitt, who made a face and laid them down in a wad on the counter by his cash register. He added up the items and subtracted the money he was paying for the eggs Granny brought in and announced the total. Granny argued with him about the total, especially what he was charging for the spices ("it aint but a little sack full!") and Levitt knocked off a little which made Granny smile. They were about to start out the door when Sadie saw Aunt Lilly and her momma coming off the road. She ran into the back and Granny Grace followed her.

"Best tell them the truth, child. You done nothin wrong."

"I was gone all night, and when I finally woke up I didn't go home right away!"

"You was *hurt*, child! And Granny had to take keer of you. Then I had you come in the store with me fer my pay. I'll tell them!"

"I'm sorry, Granny, but my daddy'd have a fit if he knew I was out in them woods all night with you! No telling what he might get in his head to do!"

Granny didn't say nothing at first, her eyes unfocused, considering. "Well then," she finally said, "I aint goin to argue with that, so I'll just let her be. But iffen it gets too hard you tell them about Granny Grace, y'hear? I aint goin to have you on my conscious, no sir!" Sadie gave her a fierce hug, and Granny stiffened up, and then hugged her back. "Girl, you listen to me," she whispered into Sadie's ear. "The future aint here till it happens. True nuff we're all headed in that di-recshun, but we go thar one step at a time, and lots ken happen between them steps!"

Sadie peered through a stack of buckets and farm equipment parts as Granny Grace headed toward the front door. As Lilly and her momma came in Granny Grace grinned her broken grin and bowed deeply before slipping out. The two women looked surprised. Sadie noticed that Momma was carrying a long list.

There was some used furniture for sale in the back room. Sadie found a floor length mirror and used it to straighten her dress up. She had a little piece of rag in her pocket she spit into and used to work at some smudges on her dress and to clean off some of the dried blood and whatever it was that Granny had smeared on the side of her face and her arms and legs. She still smelled some, but there wasn't much she could do about that. Mr. Levitt had a small selection of toilet waters nearby, and she stared at them with a kind of hunger, but her days of stealing were over, no matter what the need be.

"I *know* we aint got no more credit! You can thank my shiftless husband for that!" Sadie peeked around the corner. Her momma was waving her arms and stamping her feet. It wasn't like her — she must have been feeling especially aggravated today — usually she just frowned awful deep at folks and held her peace when they made her mad. Mr. Levitt was backing up like he might just decide to run out his own door. "But it's the Grans' birthday on Saturday and the whole family pitched in some cash. So dont you be whisperin in my ear about not bein able to extend us some credit! I weren't askin for no credit! What I'm askin is that you clear out our way while we get the things on this here list and then you add them up real fast and take our money for them so we can get out of this sorry excuse for a mercantile!"

Sadie felt shaky all over. The way her momma was this morning she was liketa kill her before she even had a chance to come up with some sorry lie.

"Sadie!" It was a thunder of a whisper. She looked down to see her aunt's wide eyes before Lilly pushed her deeper into the shadows. "Where you been? Your momma and daddy are fit to be tied!" Then she stopped and touched Sadie's cheek. "I saw you run out the service. I shoulda kept you from goin in the first place. What happen to you after that?"

"I dont know." Sadie started crying. "I ran and I ran, and I kept running into things — it felt like them snakes were biting me over and over again! I fell and I got up and run some more, and then I crashed through some trees off the trail and fell and I dont know, *hit* something. Granny Grace… she took me in and nursed me. I *shouldn't* a gone into that church! And I aint never going to go into that church again!"

"Ah, Sweetie." Aunt Lilly patted her on the arm. "It aint that simple. Why do you think *I* still go? Or your Uncle Jesse? It dont matter we're family, the preacher does just what he wants. He dont let *nobody* quit *his* church. You go just once and you're a member for life far as he's concerned! You just got to make the best of it."

"No! I cant! Aunt Lilly I *cant* go back in there!" She was crying so hard now she couldn't see, and she couldn't hear, and Momma was going to come around that corner any second now and slap the crying right out of her for what she done.

Then she knew red was leaking into her crying. It ran into her eyes. And when she tried to open them the thick, sticky blood stopped her, glued her eyelids and her lips shut, but she managed to see just a little, and what she saw was Aunt Lilly on the floor, drowning in red and staring up at her, and all leaked out of her own body.

Sadie screamed, and fell again.

Chapter Eight

THE TELLING HAD exhausted his grandmother, and almost immediately afterwards her head fell forward and she could barely raise it again, or help herself in any way. Michael was severely drained himself, his nerves raw and electric. He was beginning to wonder who her memories were going to kill first. Still, she was a sick old woman and he had to do something. After a couple of struggling attempts he managed to pick her up gently enough and carried her to her bed.

The way he'd been with her the past year embarrassed him. She deserved better. He had no aptitude for care-taking; he could barely take care of himself. And although he believed in patience, that quality had always eluded him. But he'd come back here when he'd needed to and she'd welcomed him. He owed her everything. He always had.

He remembered the first time he saw her. He'd been sitting on that cheap little cardboard suitcase his parents bought him before the first so-called "vacation." It was the first time they'd dumped him on Grandma. It wouldn't be the last.

"Dont sit on the suitcase. It's brand new and you're going to ruin it already." That was his dad, who he barely remembered, except as this nervous, fussy presence, always telling Michael he was doing something wrong, but immediately flitting off somewhere else, not following through. A few years later he would leave Michael's mother and fly to Asia, never to return.

Michael could see that the suitcase was splitting underneath him, but he didn't care. He was fat, always had been heavy, like everything in him weighed too much. But he didn't care. The suitcase shouldn't have split like that — it was a cheap piece of crap — but he didn't care. Let it split. Let them see how crappy it was.

His grandma was standing right over there, but he wouldn't look at her. He knew this was no vacation — he knew what was up. And he didn't want to be here with that old lady.

"It'll just be a few days, Ma," his dad was saying. But it was a lie. He knew it was a lie, and for some reason he thought Grandma did too, but he still wasn't going to look at her.

"I'll do right by him," Grandma said, and he knew she was looking at him, figuring him out, because they both knew she'd have him for a while. He remembered his mother crying in the background, and rubbing her hands and arms like she had bugs crawling on them. That was near the beginning. She got worse every year until they had to put her away.

It would be five years before he saw his mother, and oh, she'd been so much worse. He never saw his father again.

"Come in child. I got a place for you," Grandma had said after they'd left, but still he hadn't moved, hadn't even looked at her. Later she brought out a plate with steak and biscuits, gravy and beans. He'd never said thank you, in fact rarely said thank you the whole time he'd lived here as a child, because he'd had no thank yous in him. Sometime after dark he'd gone in, and taken the bedroom she'd left open, a green towel on the bed for him. He'd always liked green; how did she know?

All those years she'd never told him about the Grans, or the preacher either, or anything more than the average, boring details of family and lineage. That dark fellow in the photo was his great grandfather and that sour looking lady his great grandmother. There was that one photograph of Lilly, who'd been gorgeous even by contemporary standards. Not that he had paid much attention to any of it at the time. He'd felt agitated most days, had bad and busy dreams, went through periods of lip biting and scratching his own arms, and his grandmother hadn't been unkind, but she'd never helped him, never told him anything. What she did do was watch. She'd always been watching. And sometimes she'd ask questions; she'd asked him about his dreams, or if he had any "worries," but he always lied, and understood that she knew he was lying, understood how she felt about a lot of things without her telling him with either word or expression, but didn't at all understand how he could know.

Sometimes he came home from school crying, upset for no other reason than that he knew something about what was going on in another kid's life, or that he felt something, something soul destroying about some other child.

They never talked about it, but now and again she would announce, out of nowhere and with no context, "some folks round here have bad lives — aint no other way to say it. It aint your fault and there's nothing you can do about it."

But the worst thing, and he couldn't have explained it if he tried, was that just because he saw those things and felt those things didn't mean he cared sufficiently, not really. He'd witnessed too much, felt too much, and just wanted them all to leave him alone — he wanted to know nothing about their problems. Some days it was all he could do to control his anger at everyone he met.

After he got his grandmother into bed this night Michael tried to get some sleep himself, but his head was too full of her life, the preachings and the snakes and the raw red violent griminess of it. He felt sorry for her — her childhood had been far worse than his — but he didn't want to know any more about it. He could walk away, but he understood that the stakes were high; he just didn't yet know why. What was he supposed to learn from all her stories?

Not that they were simply her stories anymore. The worst thing about her memories, the most persistent thing was they were no longer just her own. It wasn't like listening to stories. It was like remembering something that had actually happened to you a long time ago and far away, when you had been very different from what you were now.

He didn't remember falling asleep. He had been trying to recapture Sadie's last vision of her Aunt Lilly. Sadie hadn't described it to him — she hadn't even tried. Michael had seen it through a cloud of red, but he hadn't understood what he was looking at. And now apparently it was gone completely from his head.

The lines of the room eventually began to waver, to lose the vertical, the horizontal, to break and bend and travel, to dangle from the window sash, to sway and drop from overhead. It was almost as if he was running a fever and things were dripping, drifting apart. Those moving lines began to hiss and snap.

He bolted awake then, his body vibrating. And the snakes he had just seen in his dream were still there: a complex tangle of rattlers sprawled over the folded quilt at the foot of his bed, a bloated copperhead hanging from one of the brass loops of the overhead light fixture, liquid lines of black-smoke water moccasins weaving themselves into the texture of the bedroom rug, snake curves gathering along the back and arms of the overstuffed chair. He held back a shout until it became a sigh, and the snakes gently faded into shadow and folds, metal and wood. Except for the thin S-shape uncoiling from his window, extending its reach and trolling for anchor.

A couple of times in his life, after a long week of poisoning himself with alcohol and whatever, he had had visions like these, the DTs. But he hadn't had a drink in some time and these felt far more than visual. He could smell the snakes in the room and hear their quickening rattles.

Michael slipped his feet into decaying flip-flops, grabbed a flashlight, and ran out into the yard in his boxer shorts. In the misty dawn light long tendrils of kudzu dangled from the front porch roof. He walked carefully around to the side of the house. Ropy vines had layered the boards under the eaves, their runners tasting whatever moisture lay in the rain gutters. Other runners lay poised beneath the upstairs windows as if waiting for the signal to break and enter.

He hadn't been around to the side of the house, or the back, in a week or so. He knew that kudzu could grow as much as a foot in a day, but still, this much spread was impossible, wasn't it? He shone his light on what appeared to be the main trunk, following it back to where a mass of leaves and vines obscured that entire corner of the house, a ragged cloud of green, devouring. The leaves at the end and sides of the runners were about the size of his hands, two- and three-lobed. There was something inexact about them, dreamy and incomplete. He tried to avoid them but one of them brushed the back of his hand. It was furry — not animal furry, really, but insect furry perhaps.

Turning the corner into a sea of leaf and vine, he had to back up to get a more complete sense of it. The kudzu had flooded in from a sparse gathering of trees behind the house, the larger vines woody and as thick as his wrist, crossed the lawn and risen like a hand with dozens of green fingers to clutch the back wall, the two chimneys, and the roof. It looked ready to pry off the top of the house in pursuit of whatever hid inside.

He didn't want to step over, or on, any of the web of vines. They lay unmoving, and the fact that he'd even have cause to notice a lack of movement was alarming. Some of the smaller leaves and narrow stalks drifted as if floating in water. He followed the stream of vines back between the trees and out to the narrow road where they funneled into and filled the corrugated drainage pipe that lay under it. The edges of the old metal pipe were bent and split. On the other side of the road the vines reappeared from the end of the pipe and made their way into the larger woods. Here and there he could make out the hulking shapes of green where trees had been mounted, covered, and starved of light. He stood still and listened to the silence, broken now and again by tree limbs shifting and cracking beneath the weight of vine.

The next morning Michael called Clarence Roberts. "I need you to come back — the vine's worse, I'd say a lot worse. Bring more workers. I... my grandma will pay them whatever you think is fair. As many as you can get."

There was a long pause on the other end during which it sounded as if Clarence was breathing with some difficulty. Finally he said, "I can do that, and I reckon I can round up some helpers somewhere, but just so you know, I wont be bringin my boy round this time."

"Well, sure." Michael wondered why the man was telling him this.

"Now I know yer good people and yer grandma, she's always been kind to me and my kin. But not everybody in yer family was always thataway, and there's all them stories, hell, Mr. Gibson, I'm sorry, but he's my *only* son."

Michael was embarrassed — Clarence sounded on the verge of tears. "Well of course, whatever you need to do. I'll pay you well."

"You pay me same as always. I dont need no extry, and whoever I find, you can pay them regular, but only if they do a good job, and I'll be tellin you if they dont do a good job."

When he got off the phone his grandmother was standing there, staring at him. "My window was full of green this morning," she said. "It aint never been full of green before. I reckon that aint just a big house plant out there."

"Grandma, are you making a joke?"

She blinked at him, then said, "Dont remember how."

He made her breakfast — bacon and eggs, tea, a piece of toast, and a couple of sliced oranges. She didn't normally eat fruit, and she wrinkled up her face when she put it into her mouth, but she ate it all anyway. He explained to her about Clarence Roberts coming out with some workers, and how he planned to help out, and not to worry because he'd make sure she'd have the house back the way it was before.

She stopped sipping her tea and looked at him. "You know kudzu dont grow like that, dont you? Not even at its worst. Aint nothing natural about it growin out there like that. A person might dream it happens that way, I reckon. So maybe that's what's going on. That kudzu is somebody's evil dream. You think you can cut down something like that?"

"I dont know what else to try. I know it's not natural. Clarence knows it too. He says the roots come together into these crowns, just under the surface. He says that's what we have to dig up and cut out, all those crowns. He's going to show me how it's done."

"So you feelin it?"

"What? What do you mean?"

"I mean are you feelin *him?*"

He knew she wasn't talking about God, or the Lord, or whomever. "Maybe," he said. "I think so."

She nodded, put her cup down and leaned back as if exhausted. "Thought so. I know I aint done much to get you ready for him. I'm truly sorry about that."

"Grandma, you hardly told me anything about the family while I was growing up. And nothing about this *sense*, or whatever it is, we have of each other. All you did was stare at me, watch me. There were days when I was a kid, I bet you didn't say more than three words to me. How do you think that made me feel?"

"Terrible, I know. Made me feel terrible, too. But I was afraid. I had to be sure."

"*I* was afraid, Grandma! I thought something was wrong with *me!* I should have found myself a wife by now, had a family…"

"Oh, no, Michael, you wouldn't want to do that, not till you was sure."

"Sure of what?"

"Sure you wasn't goin to be like the preacher. That's what I waited for, watched you for, to see if you was goin to turn out like me, or like the preacher."

He stared at her. "I'd *never!* I was angry sometimes, sure — I was an angry kid, but I never did anything *mean*. I'd never *hurt* anybody! What would you have done, anyway, if you thought I'd turned out like him?"

She sighed. "Killed you, I reckon. Killed you dead and then some."

Later that morning Clarence Roberts showed up with three other beat-up pickup trucks full of men, strangers to Michael. A couple of them looked slightly drunk and dangerous, but Michael figured Clarence would handle them as necessary. They all brought plenty of tools — axes and picks and shovels and big two-man pruning saws and saws smaller but with wicked teeth and ladders to get up the side of the house and onto the roof.

"I'd been here sooner but I'll tell you true couldn't find a soul here local willin to come. These fellers..." The back of his hand swept around as if he wasn't too impressed with what it was pointing to. "They're from over the mountain, down near that Crossroads Hotel. Rough as grits, but I reckon I can get them to work alright."

"What's the word in town," Michael asked, "about all this?"

"I guess some of them folks weren't all that surprised to hear of your problem. They figure it's cursed ground, I reckon, but most folks dont much like clearin kudzu anyways."

The men started on the house, simply pulling the furthest, smallest runners down by hand, snipping them, and rolling them into sacks. Three fellows climbed up on the roof and began peeling the mass of green off the shingles. Sometimes a vine would snag and break off in a crack, or maybe it had already attempted to root. Clarence sent men up the ladders after these, determined to remove every scrap of vine. "If you dont get it all it's likely to come back. It finds a place it likes and it wants to stay. Too bad people's cash crops round here aint that stubborn."

They rolled up the vine until it got too big and stiff to bend, and then switched to cutting it into sections and then hauling each section, as best they could, to the trucks. All afternoon the trucks took the cut-up vine away to some location where Clarence said they'd burn it. Since big burns like that were illegal in the county Clarence didn't want to tell Michael where the location was, "less'n you want to watch." Michael gave his regrets thinking there'd be a lot of drinking involved and he didn't want to be with this bunch when there was both fire and liquor around.

Clarence kept yelling at the men not to do any rough chopping at the vines and the argument came to a head when they started digging into the ground to expose the crowns that formed the nexus for each network of roots.

Clarence had several of the large brown masses exposed and kept staring at them as if he wasn't sure what to do. "It takes them a long, long time to get this big," he said. "Years I reckon. But I was just here less'n a week ago, and there was nary a plant I could see."

They were about the size of basketballs, but not so round. Shaped almost like a brain, if the brain had been injured on one side and swelled up lop-sided. Several wrist-thick shafts of root came out of each crown parallel to the ground. Like water pipes, vegetable pipes. One of the men prodded a crown with a large axe.

"Hold on now, dont be swingin that axe at them crowns!" Clarence walked between the man and the excavated kudzu. The man looked angry, but stepped back and bowed his head a little. Clarence turned to Michael. "You got to take them out whole and get rid of them somewheres else," he said. "You chop them up an you dont manage to pick up all them pieces of the crown, you just get more kudzu. And when you take it somewheres to get rid of it, you best get rid of it all or you're just movin your problem around."

Clarence got two men on each saw to cut out all the crowns as they were uncovered with about two feet of root sticking out on each side. Then they carried them to the trucks and went back for more, and where any of the runners had rooted they dug those out too to join the pile.

When a fellow brought a gas can over to Clarence there was another argument. "You want that fire to take the house and god knows what after?" was all he heard. The worker looked both embarrassed and angry.

A little way down the hill from the house were the remains of the preacher's church. Growing up there Michael'd always thought it was just the ruins of some old barn. Instead of tearing isolated buildings down they just let the vegetation take them. The results were rather beautiful, he thought, but contributed to an overall feel of decay and extinction. When he'd asked his grandmother about that building she'd said, "Jest an old buildin. You keep outta there, boy! There's rusty nails what give you the lock-jaw in there iffen you step on them. Spiders and coons and likely some snakes. Likely a lot of them snakes the poisonous kind. They swole you up dead most likely before I could even get to you!"

But once he'd heard his grandma's tale he knew exactly what the building had been because of its location. And the fact that she would make up a warning about snakes to keep a child out of there now seemed gutsy, given its history. Unless it were true. He'd seen no snakes around the property, not ever. Still, he couldn't see himself ever going in there. Not then, not now.

On the outside of the building there were no signs of the writing she'd described — any paint had long worn off. It was all splintered gray board now, with a few dark crumbling posts poking up through the wreckage of the rusted tin roof. The doors were gone, probably scavenged long ago, but the frame had held up enough to keep a lopsided dark cavern open at the ruin's center for any child foolish enough to venture there. Most of it was covered in vine — not kudzu, probably oriental bittersweet — and here and there small pines or a foul-smelling tree of heaven filled some of the interior space. Sometimes rain beating on what was left of the roof made a continuous hollow sound like singing, if the singers had forgotten the words and made up their own language.

From where the stream of kudzu had poured out between the trees behind the house Michael had a clear view of the church ruins, and as the men worked their way back through the trees removing the thick web of kudzu he still had an unobstructed view of that structure almost as far as the road. There the stream of vine turned and narrowed to enter the corrugated drainage pipe.

Michael gazed at where the kudzu had abruptly changed direction. There was no accounting for it. The woods were sparse enough here they provided no barrier at all to the encroaching vine. The kudzu should have just travelled straight on and filled the space. There'd been no reason for it to turn. There'd been no reason for it to restrict itself to the drainpipe either. It would have gone through the drainpipe certainly but it should have flowed over the road without anyone there to trim it back. Unless what it wanted was to hide itself until just the right time.

He watched as the men dug and exposed more of the crown and root system. Two of the crowns nearest the drainage pipe were a good three times larger than the rest, broad and flattened like rough, scarred palms, roots coming out like fingers that reached on and on toward the house until the point where the workmen severed them, hoping to keep them from going any further. One of the palms was darkened, twisted and mutilated on one side.

Michael watched as they removed the fingers, the palms, the roots that trailed into the pipe. The vine was so thick inside that the metal had ruptured, and as they pulled out each vine individually Clarence had to insert stakes to keep the pipe from collapsing completely and leaving a deep gulley in the road. As it was Michael would have to hire a crew someday to come out and fix the damage, if he ever could find a crew that was willing after this. His grandma had a lot of money saved up, but she might need it for other things.

They worked late into the night by flashlights, truck headlights, and lanterns. Grandma was up, having slept most of the day, and insisted on providing coffee. The men accepted but kept their distance from her. At one point a section of the kudzu curled up after it was severed and snapped at the men, slapping one worker so hard across the face he bled.

Michael lost some time then, watching Clarence bandage the man's face. He saw the huge snakes striking, the boy and the girl pursued by the preacher in his black coat flapping through the woods. When Michael came out of it he left Clarence and the men to finish on their own, found his grandma sitting by the window staring into the inky dark, and asked her to tell him some more.

Chapter Nine

"BIRTHDAY GRANS... THE fog, oh that fog!" Sadie stared at her grandson, the words difficult to find and to choose when she did find them, so that although they came out infrequently, they came out strongly. "Gray ladies... those poor... those poor... gray ladies! They just... just faded away!" Just as her grandson faded away now, and her body grew smaller, and better formed, and without the physical pain that had plagued her for years. Not that that young girl didn't have troubles. She did, and Sadie knew she always would.

The day of the Grans' birthday began with a stubborn morning fog, catching on the ragged limestone spines of the hill slopes, and still clinging hours later like torn slips among the low scrub trees as the picnic spread was being served. Sadie guessed that meant there were cold patches where maybe the sun didn't always reach. She'd found those places some early mornings herself, and they always made her feel bad, like some things never got better. Sometimes folks had to make do with sorry explanations because those were the only ones they had.

They'd set up the celebration at the campground, and she reckoned everybody she ever knew was out there on that knobby field that fell back behind the buildings on main street. The field was surrounded by trees, most of them too far away to give much shade, but there were a couple near where the big shelter used to be, and they planted the Grans there to keep their heads out of the sun. Folks treated the old people sometimes like they were fragile little baby birds you could scarce breathe on but if they were *that* delicate then how had they lived so long?

There was a clump of three or four crippled up maples about a hundred feet past, there where the old Mullins farm began, the wide trunks and the twisted limbs all tangled up in wild strawberry vine, and under and through it all the weeds that hadn't been mowed in ages. That overgrowth was a long way from Sadie, so she couldn't see much detail, but it looked like there was still some fog trapped in there by the vines. People stayed away from that area, she reckoned because of the mess, and whatever critters it hid, but her eyes kept going back there, as if they expected to see something.

Back in the old days they'd used this field for camp meeting, evenings of travelling preachers fighting to renew the faith of some but mostly hoping to bring new sinners into the loving arms of Jesus. There'd been the one big shelter with the roof and a raised floor in case it rained, and the smaller ones, for the church camp kids and little get-togethers.

She'd heard her mama say that all stopped ten years back when the preacher insisted on being a part of every service, and since he was the local minister those visiting men of God must have felt obliged to humor him. But give the devil an inch and you'll wish you hadn't because before long the preacher ran that whole camp meeting tradition into the ground. He wasn't handling snakes back then but you couldn't get him to stop once he got started talking, and sometimes he preached mean and sometimes he preached angry so the traveling preachers stayed away after a while and anybody not in the preacher's own little group stopped coming. After a couple of years pieces of the shelters started disappearing, boards and tin roof and even posts, about the same time the preacher's new church started going up. Nobody accused him but pretty much everybody knew what was going on. Nobody did nothing about it though, nobody did nothing about nothing in the hollow, and pretty soon most of those shelters were gone, and now all that field got used for was the occasional church picnic and maybe a game of pickup ball.

The only signs those buildings had even been there were a few posts too buried to move and some scattered piles of stones they'd used to shore up the old floors. Today folks were sitting on those stones and hanging baskets of flowers from the posts. What was left of a few steps now led up to nothing. People sat on those, too, even though they were wobbly. Sometimes the little children would take those steps up to the nothing and then jump off into giggles.

While everybody else was congratulating the Grans and finding their sitting place Sadie held back, standing under the trees behind Levitt's where she could see pretty much the whole picture, how it was all laid out and who sat where. She wasn't ready to commit herself. Sit by the wrong bunch and she'd get stuck in a bad place all day. She looked around for her granddaddy Simpson but it looked like he hadn't got there yet. Folks had started eating and the younger ones were choosing up for games.

"Hey, Sadie."

She looked around at him, staring at her, making her jittery inside with those wet eyes of his with the long girly lashes. "Oh, hey Mickey-Gene." She turned back to the picnic. She could hear him moving up behind her. She tried to ignore him, but he felt really big beside her. Even though he wasn't very big, he felt big.

"It's like a painting, aint it? A painting that moves."

Something hard loosened up inside her head. That's exactly what she'd been thinking, only he'd said it better. "What you mean, Mickey-Gene?" She didn't look at him.

"Well if you squint your eyes a little, and look at it all just so, they're like dibs and dabs of color, paint maybe, or pieces of cloth. Real pretty. But it's better cause they move around, like butterflies, or bees gatherin their honey. They get pulled this way and that, like there's a river of them, and you can see them flowin along, and changin course, and some of the little pieces in the stream, they jump out, and then they jump into a different stream, and if you look at it all long enough, well, I think you can tell what they're going to do next. At least I can."

Sadie didn't say anything for a time, because she was too busy seeing what Mickey-Gene was seeing. Then she said, "Mickey-Gene, you aint dumb like everybody says?"

She could hear him shuffling his feet. "Dont tell nobody. But I reckon not."

She heard a sound then, a complaining, unhappy kind of sound but with no words in it. It rose up out of the field and floated over everything. People lifted their heads and stretched their necks trying to find where it came from. Sadie knew right away. It was coming from where the Grans were sitting. Addie was the one. How she knew which one was Addie from this distance when they both looked the same Sadie wasn't sure. She just knew it was the kind of sound only Addie would make.

Addie was staring across the field and pointing, her face red and her mouth drooped open, and there where she was pointing was the preacher coming down that slope behind the livery, and he had two of his big saints with him carrying this long wooden box. Sadie could hardly believe it, but there was no mistaking it was the snake box.

The crowd separated to let them through, some of the folks clearly upset. A few even grabbed up their things and left. "You reckon he's got his snakes in that box?" Mickey-Gene asked.

"That's the box I guess, and he must figure folks are gonna *think* they's snakes in there. But I cant believe he'd take them out in front of the Grans." But Sadie wasn't looking at the preacher and his box anymore. She'd been looking at the crowd, and there on the edge of it, just after the preacher passed, she saw a black-haired woman she didn't recognize, all dressed in gray. She was staring at Sadie like she wanted Sadie to know something. The woman's gaze was so intense that it made Sadie look away, and when she looked away she found another strange woman dressed all in cream-colored clothes, staring at her. This woman had light yellow hair and a pale face and eyes that looked… Sadie couldn't even find the eyes they were so pale, and no eyebrows either, but the way that woman's head was pointed her way, leaning forward, Sadie knew the woman wanted her to pay attention.

And that's when Sadie could see them all so clearly, back under the distant trees that bordered the campground, and there between some of the buildings, and there, even there inside that overgrown clump of trees, where nobody could get into, and where the silver wraps of fog still lingered, a woman's pale head was clearly visible, staring at Sadie.

"Did you hear me? Did you hear me, Sadie?" Mickey-Gene was tugging on Sadie's arm. Gently, almost tenderly she thought, like he was trying to wake her up. "I said I know where the preacher gets his snakes."

She turned around. "I figured he just trapped them here local. You mean he dont?"

"Last summer I spent some time with Aunt Mattie's people around the coal camps above St. Charles. They kept tellin me to stay away from them hills up there, said they was full of holes cause of the mines, didn't want to have to explain to Aunt Mattie why I fell into one I reckon — she's pretty quiet but she can be a terror where children are concerned. Anyways, I talked one of the older fellers into takin me exploring, figured I'd find me some treasure. Silver maybe."

"They got silver around here?" Sadie frowned, glanced back at the celebration. The preacher was standing on that box of his getting ready to preach. The thought of all those snakes wriggling around under his feet while he preached made her own feet tingle.

"Not that I know of." He looked embarrassed. "I just liked the idea of it. It gave me pleasure. Anyways, we came up over a ridge and was coming around some trees when we saw his big old black hat and his coat, even though it was hot as He — Hades that day. He was looking into this dark hole there in the side of the hill and he was reading from this big old floppy Bible what seen better days, had it clutched up in his bad hand, you know, the one what's dark and kinda tore up."

"Yep, I know that ugly thing." The preacher was raising his voice, but the people were restless, maybe because of that snake box, and maybe because they didn't want to hear any preaching. So the preacher raised his voice some more until Sadie could hear the hoarseness in it. But she wasn't hearing too many of the words, because she was looking for those pale women in the trees and in the crowd, and she spied at least three or four more than before.

"And Abraham was *old*, and well stricken in age, and the Lord had blessed Abraham in all things. And as the Lord says in Genesis, I'm saying to you now, we gots among us here Addie and Elijah, surely two of the oldest of the old in this world, forebears and ancestors, progenitors and part of the Gibson original flesh! We've come here today to honor them, and eat as much food as possible!" There was some scattered laughter, mostly among the preacher's saints, but Sadie figured most people were reluctant to laugh in the preacher's presence, not being sure how he might take it. Sometimes what sounded like a joke from the preacher was just him making a point of being cruel.

Addie was still going on in the background, her voice rising and falling, but a little softer now, like she was running out of steam. People didn't seem to be paying her any mind, or maybe they were deliberately ignoring her. It was like she was just another part of the noise of the day, like the wind blowing through the trees — dark clouds were coming in, so maybe they'd get a little rain — or like the cows mooing in that pasture on the other side of the fence. But Addie's calling made Sadie feel sad — they shouldn't ignore the old woman, especially when she'd been so important to everyone here. And Sadie couldn't tell if it was the distressed sound of a creature that didn't understand what was going on, or understood far too much.

"Sadie, this is *important!*"

She turned back and stared at Mickey-Gene. "Sorry. There's just... I'm seeing lots going on today. What is it?"

"The preacher had a *woman* with him that day." Mickey-Gene's face was redder than usual.

"Did you recognize her?"

"Never seen her before. I dont think she's from around here. She had her arm around him, and she was all pressed up against him while he was reading them words from his Bible aloud, and in her other hand she had a bunch of feed sacks. And sometimes, well, she'd kiss him on the neck."

"Kissed him?" He might as well have said she'd grown wings and flown away.

"Yes, ma'am. And the more she kissed him seemed like the louder he got, and that's when all them snakes come out!"

"Then Abraham gave up the ghost, and died in a good old age, an old man, and full of years; and was gathered to his people!" The preacher's voice was loud and harsh and Sadie's head was suddenly full of it. And why was he going on so about old people dying? "And *aint* that the usual way of it folks? Nobody lives forever, not on this good earth! If a man is lucky he gets his threescore and ten, and fourscore maybe if he be a saint! But if he live past fourscore, why I dont know if he thinks he's a god or what, but there can only be one God, praise his name, and that be Jesus, Lord Save Us Amen! To everything its season! And may the old make way for the young, Hallelujah!"

"What snakes, Mickey-Gene?"

"Rattlers and copperheads, mostly, biggest ones I ever seen. They came outta that hole from somewhere deep underground. And they wriggled on over there to the preacher and he laid his Bible down on the ground and they swarmed up on it, twisting together into one and raising themselves up on it like they were almost as tall as the preacher. Then he moved his head up on them and I swear they kissed him on his lips with those slippy tongues of theirs and he fell back sighing and carrying on such, laughing and all, and he took the sacks off the woman and he held them open and those snakes just slithered on in to them like that was their homes. Then he tied all them sacks together and he turned on the woman and he just fell on her like some kind of animal pawing at her and tearing her clothes off! That older boy with me wanted to stay but I was so scared I couldn't wait and I just run away fast as I could! He came along behind me, finally. He was pretty mad, said I was a baby. I aint no baby, Sadie, but I dont need to see nothing like that."

"That's okay, Mickey-Gene. You done the right thing. You done the *smart* thing."

"And it came to pass a long time after that the Lord had given rest unto Israel from all their enemies round about, that Joshua waxed old and stricken in age! So he had to divide among them his lands folks! He was compelled by God to give them the inheritance they *deserved*, as the Lord your God hath promised unto you." The preacher was stomping his feet, and the box beneath them was rocking as a result, or from the movement of whatever might be inside.

Addie's complaint was rising louder again, and Sadie could see the agitation flow across the field. More people were gathering up their things and leaving. The pale women had disappeared from under the trees, and they weren't as obvious to her as before, but here and there she'd catch a glimpse of them — a twist of gray or a pale stretch of face. The sky had grayed out to the color of tarnished silver, painful to look at. She saw several people around the Grans, trying to calm down Addie, trying to talk to Elijah. She saw her Aunt Lilly crouched down with her momma, holding Addie's hands, trying to cover up her balding head. Uncle Jesse and her daddy were standing up, just watching the preacher, beers in their hands. And there were saints among them, moving around, looking at the preacher, then looking down, and not at all looking like they belonged.

"Mickey-Gene, we best get down there." She grabbed him by the hand and ran out into the middle of it, dragging him through the people, not sure what she was trying to do, just needing to get beside the Grans. She wished her Granddaddy Simpson was there — he'd know what to do, or at least might know what to say to her that might calm her down. She was a little angry with him that he hadn't shown up.

She felt a few drops of rain on her arm, and it was like it poisoned her, because in just a few seconds her entire body was cold. She saw the short, frail form ahead of her also headed for the Grans, and knew at once it was Granny Grace, who she hadn't seen all day, and it was like she'd just popped up out of the ground, and now was running for all she was worth. And that made Sadie scared, so that now she was running too, and dragging poor Mickey-Gene with her.

"As they tell us in Job," the preacher's voice bellowed behind them, and above them all, "You shall come to your grave in ripe old age, like a sheaf gathered up in its season!"

She wasn't thinking about those gray women then, but she kept getting glimpses of them, pale dresses and faces fluttering like moth wings, in and out between the townspeople. The rain had picked up, and Sadie's hair was sticking to her face. She felt like a fish in a net.

"As for yourself, you shall go to your fathers in peace; you shall be buried in a good old age. As the Lord said in Genesis, so it is now. There is a power in our people, but it is a power we have to seize. There is a greater destiny out there for the Gibsons, but only if we let go of our past and march on!"

By the time Sadie got to the Grans, Granny Grace was already sitting there between them, patting Addie's hand and whispering to her. Addie was still making that noise, but Sadie could barely hear it now, it was more like a gentle babble, and Addie was rocking.

Uncle Jesse was so drunk he could barely stand. Daddy and Aunt Lilly were talking to him, trying to get him to sit down. He staggered toward Sadie and Mickey-Gene pulled her out of the way. The rain was coming down hard now, and everybody was grabbing what they could to leave.

"Then he died at a good age, full of days, riches, and honor. And Solomon his son reigned in his place." The preacher was right there on the edge of their small bunch of family, staring at the Grans, speaking firmly as if lecturing children, the rain pouring down his face, his hair like dark vines tearing across his skin and curling around his neck.

Seeing the preacher Uncle Jesse raised his beer and stepped forward. Aunt Lilly tried to grab him but it was too late. Uncle Jesse slipped and fell right in front of Elijah, whose eyes went wide in surprise at the near-miss. Then he started to cackle, then laugh hysterically as Uncle Jesse tried to get himself up but couldn't. Finally Uncle Jesse fell back and lay there, saying, "Ah Lilly, I'm dying. I'm gonna *drown* out here!"

The preacher stepped forward and slammed his boot down into Uncle Jesse's belly. "Have some respect!" Jesse howled until Granny Grace leaned forward with something hidden in her hand. The preacher yelled and stepped away. Sadie could see blood running across the preacher's pants just above the boot. "That's the last time you'll be touchin anybody, witch!" the preacher shouted. Sadie watched as several of the saints entered the circle, their fists raised.

Mickey-Gene stepped between her and whatever might happen next. "Preacher," he said, voice wavering, "dont you always say there should be peace in a family?"

But the sky exploded then, the rain coming down even harder than before. Somebody helped Uncle Jesse up and Sadie and Mickey-Gene and some others went to pull the Grans out of the flood.

A few minutes later the group of them stood in the sheltered lane by the livery where they worked on the wagons. All except the preacher, who was standing out in the rain, staring at the rest of them, now and then looking straight up at the sky, sometimes opening his mouth and letting the weather inside. Daddy told him he should come in, told him he couldn't do much preaching if he was sick in bed, but the preacher didn't answer. Granny Grace squatted on the ground like a toad wearing a scraggly wig, staring back, looking like she'd bite his throat if he did decide to come in for shelter. Sadie noticed how she kept rocking back forth, moving side to side, and ready to do whatever to protect the Grans.

The box was in there with them, a couple of saints standing at each end, but Sadie didn't think there was anything in it after all — she couldn't see any movement on the other side of those holes. Had he just brought the box to stir things up? Just like she knew what Sadie was thinking, Granny Grace reached out her hand and stuck her forefinger up to the knuckle in one of the holes, grinning at the preacher the whole time.

Sadie heard a hissing. It made her heart stop, but Granny didn't even flinch. There was that hissing again. She looked around. There was Elijah looking at her with eyes like wet stones, his finger to his lips. She went over to him and crouched.

"It's *time*," he said to her, his voice eked out and thin. "Too big for his britches… he always were, but *now*." He spit toward the ground, but as far as Sadie could see nothing came out. "You're the only one… the only one who'll see it, who'll do something when the time comes."

"Gran, I dont know *nothing*…" She tried not to cry.

"You dont know all you know. You just dont," he said and sighed, closing his eyes as if too exhausted to explain. "You got to get that special Bible he has, the one he writes in hisself. He dont hold it forever, find out where he hides it. Without that maybe, maybe he cant do so much harm."

Elijah tried to say some more but couldn't, and finally just fell asleep. Sadie held on to his arm. She was just a little girl — she didn't care what her body was saying. It just wasn't fair.

Chapter Ten

ON HER WAY to school the next morning Sadie stopped at her granddaddy's house. It was another cool, gray morning, the heavy rains of the day before making everything look damp, the shadows melted and spread over everything, so that everything looked flat, like something had been taken away from the world.

She knocked on the front door, and knocked on it. Granddaddy was always up at sunrise, working, but she didn't hear a sound inside. The door was locked. It hadn't always been locked, but that had all changed when her granddaddy and her dad had that falling out. Granddaddy thought her dad stole things. She didn't think he did, at least she'd never seen him do it. She hoped he didn't. She'd always liked thinking that however bad he was, at least he didn't steal.

She went around the back and tried that door. Still no answer. He was probably out in the fields, working with his cows. He'd been feeling poorly lately, and he'd gotten behind in his chores. She'd offered to help him but he'd always turned her down, said she had to put all her energy into her school work, make something of herself. He was probably out in the fields. She thought about going out to the barn, but he was probably out in the fields, and she was going to be late for school if she didn't get going.

The path up the hill to the school was still muddy and deeply rutted from the horses and the school wagon that morning so she had to climb up on the bank and walk through the wet grass. The ground was pretty rocky which was why it was good for neither planting or pasture which was why it had been donated for the school house she reckoned. She'd heard the building had been a little barn for feed in the old days and then a small group made it their church but after a bunch of them went north for jobs the children got to have it for their school. Most of those church people were back now that the jobs were drying up all over but they became part of the preacher's group or they gave up praying all together. The school was higher than the town and it made her feel like a queen looking down from the top of that hill.

When Sadie got to the school building everybody else was already sitting down. Mrs. Welch looked up at her, and didn't smile her usual smile, but she went back to helping Little Jamie Collins with his arithmetic, and she didn't say a word. Mrs. Welch was like that — she didn't yell at you, but she noticed pretty much everything, and you felt bad if she noticed you doing something wrong. Sadie went to the back wall and hung her sweater up on a nail, then handed out the books to the first, second, and third graders like she was supposed to every morning. Some kids were assigned the stove and the coal bucket there in the middle of the room (everybody thought that was the best job because you got to be called "the fireman"), and some kids had to carry in the water pail, and some of the smaller kids had to do things like sweeping, but Mrs. Welch thought Sadie was the best reader, so she got to handle the school books.

The children Sadie's age were supposed to read while Mrs. Welch worked with the third graders in math. There was a shelf of donated novels at the front of the room, mostly ones that belonged to folks who had died and then the family gave them to the school. The older kids were supposed to choose one and read it and maybe answer some questions Mrs. Welch would ask about it. Some of the children gave a report to the class, but Mrs. Welch didn't make you if you were too shy. Mrs. Welch was nice enough, but that was the only time she seemed especially nice.

This last time Sadie had chosen *Papa's Little Daughters* by Mrs. Mary D. Brine. It had shown up on the bookshelf just two weeks ago, she didn't know from who or where. Like most of the books it was old — the front page said 1882. It was all about the nice Moore family who lived in a fine house in the city. She didn't think they were supposed to be rich but they were surely rich by Morrison standards, what with their library and sitting room and a chambermaid named Betty and nice dresses and a daddy who worked in an office downtown and put on a fancy coat every morning and read the newspaper. They even owned a canary in a cage with his own little dish for food. But for all that they seemed like just the nicest people and she was sure they'd be nice to her if she ever met them one time even if she was poor and shabby.

It was sad because their mother died right at the first of the book — the poor woman's pale skin and her blue veins showing — and the little girls Madge and Marjorie (the one with the lovely curls, and the one with "golden, flaxen" hair like Sadie had never seen and could barely imagine) were left alone with their dear sweet papa who laughed a lot and said things like "Goodness gracious!" and put them on his knee and hugged and kissed them all the time.

And then Papa's sister came from out west, the dark-eyed Aunt Grace, who was so nice and the daughters "were as fond of Auntie as though they had never known a dearer love."

The strange thing was Sadie could get so wrapped up in the lives of these two little girls and their worries even though their worries were pretty small when she thought about them, especially compared to folks living in the hollow — worries like what they were going to wear and what papa's big secret was and why one of them was being cross one day and all that.

Sometimes when she read that book she would look around at the other students — their shabby clothes and their broke-down shoes, their burnt skin, their spreading bruises, the way they coughed too much or sneezed too much, how skinny some of them looked, how pale — and she'd gaze out the window at the gray board shacks and the fallen down fences and the broken things in folks' yards and just how dirty everything was. Most everything she saw was messed up, forgot, or just uncared for. She wondered how it was that authors could write about a different way of life, a different story of what a person could be, but no one she knew could do that in the real world outside of them books.

Today it was hard to read because she was still thinking about the Grans' birthday and how disappointed she was that she hadn't been able to talk to her grandpa about it and because Mrs. Welch had to paddle some little boy in the first grade for misspelling "meadow."

She took her book outside at recess and watched the other children playing Round Town and Anty Over and Fox and Dog. She wasn't popular mostly because of her daddy and the rest of her family and what people thought about them. But she was pretty shy herself anyway and had never been too good at making friends. Momma always said she was too *sensitive*. Maybe she was. She always seemed to know when people didn't like her, or were annoyed with her, or were suspicious of her. They didn't have to say anything to her; they didn't even have to look at her. She just knew, and knowing was a hard thing sometimes.

She sat on a rock and ate her biscuit and jelly and her corncob. She read another page and then she heard some of the children yelling and there was Mrs. Welch dragging Andy Carter down to the toilets by his ear. Jane Gollaghon came up to her all out of breath. "He done dropped his reader into the toilet hole *on purpose*. Teacher says he's got to fish it out and take it down the creek for a bath!" Then she ran off to watch. Jane was the biggest gossip in school and only spoke to Sadie when she had news and needed somebody to tell it to, but Sadie was still glad to be included.

Something turning in the edge of the woods caught her eye. She stared at it and just like she thought it was one of those gray ladies again, looking at her. The way they kept bothering her made her mad and she tried to look back with hardness in her eyes, but that only made her see more of them, two more behind the first and another one to the right a few feet, that one particularly bad because her neck was bent to the side and she had blood trailing out of her mouth and onto her pale see-through dress. Only it wasn't like see-through naked. It was see-through like Sadie could see through to the trees standing behind that woman.

There was a sound coming out of those woods. It was long and lonesome, kind of like the sound poor Addie had made at the picnic. But with something extra, crying maybe but worse than crying.

She wondered if one of those gray ladies was the woman Mickey-Gene had seen that day up by the mines. But that was an awful thing to think about and she didn't want to think about it right now. She opened up her book and tried to read some more.

The words had changed so Sadie couldn't read them. They were wiggling around the page like worms, or snakes. Somebody had written on the page, doodles and drawings, pictures of such terrible things. There were some Bible verses and a house with a woman in it and bones and snakes and such. She wanted to look away but she couldn't help studying it. There was a room with a Bible in it and there was a church nearby. That was when she knew the preacher kept his special Bible in his house in its own special room.

SADIE WENT BY her granddaddy's house again right after school. The front door was still locked and there was still no answer, but when she walked around the side she was relieved to see the big barn door wide open. "Grandpa!" she called. "Grandpa!" maybe a little too loud and a little too excited. She started walking fast and by the time she reached the barn door she was running.

She couldn't see much at first, and when she heard a woman singing softly it confused and scared her. "Grandpa?"

"Over here child," the woman said.

Sadie walked around the edge of the first stall. Granny Grace was sitting there in the hay with her granddaddy. For a second she was embarrassed, not sure what she was seeing, not able to put any of it together. She didn't think she'd ever even seen her granddaddy lying down before. Her eyes went to his feet. He had his work boots on. They were fallen over, one to each side, like his feet couldn't handle the weight of them. His overalls were stretched tight over his skinny legs. The tail of his checked shirt had come loose, and one corner was now poking outside. He'd hate that. He'd always liked things neat and tidy.

Granddaddy's head was in Granny Grace's lap. She was stroking it lightly. His eyes were closed and his lips hung loose. He might have been sleeping but Sadie knew he wasn't.

"Used to buy my eggs," Granny Grace said smiling. "And he'd trade me for things. He'd ask me to make a powder for his feet, or something for his sore muscles. He didn't need it I dont reckon, but I made it like he needed it. He'd give me vegetables and meat, all kind of things. Once he asked me to make him a poultice for heartbreak, said he might need it someday. I told him not to use too much, might make the womens run after him. A good man, your grandpa."

"What happened?"

"Stroke, child. They used to say that's what the fairies did, touch your heart with they magic and make it stop."

"Cant you do something?" Then she was crying so hard she couldn't talk.

"I aint no fairy, honey. Aint no witch, neither, not really. I knows a few things. But aint no comin back from where your grandpa gone."

Chapter Eleven

MICHAEL WOKE UP on the couch twisted and sore, his head coming apart. He'd fallen asleep there listening to his grandmother's story. He staggered into the bathroom and stared at himself in the mirror. The right side of his face was deeply creased by the cushion. His eyes were red, inflamed, and there was a yellowish cast to the whites. He felt as if he'd been crying for days.

Of course he hadn't known his great great grandfather except through her memories, but when she told her stories they weren't like *her* memories. They became his rage and despair and sweet love, each a charge of pure emotion that ran through his veins like a drug, in fact so like a drug that he felt muted without it, disconnected from his primary sources of feeling. Almost immediately, when her stories stopped he felt in withdrawal. Having once been so reluctant to have her begin, now he didn't really want her to stop, didn't want to eat, sleep, dream on his own as long as she was talking. Even though her talking seemed to steal everything out of him, as if he didn't have his own life anymore.

As overwhelming an experience as it was listening to her stories of her long ago days, he couldn't recall many of the actual words she'd used to tell it. He'd begun to realize that she was using fewer and fewer words to tell these stories, didn't have the strength or the energy for any more. And yet his visualization of that lost year in Morrison had grown sharper with each of her tellings.

And there were other stray, trace images he didn't think had ever been conveyed by her, but which he had seen on his own. Whether they were real, whether they had actually happened, or if they were merely the random generations of his own over-reaching imagination he had no idea.

Lodged in his head like a stake was a vision of the preacher surrounded by several young women and numerous writhing, aggressively moving snakes. The women ran, but they were unable to escape being bitten, by the man, or by the snakes. The women fell to the ground around the preacher as the snakes returned to him, climbed his legs and encircled his body. Several bit him but he appeared unaffected. He seethed, near out of his head.

Michael looked at his watch. It was ten AM. He never slept this late; he was surprised his grandma had let him. "Grandma!" he called, running into his bedroom to change shirts. "Sorry! I overslept! Wait right there!"

He knocked on her door and went in — she wasn't there. He couldn't tell if she'd even been in there to sleep; she seldom fully made her bed anymore. It was something he should do for her, but she'd always seemed reluctant. "Grandma!" He went back through the house and paused at the door of the sitting room where the two of them had been chatting the night before, where he'd fallen asleep, but still — he now realized — hearing her. Had he even missed a word? Was she inside his dreams now?

She was still sitting in her rocker, but slumped over. He ran to her and gently grabbed her shoulders, pushing her upright slowly. "Grandma, wake up. You fell asleep in the rocker. Grandma? Grandma are you okay?"

She moaned softly, but didn't open her eyes. "Come on, Grandma, wake up!" He moved her shoulders, afraid to shake her much more. Her lids opened slightly. Her eyes looked pale, silvered. "I'm too tired," she whispered, so softly and with so little lip movement he wasn't really sure it was her speaking. "Cant do my chores."

Michael bundled her carefully into a blanket and carried her out to the car. His leg throbbed terribly, almost more than he could bear. He assumed someone at their small regional hospital could get her inside because he could already tell he wouldn't be of much more physical assistance the rest of that day.

As Michael was closing the car door a long skinny gray house cat crept out of the woods a few yards away. Michael stopped, trembling. Part of the left side of its head had been shaved, as if for some medical procedure. There was a long scar that ran from just below the left eye almost all the way to its mouth. It was the ugliest cat he'd ever seen — there was no way he'd ever forget it. But it was the same cat he'd seen in Denver a few days before deciding to come out here. He felt sure of it, except he couldn't be sure of it of course because it was impossible.

He hadn't been out driving in several weeks and it was painful to step on the brake. Still, he found himself tapping it almost immediately as he was leaving the yard. Down the hill in the overgrown ruins of the old church something had changed. Michael leaned over the steering wheel and stared: a section of the rusted tin roof appeared to be floating unsupported in the sky. He climbed out of the car and stepped in front of it, leaning back against the hood, wanting to go down for a closer look but not daring to leave his grandmother alone.

He wasn't sure when was the last time he'd looked downhill from the house. The last several days he'd been inside, taking care of his grandma or simply consuming her story for hours at a time. Probably the last time he'd given the abandoned church building a good stare had been when the crew was removing the kudzu from around the house, and that had been no longer than a week ago.

The mass of growing things inside the ruins had expanded an unlikely amount, branches and vines shooting out of every break in its shell, and the tree of heaven at its center had multiplied in size, outwards and vertically, and it was a branch of that tree now supporting the tin roof panel from behind. Michael didn't see any signs of kudzu in the ruins, but he didn't have time for a closer look.

Random sections of wooden wall drifted slowly into view, ensnared in vine and branch and pushed by what... wind? He couldn't imagine what else might have caused it.

The erased words had reappeared on these pieces, as discoloration or mold replacing the paint. *these signs* on one piece. *devils* on another. *tongues. serpeants*, that misspelling forever preserved. *shall recover.*

At the end of their lane where it met a larger but unpaved road of gravel and dust Michael smelled acrid smoke, with something green in it, like beans in a pot left on a stove to burn. The stench made his stomach turn. In the next field over men with kerchiefs over their mouths were setting fire to a massive wall of vine. The various ends of this vine wriggled above their heads as the vegetable pulp swelled, shrank, and collapsed. He turned onto the road and drove away toward the main highway and town, frustrated that he could go only so fast on the loose gravel.

Something about the road looked different. After a mile or so he realized it was much darker in the road bed than he remembered, more shaded. He leaned forward and peered through the top edge of the windshield. Long streamers of kudzu vine knitted the row of trees that ran alongside the road, with occasional screens of the vine dropping down and disappearing within the fields full of tall grass on the other side. A county road crew was busily chopping on the vine where it had attempted to cross the road. Other workers in the adjacent field were setting fire to it in sections. An old man in a tattered baseball cap and an orange vest waved him down, sliding off his cap as he approached.

"If yer going to town you'd best keep right at that branch up ahead. They gots things pretty tore up the other side. Kudzu rooted right there in the middle of the road. I never seen the like."

"I didn't think burning would do any good. I thought you had to dig out the crowns," Michael said.

"Knows your kudzu I see. Well, that's exactly right, but diggin up the crowns takes time, and we aint got enough. This crap's everwhere. Gots to keep the roads open first."

Michael did as he was told and eventually reached a cracked, but fully paved road where he could pick up speed. Every now and then he twisted around and checked on his grandmother. She still dozed, her breathing shallow but steady.

The road took them through the old part of Morrison. Most of the dilapidated buildings had been torn down. Levitt's Store was now supposedly an "antique emporium" but Michael had never seen any cars parked in front of it, and it was too far from the relocated downtown to catch any tourist trade. A couple of other buildings had been turned into barns; a couple of others had been partially demolished. A small house still had a board with *Miss Perkins' Dresses & Notions* etched into it and nailed up under the eaves, but Michael had heard it had been many things since Miss Perkins' day and now it appeared someone was living there. There were curtains in the windows and a child's swing set in the side yard.

A steep incline took them down off the hill and into a flat area where a relatively new metal sign proclaimed "Welcome To Morrison, Virginia. Please enjoy your stay." But there were no motels in Morrison so he couldn't imagine where these visitors were supposed to stay.

At least here there were a few signs of modern life: a grocery and drug store, post office, and gas station with a mini-mart attached. Back from the road a scattering of new houses with tiny lawns filled the area before the hills became steep again.

A little past the gas station a nice shaded lane lead him to the regional hospital with a park and picnic tables across the road. It all appeared peaceful and only lightly used. He pulled in front of the emergency room door and ran inside for help.

After an hour or so a Middle Eastern doctor with a heavy accent came out and explained they were going to admit her for a few days. It was probably just dehydration and they'd be better able to control her fluid intake if she stayed there. "And given her age. Does she have a regular physician?" he asked.

Michael was embarrassed to admit, "I dont know."

"Has she had any difficulty sleeping?"

"Excuse me?" The man's accent was so heavy Michael had some trouble understanding him.

"Has she slept?"

She'd been telling him her stories daily for several weeks. Neither one of them had gotten much sleep. "No," he replied. "At least not well."

While his grandmother napped Michael walked out to the park across the street and sat at one of the picnic tables. The grass was neatly trimmed, the trees perfectly, almost unnaturally, shaped. No one else was in the park. In the distance, above the treetops, was the raised dirt and rock embankment of the interstate by-pass, now thick with some more civilized vine than kudzu. He couldn't see the cars, but he could hear the susurration as they descended into the lengthy elevated stretch crossing several low valleys where the highway entered eastern Tennessee. He looked down at his hands. When had they scarred up like that? It must have been the day they'd taken the vine down from around the house.

He wondered if there was someone he should call about Grandma, but there really wasn't anyone left to call, was there? His parents were gone, and most of those Gibsons from her generation as far as he knew. Perhaps those people had had children who still survived, but it seemed doubtful any of them would even know who Sadie Gibson was. If any of them had that mysterious Gibson feeling — a small family within the family — then they wouldn't need to be told. They'd already know.

It was such a terribly sad thing, though, not having anyone to tell, not only for her, but for himself as well. He couldn't call Allison, and he'd burned so many bridges with his self-centered behavior, he had no one else to tell about the things that had been happening in his life. He was in a sense as unreachable as his mother had been the last few years of her life.

The one time he'd visited her he'd still been in college, and when he'd first driven up to Southwest Virginia State Hospital in Marion it had struck him how like a school it looked, like a small college or boarding school. "Reality School," he'd thought, a little embarrassed by his own flippancy. They'd brought him along with the other visitors into a large room with floor to ceiling windows. The walls were a pale green — they probably called it 'sea mist' or something like that. He supposed it was meant to be relaxing. He didn't imagine the walls ever looked completely clean in that color. And it made him think of drowning in a public swimming pool.

His mother had taken one look at him and ran into the corner whimpering, unwilling to come out. He never found out who she thought he actually was.

A statue of a miner was a few feet away near one of the park's many picnic tables. The plaque underneath was inscribed "To All the Ones Who Died." The nearby mines had been closed down decades ago. He wondered who around here besides his grandma still possessed first-hand knowledge of those times.

Hobbling his way was an almond-skinned guy with a wide jaw. He had a stick with a nail in one end he'd been using to pick up trash and drop into the black plastic bag in his other hand. When he was right up next to him Michael looked into his wet, dreamy eyes.

"I think I recognize you," he told the man.

The elderly fellow nodded. "I'm Mickey-Gene. So pleased to meet you. I'd been hoping to sometime. But I couldn't get up the nerve. Is she there in the hospital?"

They went into Sadie's room together. She was sitting up, looking all too bright and all too eager. "I waited," she said. "I got lots more to tell I reckon."

Chapter Twelve

HER GRANDDADDY'S FUNERAL took place on a Sunday afternoon. The sky was unusually blue that day, the few clouds hiding enough of the sun to keep things pleasant. Some of his people made the long journey from Wythe County way out on the other side of Walker's Mountain. A sister and some Simpson cousins, and a few of the cousins' little children and grandchildren who never even met her granddaddy and had no idea how to act at a funeral. They were a conservative, tight-laced bunch, and Sadie had never met any of them. Her momma hadn't seen them since she was a little girl, but she invited them to stay in Granddaddy's house. They told her that would be convenient, since they needed to go through Granddaddy's things. That made Sadie furious, but Momma told her, "that's just the way things are done, girl. It's the depression, or so they tell me, and the only way some folks can get ahead is taking whatever they can get offen their dead relations."

"But you're his daughter!"

"Ah Sadie, I wasn't much of one. He didn't want me marryin your pa, and he was right I'm sorry to say, but I always held it agin him. He tried to make up, but I wouldn't let him. Hold on to the ones what love you cause none of us'll be here forever. I dont deserve none of my daddy's things — they can have it all, if you ask me. Now, if you want something special, speak up now — I'll make sure you get it." The only thing on Granddaddy's farm Sadie ever cared about was Granddaddy, so she didn't even bother to answer.

Momma held up pretty well then fell apart at the funeral. Aunt Lilly might have been a help to her but she never showed up. Aunt Lilly didn't show up to a lot of things if Uncle Jesse was having a bad drinking spell. Sadie was shocked that her daddy came — even more shocked that he dressed up for it and even held Momma's hand when she was crying especially hard. But Sadie couldn't watch for long, afraid she'd start crying too, and the one thing she wasn't going to do was cry in front of that bunch. But she couldn't just leave her grandpa's funeral either, out of respect for him, so she just walked away from the bunch of them, and went out there among the headstones to think.

She didn't know how long this little patch up on the mountain had been a cemetery, but most of the dead people she knew were buried there. Folks said it was because of the beautiful view, like the dead would care, being in the ground and all. But people liked to have a picnic on Grave Decoration Day, and this was a plum spot for a picnic.

The headstones were all made out of limestone, which was everywhere in the hollow, used for foundations and wells and paths and such. Sharp ridges of the pale gray stone traced the hillsides like the exposed spines of giant skeletons, and from a distance this cemetery, too, looked like nothing more than a field full of rocks. She stopped to read a few, but the lettering on most of the old ones was practically worn off, the wind and the rain wiping them down to a collection of shallow bumps and soft grooves. She guessed folks didn't have much choice about what kind of rock to use but it seemed a shame to have gone to all that trouble to mark your last place in the world and all anybody would ever know was that there was a bunch of unknown bones under their feet.

Some of those older stones had a circular piece at the top with a star or a flower inside, and a few of the fancy ones had a carving of a vine or a rose bush growing out of a big heart. She didn't know what kind of vine that was, but reckoned it wasn't kudzu.

"You aint shopping for a stone are you?"

She looked up. Granny Grace was sitting on a stump a few feet away, grinning at her. "What are you doing here?" Sadie asked.

"Why howdy to you, too. Same as you, here to pay my respects to your grandpa. Cept I'm over here cause I'd make your family none too happy if I was over yonder. Come to think of it, why aint *you* over yonder?"

"Dont like them people much, most of them. Wouldn't want their like to see me cry."

"I unnerstand, child. More than you might think. You gots to wear a brave face in this world, that's for sure. You can always take it off at home, cept I guess not everbody can even do that." She held a hand up to shade her eyes and peered across the cemetery to where the graveside service was still going on. "Who's that sayin the words? It aint the preacher of course."

"Reverend Billings from just over the Tennessee line. I guess he knew Granddaddy in the old days."

"Well, least the preacher didn't try to horn in. I guess that's why them gray womens aint around."

"You see them too?"

"Yep, you and me. And maybe the Grans, cept they'd never say. Anybody else round here with the sight I dont knowed them."

"Who are they?"

"Dont know past theys dead women, and dead not too long I figure. And they belong to the preacher somehow."

Sadie hugged herself. "They keep lookin at me."

Granny Grace frowned. "Well now, I see them, but they dont look at me, so I reckon they got some kind of message for you, or they need somethin from you."

"But what?"

"Oh child, I dont know everthin. We just gots to take this one step at a time. Next up we gots to get the preacher's Bible away from him."

"You know about that?"

Granny Grace laughed. "I said I didn't know everthin. But I do know *somethin*."

SADIE AND GRANNY Grace stood back in the trees a long time watching the preacher's house. The only reason they knew he was still home was because of the yellow lamp flicker they could see through a window near the back, moving a few times as the preacher carried the kerosene lamp from room to room. Sadie was cold and scared and wanted to go home. She was sure her pale dress must glow in the dark — all the preacher had to do was peek out the window and he'd know for sure it was her. Granny Grace on the other hand was so dark and dirty and woodsy that Sadie could barely make her out and she was standing right next to her.

"Let's leave," Sadie hissed. "He's got church tonight and he'll be taking his Bible. We aint got no chance at it."

"Patience, missy. He'll be goin for supper soon. He wont take that special Bible to eat. He wont carry it round like that."

"How you know he wont be eating at home?"

Granny Grace sighed like Sadie was a two year old that didn't know nothing. "Cause he most never eat at home, not his supper anyways. Not that one."

"Where does he eat then?"

"Everbody knows he goes over to the Mullins sisters for supper most nights."

"*I* didn't know," Sadie said.

"That's cause you a youngin. And that's adult business."

"They're not even in his church! Why would he have anything to do with them? And why would *they* mess with *him?*"

"Cause he knowed better than messin round with women in his own church, that's why. And some women, they look at his ugly and they think it handsome."

"I dont understand."

"Granny Grace dont understand it neither, but that's how it be sometimes."

The lamp flicker bobbed suddenly among the shadows at the back of the house, then moved quickly past the windows to the front before appearing on the other side of the wire screen in the front door. It floated there a few seconds, and Sadie imagined its burning eye watching her, then it bobbed again and led the dark silhouette of the preacher out onto the front porch. His broad hat was tilted down. It moved side to side and then he stepped off the porch and around to the woods on that side of the house. The floating light rushed down the path and disappeared.

Granny Grace bounded across the yard, Sadie struggling to keep up. "Think he locked it?" she whispered to Granny on the porch.

"Your daddy locks yours?" Granny pulled a lamp out from under her shawl.

"Not that I know of," Sadie admitted.

Granny dragged her inside the front parlor of the preacher's house and struck a match. "Well I reckon the preacher feels safer than anybody." She lit the lamp.

On the back wall of the parlor was a framed picture of Jesus on one side of the door and a little photo of the preacher hanging on the other. His face was as white as a skull under his big black hat and his body an inky streak. Granny stared at the pictures, and then looked around the room. It was completely empty. "Preacher likes it spare," she said. "Come on. Lotsa lookin to do," and they rushed into the dark spaces beyond the door.

In the short dusty hall grit crunched under Sadie's shoes. Granny Grace pushed the lantern into the dark, open doorway on their left. Sadie squinted, at first seeing nothing, or not understanding what she was seeing, just bits and pieces, an axe driven into the floorboards near the center of the room, and stacked behind it the severed arms and legs, of chair after chair, pieces of tables and drawer sets, all kinds of furniture chopped and splintered and stacked like firewood.

Granny whistled through her missing teeth. "'Do not lay up for yourselves treasures on earth,' as they say in Matthew. Looks like the preacher done took it literal."

"What *is* this?" Sadie could hardly breathe.

"I dont know, child. I reckon it's the room where he does his frustratin.'"

They crossed the hall into the next room. Something soft brushed against Sadie's face. Thinking it a cobweb she lifted her hand and felt cloth. Granny raised the lantern. Ladies' dresses, hats, lingerie, hung from the ceiling. Granny moved the lantern around, shining it on the walls layered in more dresses, nightgowns, corsets and slips, a brassiere or two, a waterfall of what her Aunt Lilly called "unmentionables."

Sadie picked up a small pile of green cloth on the floor in front of her. It was a flimsy little dress, and there was a tag inside. *Miss Perkins'* it said. Sadie thought back to that day in the dress shop when she'd lifted the pretty little celluloid box. Mrs. Walkins talking about her missing daughter Phyllis and that green dress. The dress was suddenly a fiery pain in her hands and Sadie dropped it, tried to look away from it. She started to say something but Granny Grace kept moving the lamp, finding more and more things.

The lantern light flickered past a dusty, empty chair, but when Granny's arm brought the lamp back around a woman was sitting there in her undergarments, weeping softly as she removed her rayon stockings. There was something watery about her, and the undergarments too, flowing and transparent. She looked up suddenly, staring at them as they stood in the doorway. Her mouth gaped wide, the opening rapidly growing larger as her lips and the skin around them cracked and blackened and peeled backwards and away from teeth and bone.

Sadie's mouth made a noise and then the others rushed in, a flurry of pale flesh and liquid bone, hair rustling like dead weeds and dry leaves falling into bits and filling the air with their choking dryness and perfumes gone both sour and thick with a smothering sweetness. Sadie ran out of there and into the hall and then another door, turning around when she'd realized her mistake, but maybe turned too far because the next door didn't lead her into anything she recognized but another door and another and it seemed she could hear her own footsteps running away from her into distant parts of the house.

And then she was in a room that slithered. She couldn't see nothing, but she could feel the shifting around her, the folding on top of folding, the bend and the curve of muscle, the intense focus on her, the new warmth in the room. And the sound was almost nothing, just scale across scale, punctuated now and then by a dry rattle like seeds in a gourd.

More crunches beneath her shoes, and curled debris along her ankles. The air stank, but she couldn't place the smell. It made her think of decayed things, and places that hadn't been cleaned in a very long time. Everything waited for her, but she couldn't move.

Then footsteps and a light behind her as if somebody set fire to the room. The room was full of cages. The snakes twisted as if suddenly aware, their heads coming around, eyes reflected yellow from the lantern. But some were so large they could hardly move.

"Over there," Granny croaked softly behind her. "That one."

The light shifted a little, and there it was. The cage was slightly taller and wider than the others, and the front of it was hinged on one side, latched on the other. In the bottom of the cage was that big floppy Bible. Curled up on top of it was a giant copperhead, its jaws open so wide Sadie thought she could see all the way to the bottom of its insides.

"I'm gonna open that cage and get the snake out. You get that Bible."

"What? No, Granny — how're you going to do that? Can you talk to snakes?"

Granny cackled. "Child, you must think I got the real dark magics! No sir, I'll wiggle a little, sing a little. I seen the preacher do it oncet. Cant see why I cant do the sames."

"No, Granny, I cant…"

But Granny Grace had already started moving, gliding back and forth toward the cage and wiggling herself so hard bits and pieces of all the stuff she carried with her all the time started falling off and knocking and clanging on the floor. She was saying words, too, or saying/singing them, words like bugga loo and Sally too hedaya heyday hoo so sad so sad and lonely my my body and soul, sad words and excited words and speaking in tongues kind of words and words like in that song she heard folks said was popular a year or two back.

Then Granny reached out and slapped open the cage door and that copperhead flew out its entire length mouth open like a stocking chewing its way up a leg. Sadie shook and squealed and Granny backed up against the wall swinging the lamp back and forth between her and the snake. "Move girl!" she cried and Sadie did, though it confused her with the light swinging back and forth so her hand missed the cage the first time. "Sadie Gibson! Get that Bible now!" And then she did, clutching the thing to her chest and turning around. Granny made a final low sweep with the lamp above the floor that caught the snake and sent it flying like a broken stick and the two ran through the house and out the screen door onto the porch and into the yard and almost to the woods before Sadie stopped.

"Wait!" Sadie said, bent over and breathing hard.

"You okay, child?"

"What if it isn't the right Bible?"

Granny snorted. "It's a Bible, aint it? Big and floppy like a dead bird or somethin. I seen him carry it around."

"What if he has more than one and this one isn't the same one, the special one?"

"Well come here, then. You take a look and say what you think."

Sadie shook her head. "I dont know. How would I know? You're the special one, Granny."

"Child, I'm also the one dont know how to read. Just bring your eyes over here and tell me what they see."

They sat down together in the grass and Sadie opened the Bible on her lap. There were all kinds of strings and ribbons and strips of newspaper and such marking places in the book, and she went to each one looking for something that might tell her what she was really looking for. The preacher had drawn lines under a lot of things and drawn boxes around certain sections, and there were words written in the margins and between the lines she could barely read. Real words and nonsense words and made-up words that still made her agitated and sick in her belly. The words eventually gave way to doodles — circles and targets and crosses and such that got more and more complicated, smooth lines leading into crooked lines that spiraled down into and around the words. Then there were all these animal drawings with their heads and legs cut off, the blood dripping down and pointing to certain words. There were faces, too, faces with three eyes, then four, then six, horns and wings and long skinny tails coming out of the heads as if the heads were their own separate animals. Then there were these crude drawings of naked people, especially women with their breasts and that place between the legs exposed. Pictures that weren't very good, more like what a naughty little boy might draw and not like a grown man at all. But that made them even worse and she was ashamed to look at them how dirty they made her feel and thinking that was the way her own daddy looked at her body.

Then there were the drawings of snakes, snakes everywhere of all different sizes crawling up and down between the pages and along the tops and bottoms, and big long snakes that would wrap around two pages together all at once, and then that naked man with the big black hat and that snake where his man thing was supposed to be.

Then there were the painted pages, done with what appeared to be nail polish in bright reds, greens, silver and gold, the polish making hard, stiff areas and wrinkled areas in the Bible like small creatures had crawled in between the pages and died.

These painted areas made mouth shapes and head shapes and sometimes wings, sometimes horns and tails. And sometimes the preacher had left a Bible verse or two exposed and highlighted inside one of the mouths or maybe inside a belly as if the words had been eaten by a demon. So sometimes when she looked at a picture he'd made Sadie would read the passages out loud as well so Granny Grace could hear them.

So in Peter she read that "the day of the Lord will come like a thief, and then the heavens will pass away with a roar, and the heavenly bodies will be burned up and dissolved," and there was all this fire on the page and all these screaming faces. And "the heavens will be set on fire and dissolved, and the heavenly bodies will melt" as the colors ran down the page onto the bodies that burned or vanished below.

In Matthew "there will be great tribulation, such as has not been from the beginning of the world until now" and there were the golden gates painted across a spread of pages, and the fire that rolled out of them to burn the world.

And in Revelation, "the great dragon was thrown down, that ancient serpent, who is called the devil and Satan, the deceiver of the whole world — he was thrown down to the earth, and his angels were thrown down with him," and the painted fire destroyed page after page, and rising out of that fire the form of the dragon with his great black wings, his snakes riding upon them.

She handed the Bible over to Granny Grace, not wanting to touch it no more. "I'll keep it safe," Granny said. "The reglar church meetin is startin soon — you'd best be down there."

Sadie shivered then. "But why? I dont want to know one more thing about what that man thinks!"

"He dont let you quit, member? Least not without a fuss, and right now you dont need the attention of a fuss. Less suspicious if you're there. After all, we're takin his Bible away from him, and that's his mind and his heart writ down in there, his whole bein and his whole plan about what's to be. He aint gonna be none too happy when he finds it missin!"

Chapter Thirteen

SADIE SAT AT the back of the church in roughly the same spot as before, watching the people fill the benches, waiting for the preacher, sure that if he laid his cold eyes on her she wouldn't be able to bear it. She would stand up and confess everything and try to accept whatever he decided to do to her. But the time rolled on and the preacher was late and later still, so that unless please God he'd been killed out in the woods she was sure he must be up in his house searching for his missing Bible. The people got restless and started talking to each other, wondering about the preacher because being late wasn't like him. So they worried, and some of the men talked about getting up and looking for him, but they never did, because getting on his wrong side was a risk they clearly didn't want to take.

Uncle Jesse staggered in, bumping against people and saying a loud "Excuse me, praise God, Lord help me Je-sus!" every time, again and again, repeating it even when he didn't bump into nobody, and still saying it when folks shushed him, just saying it a little softer when he finally sat down.

Aunt Lilly rushed in after him looking really upset. She grabbed his arm and tried to pull him out of the pew. "Please, Jesse! Let's just go on home!"

"Woman get off me! I'm here to listen to some mighty fine *preachin!* I told you one of my kin was a preacher didn't I?"

"Jesse, please! Dont let him see you like this!" She looked over her shoulder at the open church doors and the empty hill. No signs of the preacher — he was late. Several men tried to help her get Jesse to his feet but he fought them all off. Finally he got up and ran around to the front of the church. He stared at the cross as if he didn't recognize it. Then he turned around and glared at the congregation. Then he smiled a little lop-sided. "Preacher's runnin a little late tonight looks like," he said. "Did I ever tell you all he's my kin? A brother in Christ, a brother in blood. He says they're the same — I aint so sure. But as his kin, I reckon I'm next in line, so here goes the first part of my sermon."

His eyes rolled to the top of his head. Sadie thought he was going to faint, but then he said, "Oh Lord, bless this here mess! I know I'm a big old ass, but I'm your ass, I swear!"

A couple of women in the front row gasped, but there were scattered chuckles among some of the men.

Suddenly Jesse turned and pointed at one of those men, shouting, "You're wearin a smile in my church! You're wearin a smile in my church! Well *damn* you to Hell! See if you can smile with my foot up your ass!" He looked dark and furious, then suddenly smiled. "Only joshin. But *dont* let it happen again!"

Uncle Jesse tried to prance then, but could only stagger. He almost fell onto an old lady in the front pew, ended up sitting right next to her, his head lolling onto her shoulder. He appeared asleep, but suddenly jumped up swinging his arms like he was ready to fight somebody. "Holy! Holy holy holy ghost hallelujah! Dont let the Holy Ghost creep up on ya! Dont let him stick his hand in your pocket and steal your money! Dont let him kiss your wife or do none of that nasty stuff to her naked heavenly form by God Hallelujah!"

"Jesse!" Aunt Lilly yelled from the congregation.

"Hey now!" He waved his finger. "Dont interrupt the preacher while he's a-preachin! We dont allow no interrupters in this here church! No sir! We dont allow no retrobates, ingrates, crazy eights, or yellow apes who masturbates! No sir! We only want good clean Christians in this here church! No irritatin masturbatin stay up late-in scoundrels wanted here! No sir!"

Some men were still chuckling, but most of the congregation looked disgusted and angry. A stern looking saint came up the aisle with his fists balled. Jesse managed to stumble out of his way yelling "Bring out the snakes! Bring out the snakes! *They'll* protect me!"

Aunt Lilly came up out of the congregation, crying and shaking. "I'm so, so sorry. Oh Lord, please forgive this drunkard of a husband I've been saddled with all these years!"

"Hey, woman, a little respect! Aint I a man of God? Dont I have me a big black hat?"

Some more men came up to the front, their hands raised, mouths set. "Oh please dont hurt him," Aunt Lilly cried. "Just let me get him home, let him sleep it off?"

"Where's my snake box? Oh, Lordy, somebody done stole my snake box!" Jesse started lifting women's skirts, looking under benches, saying "Have you seen my snake box? I think some devil done stole my snake box!" And "Dont worry, ladies — I might a-been lookin at your undies, but I swear hit twere for Jesus purposes only!" Then he ran to the front doors and closed them. "I know my snakes is in here! Ladies you know what a preacher's snake looks like, now dont you?"

The doors exploded open. The preacher stood there glaring at the congregation as if he blamed every last one of them for what had happened during his absence. He wore his broad hat firmly on top of his head, but his white shirt was loose, sweaty, hanging out of his pants on all sides. Sadie found it a little shocking to see him at church that way, so sloppy and uncontrolled. His upper body looked swollen, and writhed beneath his shirt when he moved.

He grabbed poor Uncle Jesse by the throat and lifted him up on the toes of his boots. Uncle Jesse turned pale, then red as he struggled to breathe. Aunt Lilly came running over and pulled on the preacher's arm. "He's just drunk. He dont mean no harm. You know when he gets the drink in him he has no idea what he's doing! Please! He's your own *kin*. You're gonna *kill* him!"

The preacher turned his head slowly and stared at Sadie. It was like he was asking her "Do you want this? Do you really want this?" and Sadie felt like telling him where his Bible was, who had it and why, but she couldn't make herself move.

The preacher dropped Jesse. Aunt Lilly ran to support him so he wouldn't fall to the floor. Then the preacher tore off his white shirt and threw it down.

He had a giant rattlesnake curled around his belly and wrapped up over his chest and under one arm. His skin was something terrible to see, slashed and torn and bitten, a lot of it old scars but some of it fresh wounds. In places the muscle looked torn away, and the spaces left behind were dark and twisted up, ridged with gray scar lines. He stepped forward and grabbed Jesse by the back of the neck and pulled him toward him, dragging Lilly with him when she wouldn't let go.

"Is this what you're looking for Brother Jesse?" the preacher screamed, as the snake darted forward and opened its mouth into Jesse's face.

Jesse went rigid. As the snake came closer he closed his eyes. Aunt Lilly screamed. The snake kissed one of Jesse's eyelids, then the other, but did not bite.

The preacher pulled Jesse into his embrace and the rattler crawled over them both. Aunt Lilly jumped back, hand over her mouth. The preacher put his lips to Jesse's ear and talked rapidly, but so softly no one could hear what he was saying. Finally he kissed Jesse on the lips and stepped back. The snake slid lower along the preacher's body and clung there perfectly still.

"Take your man home, Sister Lilly!" the preacher commanded. Aunt Lilly grabbed Jesse's hand and started to lead him away. Then she stopped and looked at Sadie.

"I need you Sadie. Somebody needs to help with the kids while I get him straightened out."

Sadie jumped up and ran ahead of her aunt and uncle out the door. She avoided the preacher's eyes. Out in the cool dark air she felt relieved, and suddenly free.

Chapter Fourteen

UNCLE JESSE SAID nothing on the walk home. Sadie would steal a glimpse of his face now and then, and every time she'd be sorry she did. His jaw looked stiff and frozen, but he kept twitching his lip side to side, like he was trying to work something off the skin there, but he couldn't get it off, and he was suffering for it. It was there in his eyes, a pain in just seeing. Aunt Lilly would ask him questions, and all he would do was curl and uncurl his fingers, like he needed to grab something but there was nothing around to grab.

Their little shack was even worse than the one Sadie's family lived in. Uncle Jesse had never been much for work, or doing repairs. So Aunt Lilly took on most of the chores herself, but what with three kids to take care of she could never keep up, and their house just got worse and worse. When the three of them arrived one of Aunt Lilly's own aunts was watching the kids — she had about a hundred aunts on her momma's side. She told the old woman to go home, but the aunt hesitated, watching Jesse go back into the bedroom without a word to nobody, sitting on the bed inside and staring at his hands, still curling, uncurling like he couldn't stop them.

The aunt looked at Lilly but Lilly just shook her head. Sadie had heard before that Lilly didn't like sharing her troubles with kinfolk on that side of the family. "Are the children asleep?" she asked.

"In bed, not asleep. You know they dont fall sleep till you're home."

"How come you dont bring them to church?" Sadie asked, but knew right off it was a stupid question.

"Aint the type of church you want to bring younguns to. Bad enough we have to go. Sadie, go in there and sit with the children while I talk to your uncle."

Sadie opened the bedroom door and went inside, closing it as snugly as she could behind her. There were spaces between the boards around the door so you could still see a sliver or two of the living room. Sadie stood in front of them so the kids couldn't even see that.

A lamp burning in the room was turned down low. Three little heads popped up from under the covers and stared at her. "You're Sadie," the biggest one said.

"And you're Joseph. We've seen each other lots of times before. Like probably ever day of your life."

"You're just our cousin so we dont have to do what you say." The other two heads nodded.

Sadie tried not to smile. They were so cute. Their skin was like a dark yellow color and their eyes enormous and black. "I guess we'll see about that. I'm not telling you nothing, but your momma says you got to stay in bed."

"Why dont she come in and tells us our story?" the littlest head, Abigail, said.

"She's busy talking to your daddy right now. But I can tell you a story." She heard Lilly speaking in the other room, softly at first, then sharper, angrier. *Why you drink when you know where it always goes?*

"What *kind* of story?" the middle one, Bill, asked.

"Your momma ever tell you a Jack story?"

"Jack and the Beanstalk? That old thing? A thousand times!" Joseph declared.

What's wrong with you? Dont look at me that way! You're the one messed up with your drinkin and your foolin! Nobody thinks you're funny, you know?

Sadie spoke louder, moving her hands around. "Well that sure is a Jack story, one of the most famous! But there are others. Let me tell you another. This one is about Jack not working.

"In fact Jack was just the laziest, the sorriest thing. His ma and pa needed all kinds of work done round the place but he wouldn't lift nary a finger!"

Joseph said, "I like old Jack" and all three children giggled.

Out in the other rooms Sadie could hear a loud slap and Lilly crying. Then Uncle Jesse started talking, but it wasn't exactly his voice. It was a rough voice full of hate and sour spit, kind of like the preacher's voice but not like the preacher's voice. Maybe it was like Jesse's voice would be if he'd been swallowed whole by the preacher.

As they tell us in Proverbs, if a husband can trust her, a wife will greatly enrich his life. She'll bring him good, not harm, all the days of her life. That aint too much to ask is it — it's in the Bible!

Sadie tried to keep the shaking out of her voice. She couldn't quite manage it, but maybe the children wouldn't notice. "Jack was just so very lazy. His parents kept on telling him they needed him to work but he just flat out refused! But maybe if he got a job somewhere else he could still live at home."

Doesn't Peter tell us you wives must accept the authority of your husbands? Isn't that your duty to God? Peter tells us that submission makes us the kind of person God designed us to be!

"Is that Daddy? Did something happen to Daddy's mouth? What's he talkin about?" Abigail asked.

"That's just adult talk, honey. It aint for us younguns."

Obey the voice of the Lord your God! Jesse's voice was like thunder. Aunt Lilly began to wail.

"Sadie?" Joseph sat up in bed and stared at her.

"So his mother fixed him a snack for the trip to find himself a job somewhere else. But he ate the snack before he even left the house!"

Out in those other rooms Jesse's voice continued to distort, rising louder and louder and drowning out Lilly's screams. Sadie thought maybe she should go out and check on her but she was too scared and besides she couldn't leave the kids. Clearly her uncle was under the influence of a lot more than alcohol. It was like his voice and his head and everything else had been turned inside out.

Man's gotta run things his own, that's what my daddy always said. Lord knows it's in the Bible, just using fancier words. Dirt's his work, farmin it, hell — it's his life an family too. Cant show no weakness in your muscle or the death'll creep in. Weaken ya, like a hook worm suckin on your bone growin and eatin. But what can a real man do bout it?

Nothin, I'd say, but what do he do with it? Start gettin old, wind take the fire outta yer dirt, not much growin no more, not your corn, not your tobaccy, or your pecker. Ya wring your hands, your snake, ya cry in the dirt afore that plowin gets done, goddamn it's a hard life!

Abigail started crying and Sadie picked her up and began stroking her hair. "So Jack, he walked for a long time and he got real tired and hungry. Then he came to a big stone house with golden gates. He walked up to the gates and a man came out and asked him kind of unfriendly like, what do you want? He told the man that he wanted a job. And the man said, well, I do have this one job. It's killing giants!"

My daddy used to say yer woman's gotta be quiet, she takes it all in, holds it fer ya. Member when I met you? I picked up that stone, bout thirty pound threw it in the pond just to show you how strong I was, reglar hoss. Only a few days later we was married. Takes a strong man to win a woman like you.

Member how we used to work the fields together, two yoked mules, my arm aroun you, yer brown skin gettin browner, so's after years I could hardly tell you from the earth hitself. Sweet, under the loam, after chores, yer skin would shine through all yer sweat, just like the sun. To have a purty woman to talk to, it's alright. Yer body, she made me fly, but you never said nuthin, didn't go nowhere. You was just dead in yer eyes!

The other children now clung to Sadie and she was rocking them all. "And then the man told Jack that these giants were ten times bigger than a real man and had many many heads! What was he going to do?"

Tryin to be a man, it's a hard thing. Daddy never told me it'd be so hard. Bein a man, ya gotta take it all on, pretend them muscles dont hurt, that rheumatiz. And when yer woman's got misery, and gets all sour with you, well you gotta pretend it didn't even happen. It eats you up inside! So's ya gotta bitch bout something else. Dammit, ya know ya gotta be some kind of a king, even when the throne's just some shitty hole.

Cant let yer woman beat ya. Aint gonna be no woman's dog!

"The man gave him good food and told him to go cut some wood with an ax." Sadie couldn't keep the tremble away from her words. The tremble came out and it took over everything she tried to say. "But Jack knew if he cut the wood, the giants would hear him and come, so what was he supposed to do? How was he ever supposed to keep those giants away?"

Whatya gonna do, when yer hurtin? Daddy didn't tell me that. Drink some turpentine, some sugar, dont help. Man's gotta have somebody ta talk to. But ya just cant let her know yer down. Woman's gotta obey, less it be a crime. Dont milk the cow, she dry up. Dont spread the manure, fields dry up. Dont can nothin, aint got nothin fer winter. That woman dont obey ya, ya aint got no home. But hell, what ya do? Damn if she dont take you all inside. She dont open her mouth, she dont let you out.

Daddy'd say a woman gots magic, an I'd believe him. Her flesh'd cure all yer ills, she knows things a man dont. Look over an the woman be watchin me, quiet, an I knows she beginning ta find me out, takin me inside, knowin me, hidin me, ever night, stealin what I got, takin it, inside her an she never let it out again.

She's gonna take what I got an beat me with it. I'd beg her ta give it back, cryin, then gettin madder, cause she made me cry, wouldn't say, wouldn't give it back.

Uncle Jesse's voice kept changing. Sometimes he sounded like himself, and sometimes he sounded like the preacher, possessing him. He sounded like all the men in her life full of their weakness and delusion and unaware of the pain they caused everyone around them, instead blaming it on the women, persecuting the women, killing the women out of that terrible, devouring rage and emptiness she would never understand even if she lived into her eighties.

So's I hadda knock her down, rip open that purty pink robe, reach down where she kept it all, them things she wouldn't say or do for me, and I saw myself, all red and angry, bleedin, an

Lord I just had to rip it out!

Sadie heard the rapid climb of Jesse's voice on the other side of the door, until he was screaming, and Lilly was screaming too, first in terror, and then in pain, her throat finally making a sound unlike any human being should ever have to make. The kids were crying and screaming now, and Sadie pushed herself against the door in case he decided to come in after them. She didn't want to look, she didn't need to, having seen it all before in that vision at the store several days ago. She held onto the children and whispered to them, telling them it would be all right even though it never could be, and despite herself she turned her head and with one eye at the crack watched as Lilly's screams reached their peak, and all that blood filled the room, and Jesse curled and uncurled his fingers, casting that bloody bit down like a dirty rag, and howled.

Chapter Fifteen

MICHAEL WALKED OUT of the hospital and crossed the parking lot slowly, feeling as if he might break into a run, but not trusting himself enough to do so. He'd trip and break a leg, or run into some small child. Right now he couldn't bear the thought of kids getting hurt.

Not having a regular job, he'd actually forgotten it was a weekend, a prime visiting day at the hospital. His leg still wasn't quite right, maybe never would be.

For such a small hospital, they had a lot of visitors. But southern families were close-knit, at least that's what everybody said. Home was something special, and if your loved one couldn't be at home you brought home to them until they'd recovered. Perfectly normal-looking families hung out in the downstairs lobby or on the lawn or in the park across the street. He didn't see a thing wrong with any of them. Some of the kids were crying, but even in the best of times there were always kids crying, complaining about some small or imagined hurt. The problem was, you couldn't always tell if their hurts were small or monstrous.

He made it across the lot and across the road to the well-kept park where he threw up in a trash bin, had nothing to wipe his mouth on and took a chance on a napkin someone had thrown away. A little further in beneath the trees he lay down in the grass. He could still taste the blood in his mouth, and his nose still detected a faint trace. His brief touch of that cold and angry heart would be with him the rest of his life.

He could not begin to calculate the strength such an act had required, or the insanity necessary to generate such strength.

He gazed at the sky through the filtering green of the trees, breathing deeply and allowing the fresh air to steady him, to drive out the raw taste of the past with the light and air of this fresh new day. The car was still in the parking lot and the tank three-fourths full. He could get in it and drive, maybe sleep in the car until he found some work for a room, some food, and more gas that would get him even further down the road. Eventually he could get a better job, enough money to settle in with, meet some people and make some friends, and give regular life at least another try. No one needed to know about the family he'd once belonged to.

He had no responsibility here. He hadn't been alive when these events occurred.

Why had his grandmother needed to show him this? If it was to let him know what an evil man the preacher had been, he'd already figured that out. But what did it matter now? All those people were dead.

Or was it meant to provide him with a touchstone for his own anger, his own coldness? No use denying it was there. So far he'd been singularly unlucky in relationships — he'd never found that balance between caring and needing. It was hard not to resent the one who wouldn't give back when a good and happy life seemed just within reach. And there was something about that particular resentment that seemed unfortunately male. But still, even when his mother died and he'd gone into that dark place, even there he hadn't touched such coldness. Of what concern to him was the reality that this existed in other men?

He sat up on the grass. The day had gone on without him, and now the sun was falling behind darkening clouds. An ancient black pickup truck idled in the almost-empty parking lot. The door and fenders were creased, bent and rebent, straightened so many times that the metal looked like crepe, with spider webs of rust tracing the paint. Flaking gray plywood had been used to extend the short walls of the truck bed, and then the edges cornered with scrap aluminum to make a box. A battered garbage can lid with big hinges attached was mounted on the back end of that box.

At first he thought the truck cab was empty, and then noticed the top edge of a dome of skin, textured like an old leather basketball, and of a similar color. It bobbed, and then the driver's side door sprang open, as if kicked.

A short, squat figure in overalls climbed down to the pavement. The face looked both wrinkled and swollen, and all of it liver-spotted, or sunburnt. Before the truck door closed Michael saw that figure's twin sitting on the passenger side, smoking, staring at him.

The squat figure walked bowlegged across the lot and the road and into the park and up to a tree near where Michael was sitting. Michael decided it was male when it unzipped and let loose a stream of urine on the tree. The head turned and nodded. "Cant abide a hospital toilet."

After a couple of minutes the man zipped and turned around and walked over. He smelled of tobacco smoke and lotion. "How do." The old man moved his pale pink, swollen tongue around inside his mouth a great deal. "Be much obliged if you'd join us over there. That truck? We'll be leavin soon."

Michael tried to gauge the danger of going somewhere with this stranger and decided that at least for the moment he didn't care. "Okay." He climbed unsteadily to his feet, feeling as if he'd been knocked down and dragged for some distance.

The little old man climbed up on the running board and yanked on the door handle. The door flew open and the man fell backwards and Michael caught him before he hit the ground. He made a sound like leaves crackling and Michael decided he was laughing.

"Elijah! Dont be an old fool!" the other figure said.

Michael was so shocked he almost dropped the little man. He leaned forward to get a closer look at the little bald woman smoking in the passenger seat, her matching overalls, her simultaneously swollen and wrinkled face. "You're a Gibson all right." Her left eyelid struggled to wink over an eyeball that was mostly cataract. "Too ugly to be nothing else."

Again Elijah made that dry, somewhat painful laughing noise. "Never thought to swap her," he said.

They sat in the pickup for a while, Michael in the middle towering over the Grans, quiet except for the engine, ready for a fast departure for whatever reason. He had a dozen or so questions to ask, but their manner didn't encourage questions, so he held himself back. If anything, their presence encouraged speechless awe, and maybe a bit of fear.

A narrow passage had been cut through the back of the truck cab to allow easy access to the plywood enclosure in the bed. A towel hung over the opening but it gapped enough on the side for him to steal a peek — a mattress, clothing piled everywhere, an avalanche of machinery parts, household knick knacks, papers, and food. It seemed a smaller version of their house at the top of the ridge, a place he'd never been.

"Came to visit your grandma," Addie said.

"You went upstairs?"

"No need."

"Cant abide a hospital," Elijah said.

"She knows we're down here," Addie said. "It's enough."

"We tried to help your ma," Elijah said

"You knew my mother?"

"Didn't help. Probly made it worse." Elijah sighed deeply. "We sure got our share of crazy."

"You help out your grandma?" Addie patted his arm with her tiny, narrow fingers.

"I try. I'm not sure I know what I'm doing exactly. I don't know much, about any of this."

She patted him again. "We never knew," she said. "We were stupid."

Elijah cackled. "Never thought to swap her! Just tried to figure who she wanted to be, then I stayed out of her way!"

"He aint askin bout us, old man!" She coughed, then she whispered, "I reckon he's askin bout the preacher!"

Elijah patted Michael on the knee, and after a few seconds they were both patting him and rubbing his arms as if he were a child who needed comforting. "Problem with us Gibsons," Elijah said, "is some of us go crazy, an some of us live too long, and some of us..." his voice dropping low and cracking, "are just too damn hard to kill."

And then they had no more to say. They sat there quietly, the two very old people patting him on the leg, the knee, smiling, but not saying a word. After a few minutes Addie said, "Time to say goodbye."

Michael impulsively leaned over and kissed them on the tops of their heads and climbed out of the cab, closing the door behind him.

Elijah turned and looked at him with his cloudy eyes. "Well, that's something never happened before." He smiled and drove away.

When Michael got back upstairs his grandma was asleep. Mickey-Gene sat on the edge of the bed holding her hand. He turned and looked at Michael. It was hard to tell if he'd been crying — apparently his eyes always looked that way. "You know I never forgot about you," Mickey-Gene said. "I was always wondering what you were doing with your life."

Michael had no idea what he meant. Maybe it was just this socially-awkward old man's attempt at politeness. "Thanks for sitting with her," he replied. "I... I just needed to take a break."

"Oh sure, sure. Anytime." Carefully Mickey-Gene placed her hand on top of the covers. "She's so tired. She asked me to tell you the next part. It's okay, I was there."

"I... I dont know that it would work the same. Grandma and I, well, there's a special connection when she tells it."

"I know, I know. But it's okay, really. I'll get us both back there — I promise."

Chapter Sixteen

MICKEY-GENE WENT early to the mill as he did every morning. Even with all the trees and the stream turning the wheel the building got so hot in the afternoon he usually had to quit by three. Hopefully enough folks had come by with their bushels of shelled corn by then to make it worth his while. He took a gallon of shelled corn for every bushel he ground into meal and gave back to the customer in those cotton sacks. It wasn't much but still enough to trade for what he needed, and he didn't need much. He lived with his Uncle Ralph who owned the mill but sometimes on cooler days he just stayed at the mill all day and slept there. His uncle said that was okay it kept him out of trouble but really it just kept folks from bothering him. Both Uncle Ralph and Aunt Mattie were good at keeping crazy folks from bothering them and they'd tried to teach the same thing to Mickey-Gene.

He had figured out a long time ago that the best way to survive this family was to stay out of everybody's way and not let on how much you knew about anything.

Besides, he liked it here. It was the quietest, prettiest part of the county. It was a business, but he wasn't busy all the time — he'd go days without anybody showing up. Then he could read, or daydream, or figure things out, or whatever he took a notion to. And survive. He had a box full of books he read over and over: Shakespeare's *Complete Plays*, *Babbitt* by Sinclair Lewis, John Dos Passos' *Three Soldiers*, Jean Toomer's *Cane*, Faulkner's *The Sound and The Fury*, and *The Age of Innocence* by Edith

Wharton. He liked some of Shakespeare more than others, but all of it seemed strange, set in some other world a universe away from here. And the *language* — sometimes the words were living things, full of breath and blood and capable of biting you if you weren't careful. Wharton's book was all about a life unlike any he'd ever heard of — he couldn't quite understand these people, but he kept reading the book anyway.

In *Cane* there was this one sentence, "Call them from their houses, and teach them to dream." It was about the most beautiful thing he'd ever read.

Years ago a rock slide had taken out the dirt road on the mill side of the creek. That was how folks used to get their corn to the mill. But after half the ridge came down they either had to abandon the mill or find another way, so his uncle built this swinging rope bridge across the creek, and lined the bottom of it with boards so that it was two planks wide, and the people had to carry their bushels of corn over on that narrow footbridge.

Sometimes Mickey-Gene would look across from the mill and see some child the parents had sent on the chore, or some older person, and they'd look scared, and he could feel their scare right down into his bones and he just couldn't bear it so he'd run across and tell them to rest up there on the bank while he milled their corn for them, and then he'd carry their bushel down to the mill.

Today he'd be closing early for Lilly Gibson's funeral. Of course her folks were organizing the funeral and none of the Gibson family was invited because of what Jesse done, but they were going to show up anyway because they all had loved Lilly. They would just stand back a little, down the hill, watching and paying their silent respects. Her little kids had already been taken to her sister's house in Tennessee to live. The Gibsons knew they'd never see those children again and that was a hard thing.

He didn't do well in groups of people. He especially didn't do well at family gatherings. So today he spent some time relaxing and doing the things he enjoyed most in order to armor himself for the coming ordeal. He dipped into his box of books and read passages at random. Maybe that was a strange thing to do — he didn't know because he didn't talk to any other readers. But he liked the feeling he got from it — that sense of a solitary voice singing out from a strange and unknown place, and trying to trace it back and discover where it had come from.

The Sound and the Fury was a difficult book. He didn't know how others perceived it, but he suspected that most people thought so. It seemed to him that the book was all about communication, how difficult it was to make it happen, and by going into characters' heads like that, so completely, well he'd never seen anybody do that before. It was a demonstration of empathy, and how strange empathy was, because you never could predict, could you, what went on in other people's heads.

This "feeling" the Gibsons were always talking about — Mickey-Gene had decided a long time ago that it was *empathy* they were talking about. In certain circumstances they could understand what other folks were feeling in a deep way — as if, just briefly, they *were* them. It worked best with other members of the family, but sometimes it worked with other people too. The preacher had it, Sadie had it in spades, and he himself had it, the Grans, hell, maybe all of them in varying degrees.

But the understanding didn't necessarily make you *nice*; it didn't even make you kind. You just *knew* — that was all. You could use that power to make other people feel better, or worse. Once inside their heads, you could push them anyway you wanted to.

Mickey-Gene couldn't tolerate it. He had to shut it off a long time ago — that was why he was so alone in the world. He didn't understand how most of the others used it, or tolerated it. The preacher used it to destroy people, like Jesse and Lilly, just because he could. He could control those snakes with it. The preacher could find it in the blood and push the blood however he wanted.

And someone like Sadie, she could be kind with it. She wanted to be kind with it, but sometimes she was so beset, her life was so hard, she just didn't have the will to be as kind as she might. But maybe he could help her with that. Now that she saw him as no one else saw him, now that she was the only one who saw who he was, he would do anything for her. He thought he'd loved her all his life, but his Aunt Mattie, she'd seen it in his eyes when he looked at Sadie, and she'd said, "No, Mickey-Gene, she's your cousin. That aint for you, Mickey-Gene," and that might be true, but he'd still felt it as cruelty when she'd said it, and he'd had to run away rather than hit her.

But he'd thought enough for the day. Thinking so often hurt his heart and he had to shut it off for a while. So he stood outside and he looked at the world, all the little bits of it, and the names of everything. It was important that every bit had a name he could place in his head. Everything, including people, had a color and a sound and a name he could say. Slippery elm and winged elm and scarlet oak. Wild turkey and grouse, pheasants and black ducks. The hollow was full of birds of all kinds, especially the small ones, and people would eat any kind of bird if they were hungry enough. Moles and blue tick hounds and short-tailed shrew. The chirp and saw of the late afternoon insects like a chorus of singers with something sharp shoved down their throats. The ticks of the katydids and the crickets who sounded like little tinny bells, the bright red dabs of cardinals like flying blood singing *wait wait cheer cheer*. The jays harshly repeating their own name over and over. The sad *coo-oo-oo-hoo* of the mourning doves, and on the other side of the forest the *cheer-up cheer-up* robins. Titmouse and chickadee *dee* and that friendly towhee inviting you to *drink your tea, sweet, drink your tea*.

Mickey-Gene wasn't sure when he'd started it but he could feel himself spinning. Maple and dogwood and linden. Red cedar white cedar. Maybe if he got better he could be a painter some day or an artist of an art that hadn't even been invented yet. Dibs and dabs and names and colors and explosions of sound, but knowing how they all flowed and fit together was the important thing. Meadow mouse and bull elk and mule. He spun around so hard he was getting dizzy but he just couldn't quite stop himself.

Dry brown white oak leaves crunching beneath his feet. Red, golden, and scarlet sourwood leaves. Ripe paw paws, persimmons, and wild grapes. Sweet and sour and bitter on the tongue. Bees swarming the sky between the swaying trees.

And somewhere crying and terror and the grief that will not end or even explain itself. The sorrow for a child you cannot feed or begin to teach. The wonder, the wonder about a world impossible to parse or capture in a lifetime of looks. Milkweed blossoms, yellow butterfly weed, clumps of blue violets and phlox. Possum and groundhog and woodcock, dried pumpkin sassafras tea cornbread in a pan and biscuits cut out with the top of a glass and baked brown.

"Child! Could you stop spinnin round and come hep a poor old gal!"

Mickey-Gene stopped and looked out at the rope bridge. A skinny old woman with long ragged hair was swinging there, something big and black clutched to her belly she was losing a grip on. She looked strained and unhappy. She was that witch woman, Granny Grace, the one who had protected Sadie at the picnic, but she made him feel really nervous. He couldn't begin to understand someone like her. He didn't think he could talk to her.

But maybe he wouldn't have to. He was rapidly losing balance. He was going down.

"Oh, for heaven's sake!"

He lay there with his eyes closed, listening to the world rustle around him, and then eventually rustling to him. "You aint dead or nothin are you? Then see if you cant sit up."

He did as she said, but felt like the idiot he pretended to be. "You probably think I'm like Benjy," he said.

"Who's that?"

Of course, he had no idea if she'd read Faulkner's novel, or even if she could read, or if it was too thin a reference for her to pick up on even if she had read it. He had no sense of such things, and always got it wrong. "Sorry. A character in a book…" Should he really drop his mask with her?

"I know, you read. You aint ignorant like most of the rest of us. That's why I need you to do somethin for Sadie."

"S-s-sure. What?"

"Hide the preacher's Bible." She lifted and dropped the heavy thing into his lap. "Least you could do, after I risked my life bringin it cross that thar bridge."

He stared at it. It was old and beat up and smelled bad. The leather had a slightly greasy feel to it, like maybe it hadn't been cured right, and was now beginning to liquefy, as skin would, if not preserved. "Why?"

"Because it's too dangerous for Sadie to have it, and I just went by my place to hide it, but somebody's been there lookin, and it smells to me like the preacher been through there. And no offense, child, but I dont reckon he'd suspicion you. So you got a good place to hide it?"

"Yes'm." He was thinking of that bin full of shelled corn he had. He'd been taking his share from the last few weeks and just pouring it into that bin, not grinding it or trading it or anything, just watching it accumulate because he liked looking at it in different kinds of light, and putting his hands into it, and thinking about what kind of painting he'd make of it, if he painted. He didn't need the money — his aunt and uncle gave him everything he needed. He could take some of that corn out, put the Bible in the bin, and pour some corn back over it. He put his fingers along the edge of the Bible's cover and started to open it, but Granny Grace's quick hands closed it.

"I know you like to read child, but not this. The riginal words might be okay, but not what he done to them, or what he added, or them pictures he drew all over. No sir, you dont want any of that nonsense in your head." She got up then, and ran across the rope bridge like it was nothing.

Mickey-Gene decided he believed her. The same people who said Granny Grace was crazy thought him stupid. It was the same Bible the preacher had up at the mines. It would be hard not to look into a book when it was sitting right there in front of you, so he went inside and started burying it under all that beautiful, yellow, white, and golden corn. But after he got it all covered, and was patting himself on his own back about how clever he was, he reached into the bin and lifted the book out in a shower of corn, and sat right there on the floor and opened it.

The end papers and flyleaves had been used, like a lot of family Bibles he knew about, to record births and deaths in a kind of haphazard family tree of the Gibson family. Some of the earlier names were incomplete, or had a question mark beside them, or had been crossed out and corrected. The Grans were inside their own box that floated beside the others, with no relationship lines leading in or out of it, and it was also labeled with a red question mark.

Some of the names had the symbols of stars or planets or flowers drawn beside them, but he had no idea what any of that meant. Some of the more recent names, like Sadie, or Jesse's children, were underlined, and some of those names were connected to other names with long, flowing arrows. Mickey-Gene blushed to see his name connected to Sadie's.

The last page depicting the family tree was odd in that mostly it was just lines and arrows with spaces for names. But some marriages appeared to be planned, or speculated about, between family members, and there were even the proposed names for possible offspring. Mickey-Gene traced the lines for him and Sadie, saw that one simply said "<son>," and from there the initials "MG."

Even odder was the preacher's own lineage, in which the preacher had listed himself as "Jake," with a complex list of spouses and children heavily revised then scratched out. But as far as Mickey-Gene knew the preacher had never been married and had no children.

The rest of the Bible was awash in notations, underlines, highlights, boxes and circles around certain passages, arrows connecting others. In many of the margins were numeric and text notations in a tiny, almost unreadable script, some with spirals and crude depictions of animals and embarrassingly lewd drawings of naked people doing a variety of things to each other, most of which Mickey-Gene didn't even understand.

Some of the annotations were larger, bolder, as if the preacher had put just that much more emotion into writing them down. A number of these were about John Dillinger, who had been killed recently, and other criminals such as Pretty Boy Floyd. He had entered birth dates (and in the case of Dillinger a death date), specific crimes they'd committed, even comments on their relative good looks.

Other bold notes appeared to be about foreign countries, and camps, and factories where human beings were butchered like animals. Sometimes diagrams of these camps spread across the top margin. And in several places was the notation "Gibsons=Jews." Mickey-Gene didn't understand any of this, and the drawings were dreamlike and disturbing. The only thing clear was the size of the preacher's anger, and the grimness of the visions that anger fueled. A man like the preacher was dangerous to have around, especially with any kind of following.

The preacher had used a variety of things to bookmark certain pages: strips of paper and cloth, yellowed receipts and dried leaves and pressed flowers and strings of various colors and thicknesses and in one place a huge insect Mickey-Gene didn't recognize flattened and pressed between the pages.

Then there were the missing words. Throughout some sections of the preacher's Bible individual words in the verses had been marked out with ink or blotted out with drops of blood or in a few spots actually burned out with something like a cigarette. These usually had something to do with sex, so that in Corinthians it was "But because of the temptation to ########, each man should have his own wife" and in Deuteronomy it was "None of the daughters of Israel shall be a cult #####" and in Jude it was "Just as Sodom and Gomorrah and the surrounding cities, which likewise indulged in ##### and pursued #####" and in Leviticus it was "You shall not #####."

Other pages were so heavily altered with paint and lipstick and other kinds of ladies' makeup and cutting and by other means that they resembled crude and terrible works of art concerning apocalyptic subject matter. These were mostly spread through the chapters of Isaiah, Jeremiah, Ezekiel, Joel, and Daniel. A great many of the words were obscured on these pages but the meaning was still pretty clear to Mickey-Gene.

In the Book of Daniel *four great beasts came up from the sea... The first was like a lion, and had eagle's wings... another beast, a second, like unto a bear. And it raised up itself on one side, and it had three ribs in the mouth of it between the teeth of it; and they said thus unto it, "Arise, devour much flesh."*

These creatures had been drawn in pencil across the pages of the Bible, and then painted in with lipstick or paint or blood or whatever the preacher must have had available. They obscured most of the words except for the ones the preacher wanted to emphasize. But what troubled Mickey-Gene most was their crude resemblance to other members of the Gibson family, and to people in the town, their flesh marred by terrible wounds and sores and things growing out of them which clearly did not belong.

On several pages he saw the scribbled outlines of masses of people lining up beneath a sign that said *Arbeit Macht Frei*. In some of the depictions black wolves were attacking and eating people.

And behold, in this horn were eyes like the eyes of man, and a mouth speaking great things.

The eyes were actually like a woman's, and the lipstick smeared mouth was huge and ugly and had terrible things swimming inside.

His throne was like the fiery flame, and His wheels as burning fire.

The rest of this page was consumed by flames painted in nail polish, between them glimpses of all the folks suffering and dying.

The visions of my head troubled me.

The preacher's head, bare and bloody, his scalp being torn apart by winged creatures with barbed tails and many sharp teeth.

These great beasts, which are four, are four kings who shall arise out of the earth... and of the ten horns that were in his head... the horn that had eyes and a mouth that spoke very great things...

And everywhere Mickey-Gene looked in this part of the Bible people were burning, tortured, torn apart. What he couldn't tell was whether the preacher identified with the victims, or the torturers, and sometimes he suspected both.

And shall devour the whole earth, and shall tread it down and break it in pieces.

Until finally the devil's reptilian body rose up on a page, its head the preacher's, whose face had turned ugly and insatiable, and the torn bodies of his victims hung from his many claws.

And his power shall be mighty... and he shall destroy wondrously, and shall prosper and perform, and shall destroy the mighty and the holy people.

Mickey-Gene closed the preacher's Bible. His hands shook. His mouth gulped air. He struggled to regain control over his breathing. Finally he picked himself up and again buried the Bible in the bin full of shelled corn, digging and rearranging until every last evil swatch of it was completely obscured.

By the time he got to his aunt and uncle's house they'd already left for the funeral, but his aunt had left out some clothes for him, cleaned and pressed, hand-me-downs from his uncle. He dressed quickly and left, almost stumbling in the rutted hard clay road as he hurried. He hated coming in late to anything, with everyone staring. Life was always better sitting back in a crowd, trying not to do anything that drew attention to yourself.

He hadn't talked to Sadie since Lilly's death, and he was a little afraid to be near her for the first time. And yet he wanted to be. It was like wanting to jump off one of these mountains, not knowing whether you'd land on the rocks, or into one of those more or less soft trees.

There were people on the porch of Sadie's house, some he recognized and some he did not. A couple of the faces were not complete unknowns, Gibson cousins he'd seen only once or twice. When he came up on the porch no one even noticed him. Then he saw her sitting on the far side of the porch, looking up at the ridge that rose like a wall all around them, that separated them so completely from the rest of the world he was surprised even light or air managed to get in. He went over and sat down beside her, but didn't say anything.

"Daddy wont be at the funeral," she said. "He went out early this morning, took his shotgun. A couple of the cousins came up from town a little while ago and told us that Daddy brought in that moonshiner Lowell Jepsen to the jail this morning, said he'd sold Uncle Jesse some bad hooch, and that's why he did what he did. Deputy Collins got him to put the gun down, and then he locked him up."

"Do you think your pa might be right?"

There were tears in her eyes, and she shook her head. Mickey-Gene reached over and grabbed her hand. A sudden lurch in his chest made him close his eyes. He was seeing the redness under his lids and then could taste the blood, the heavy flavor of it in his nose, and then he saw what Jesse did to Lilly, in that area of a woman's body he had never seen, and he bit into his tongue trying not to scream.

"Mickey? You okay?" Sadie looked at him, so close, her hands holding the sides of his face. He wasn't sure he could breathe. In fact he was pretty sure he had stopped breathing because the world was still red, and would soon explode into flame. "Mickey-Gene!"

She was crying. "S-s-sorry," he said. "Didn't mean to scare you." He made himself breathe deeply, and when the air proved cool and delicious, he relaxed.

"Mickey-Gene?" It was Sadie's mother. He couldn't quite look at her directly. That bothered him — he knew he looked like a dog somebody had been beating when he did that, but he couldn't help himself. She was one of those people who always looked at him with suspicion. But Aunt Mattie was standing right behind her, making sure everything would be okay.

"Yes'm," he said.

"You go on to the cemetery with Sadie. That's alright with your Aunt."

"Keep each other company. That's the best thing," Aunt Mattie said.

Sadie's momma looked at her. "Sadie, you okay to walk with Mickey-Gene?"

"Well sure. Course."

"I'll be along directly. I got to go work out something with that sorry moonshiner, get him to drop them charges."

Mickey-Gene could see the trouble in Sadie's face. "Will they charge the moonshiner?"

Her mother shook her head. "They dont charge moonshiners round here, an how they goin to prove bad shine? Ask me it's *all* bad shine. Besides, you cant tell me bad shine would make a man..." She stopped, looked away. "You kids go on. Least some of us should be on time for poor Lilly."

Mickey-Gene and Sadie had been on their way for only a few minutes when this woman in a big floppy hat came running out of her house screaming. It wasn't until she was almost to the barbed wire fence that separated her place from that little bank by the road that Mickey-Gene recognized her as Hattie

Younger, who Mickey-Gene had never met but everybody said was crazy. Sadie started running and he started running too. The way that woman was screaming it was like the very devil was inside her working her loony mouth. Mickey-Gene was terrified. That hat on her was like a live thing, something with wings wanting to bite his head off.

Then Sadie just stopped right there in the road, her shoulders pulled up like a cat's, her hands curled into fists. It was so sudden and unexpected Hattie Younger stopped screaming and came down to the fence. She bent down and looked at the two of them between the barbed wire.

Sadie turned and walked up the embankment. She reached between the two stretches of barbed wire, grabbed Hattie's dress near the neck, and yanked the shocked woman's head forward. The floppy hat caught on the top strand and flipped back off her head. Hattie's head looked tiny between the twin strands, her eyes darting at the barbs above and below her. She moaned like a cornered cat.

Sadie pushed her head up close to Hattie's until it looked like she was trying to smell the frightened woman's face. She stayed that way a few seconds, and then she said, "I'm sorry your baby died the day I was born, but I didn't do it." Then she waited a few more seconds before saying, "Did you drop it? Is that what happened? Or were you just so crazy, even then, that you threw it down?" The woman started squirming, mewling, as if there was something burning her. Mickey-Gene found himself squirming, too, tortured by something he felt but didn't understand. Sadie stood rigid, her smallish hands holding the woman still. He hardly recognized her. "Dont run after me again," she said, and let her go. The woman tumbled back and just lay there in the tall grass.

They went on their way. Behind them, Mickey-Gene heard a screen door slamming, a boy yelling "Mama!" and "Sadie, what did you do?"

Sadie didn't say anything for a long time. Mickey-Gene kept trying to get a good look at her face and she kept turning her head away. Finally he came around and stood in front of her. Her eyes and face were wet with tears. "I'm a terrible person!" she cried.

"You just wanted to get her to stop bothering you."

"She was in Hell! And I left her there!" Sadie pushed past him. She scared him, and she moved him with her regret. He was hopelessly in love with her.

THINGS FELT SO badly at the funeral Mickey-Gene was afraid he was going to throw up and make some kind of scene, and having people notice him like that right now felt like the worst thing that could happen. As it was he started crying from the tension, and couldn't stop, even when everybody started looking at him — embarrassed or hateful. Even when Sadie took his hand.

Lilly's family stood up on the hill around the grave, their backs to all the Gibsons who had dressed up only to stand no closer than forty feet or so down the hill. Lilly's family brought in a preacher from that Methodist church down in the flatlands a few miles away. He spoke quietly just to that bunch gathered around him, his voice carrying no farther. Not like the preacher at all, which was a great thing, except the Gibson bunch would have liked a few words of comfort as well, not that Mickey-Gene believed there was any real comfort anywhere in this world.

He could see the preacher, just barely, up on the edge of the woods there above the graves. It would be easy to mistake him for something else, a tree maybe or some rocks, but Mickey-Gene had always been pretty good at picking out individual pieces in any kind of picture. The preacher was standing perfectly still, watching, ready like some giant dark bird of prey to strike when the time was right. Mickey-Gene wondered if Sadie had noticed the preacher, and she did keep looking up there, but he figured she thought she might have seen him, but wasn't quite sure. After a while it seemed she got tired of looking, and just stared at her hands, or at the backs of Lilly's other kin.

The patience of his family surprised him. They all just stood there quietly, looking up the hill, not saying a word. Some of them closed their eyes, their lips twitching like they were saying their own personal prayers to themselves. It wasn't like them. He hoped the funeral didn't last any longer than their patience.

The preacher was staring in Sadie's direction. Mickey-Gene didn't think she knew, which was a good thing. Mickey-Gene felt like he would just melt away if someone looked at him that way. Sadie's mother finally got there with two of the cousins. She came up behind Sadie and started whispering. "Lowell Jepsen says he'll take eighteen dollars to forget about what your daddy did. That's the same as two gallons of his hooch he figures he woulda sold if Bobby hadn't interfered with him. We'll take care of it... after."

Then she stepped back and stared up the hill at the ongoing funeral. But after only a couple of minutes she was crying, and a couple of minutes more and she was sobbing about as loud as a person could sob. Sadie kept touching on her and holding her hands but it only seemed to make it worse. Lilly's family kept turning around and looking, some of them with angry faces, and eventually all the Gibsons had to leave.

SADIE'S MOTHER POUNDED on the jail door a good five minutes before Deputy Collins finally came to the little window. He looked really nervous and he insisted on everybody speaking their name out loud before he would let anybody inside. "I aint gettin a minute asleep till the county sheriff comes and picks up your Jesse." Sadie's mother scowled at him. "No offense."

"I aint here for Jesse." She poked her finger into his chest until he backed away. "I dont want to hear that name spoke in my presence, if'n you dont mind. I'm here for my husband. I put that eighteen dollar together for that sorry moonshiner to drop the charges."

Deputy Collins looked embarrassed. "I aint supposed to know about that. And he aint here. Maybe you could go find him."

"You're gonna take that eighteen dollar and hold it for that moonshiner to come back round for it. And you're gonna let my husband out. Unless you want me to talk to the sheriff about the local moonshining and what you aint doin about it."

"Oh he knows. Everbody knows, Mizz Gibson."

She slapped the money down on his desk and started up the stairs. "Best bring them keys," she said over her shoulder. The rest of the family waited for the deputy to pass and followed him up the stairs to the cells.

Sadie's daddy was in the first cell. It was old and a little rusty, made out of flat pieces of metal that crossed over each other in a lattice with square spaces about six inches on a side. It must have taken someone forever to build, and it was probably empty most of the time — you had to do a lot to get locked up in this town. He'd heard that Deputy Collins only locked folks up if he really had to. Mickey-Gene thought it looked more like an iron crate or a bird cage than a jail cell. Bobby Gibson grinned up at them from the stained mattress. "He lockin up the moonshiner?"

"No, he aint," her mother said. "But you're getting out."

"I tell you that moonshiner *paisened* my brother. He wouldn't done such a thing otherwise! That shine put the idear into him!"

"Daddy?"

He looked at Sadie as if noticing for the first time that she was there. "Jail's no place for a girl," he said, frowning.

"Daddy, it wasn't that moonshiner put the idea into Uncle Jesse's head."

"Girl, this is grown up business here. You shouldn't even be talkin bout such things."

"But it was the preacher. You need to leave that man alone. I was there at the church. The preacher scared Uncle Jesse with his snake, and then he whispered something into his ear, and he kissed him on the lips, like he does with some of his saints. And after that Uncle Jesse and Aunt Lilly and I went to their house and that's when he did what he did."

Then she stepped back, as if her pa could have reached through the bars and hit her. Mickey-Gene held his breath, thinking about how awful all this was, and waiting for her pa to explode.

But he didn't. He just stared at her, and his eyes went off somewhere, and he licked his lips, and he straightened himself up on that cot. "Daughter," he finally said. "You best just go home. Jail's a bad, bad place. And not for you."

Sadie glanced at Mickey-Gene, turned and went down the hall, and Mickey-Gene followed her. But they didn't go back downstairs. Sadie led him around the corner, to this cell they had in the back, away from the others.

It stank of sweat and alcohol and human waste. There was a big lard can with a newspaper over it in one corner, and Mickey-Gene was pretty sure that was supposed to do for a toilet, but he didn't think it had been used in a while. A ragged, sorrowful figure was shackled to an iron ring in the center of the floor, and he didn't think the prisoner had ever been let loose from that. Tin plates of half-eaten food were scattered on the floor around the prisoner, and a biscuit and a carrot on the floor between the cell door and the figure. Mickey-Gene assumed the deputy had just slid the plate across the floor rather than get too close, and occasionally something would tumble off. The cell door wasn't even locked — that iron ring and those shackles would have held an elephant securely. The deputy was a nervous, cautious man, and Mickey-Gene didn't blame him for a certain caution after what Jesse had done.

Before he could stop her Sadie was inside the cell approaching her Uncle Jesse. At least she was walking slowly, talking softly. Maybe if he suddenly went crazy she could get out in time.

"Uncle Jesse? It's Sadie. Oh, Jesse, I'm *so* sorry."

The figure stirred, uncurled, shook. Mickey-Gene saw the shiny spots on Jesse's clothes where he had fouled himself. The stench was worse now, terrible, and yet Sadie showed nothing in her face. Jesse turned around, squatting because the chain was so short. Like a duck or a frog. His eyes came around from under his matted, greasy hair, slick gray stones at the bottom of pits dug out of the mud by hand. His mouth looked broken. Somebody had hit him a few times between then and now.

"Jesse?" Sadie crouched a little, on her uncle's level. "Do you remember?" She paused. "What did the preacher say to you, back there at the church?"

He stared at her. "Sadie? Sadie, how's my Lilly?"

Mickey-Gene could hear the little gasp she made. In the yellow light of the one narrow window her face looked damp and shiny. "Do you remember, Uncle Jesse? The preacher had that big snake wrapped around him, and he whispered something to you. Just between the two of you — no one else could hear?"

Jesse shook his head, shook it again, like a dog that had something crawling around in his ear and he couldn't get it out. "Said she were a demon." His voice croaked like the creature he resembled. "Women, they all got secrets. He said that, and I know it too. They know what you need to hear, but they dont always say it. They know things you never will, but they dont want to share none of it. I seen it myself, I just didn't know it was because they had a demon in there. That preacher, he knows all about demons, always did." He shook his head again. "Used to be my brother. Now he's... more." He shook it again, this time with fury, as if he might snap his own neck. "Lilly okay? Why aint she visited?"

Sadie was sobbing. Mickey-Gene eased himself into the cell, more terrified with every step. He could smell the blood again and there was this roaring in his ears, his own panic and a woman's screams, drowning in red.

"Sadie?" Jesse's head went up, his eyes wide and staring. Mickey-Gene began pulling Sadie slowly out of the cell. He could feel the world breaking apart around him, dibs and dabs of color and sound, and all of it flowing and making new patterns in the world that spread and divided through time. "Sadie!" Jesse screamed, pulling against his chain, and the both of them ran, flowing past the deputy and the running Gibsons, down the stairs and out into the town.

Chapter Seventeen

MICHAEL FLUTTERED HIS eyes as the town faded from his view of the hospital room. Increasingly it had become difficult to tell if he fell asleep during these tellings, or if he simply entered an intensive and altered, listening state. He looked at the chair across from him where Mickey-Gene slept. It jolted him. Had Mickey-Gene fallen asleep just as Michael was entering normal awareness? He couldn't make sense of it any other way, because if Mickey-Gene had fallen asleep much earlier then who had told the story?

The man sitting across from him was nothing like the man Michael had imagined when his grandmother started relating the story. When he'd been little she'd always told him not to "judge a book by its cover." She should have told him the story of Mickey-Gene instead. Michael wanted nothing more than to hear more of Mickey-Gene's life told in his own words. Or just to hear his take on what had happened to these people, and what this monster the preacher had been like.

After southwest Virginia in the thirties Michael was amazed at how clean and sanitized everything looked. Just this room alone looked so scrubbed, crisp, and perfect it might have been a dream. So when his grandmother started speaking to him again he didn't even think to answer at first.

"Michael, did you... hear me?" Her voice was dry and weak.

"Grandma? Can I get you some water?"

She started to speak, and then just nodded. As he turned to get it Mickey-Gene was already there, smiling, handing a full glass to him. She took a few sips, cleared her throat and said, "So you've finally met your grandpa. You know you were named after him?"

It was an awkward moment. Michael smiled, shook his head. "You'll have to give me a minute. You're not," he looked at Mickey-Gene, "this isn't what I was expecting."

"We haven't lived together in a long time," Mickey-Gene said. "But we were good together. After it was all over, or after we thought it was all over, we needed, well, no two people could have understood each other better."

"It was me, I reckon," his grandmother said. "Michael, you know I'm not always easy to live with." She laughed softly, and winced. "Mickey-Gene's a good man, and he knows, well he knows things I cant even dream of, and after everything that happened, it was *healing*, for us to be together. But I knew from the beginning the preacher *wanted* us together, it was something he'd *planned*. And that couldn't be a good thing. Fact is, that had to be a *terrible* thing. We just didn't know how yet. And it weighed on me so. I was the one who told Mickey-Gene to leave, after we had a child, and raised him. I thought maybe then we could pretend it never happened, that everything would be okay. But I was foolish, as foolish as I was when I was that barefoot girl running around messing in things she hadn't a fly's chance of understanding. I was just a fool, a complete *fool*. Your daddy suffered for it, and your poor mother — we couldn't help either one of them. And now it comes down to you. What kind of legacy is this for a child?"

"Grandma, I'm not a kid. I didn't *have* to be here."

"Didn't you?" She wasn't crying, but she began to shake. "I think we *all* had to be here!"

Michael decided to take a break while Mickey-Gene talked to his grandmother. But before he left he said, "Granddad? Did you ever start painting? Did you work on your art?"

Mickey-Gene looked blank for a moment, then smiled sadly. "Not really. Just in my head. I filled my head with those paintings, but they never quite got outside."

He wanted nothing better than to talk to his grandfather some more, but of course his grandmother had to be taken care of first. He walked down to the lunchroom, struggling to put it all together. Why couldn't they have told him at some point? No doubt he would have been angry about it, but at least he wouldn't have had so many questions.

Down in the lunchroom he watched a nearby elderly couple sitting and holding hands. *They are so old*, he thought, *maybe the oldest couple I've ever seen.* So old they looked like twins. One turned to him and nodded. Behind Elijah, Addie tilted her head forward and smiled at him.

"Did you decide to come back?" Michael asked. "I saw your truck leave."

"He's almost awake, I think," Elijah said.

"Awake?"

"Best get him while he still lies," Addie shook her head.

"I don't…"

"Stop him before he stands up," Elijah added. "He can be a real devil if he's standing."

"I'm sorry, but why…"

"And for sure before he strides. He's got a helluva stride," Addie said almost gleefully.

"Excuse me, who are you talking about?"

Addie stared at him, the side of her mouth drooping, as if she'd just had a stroke. "Oh, sweetheart. You haven't been payin attention. That thing in the box, of course."

The vision of the two faded even as he was looking at them. There was no one sitting there.

Clarence Roberts came into the lunchroom and waved to catch Michael's attention. Clarence walked up to him, frowned, looking down at his feet. "Fraid I cant work for you no more, Mr. Gibson. I thought I knew what I was doin, but I've been plumb useless to you."

"What are you talking about, Clarence? You've been doing great for my grandmother and me."

Clarence shook his head. "That kudzu is back, and it pretty near covers *everything*. You cant even see the house no more. I never seen the like, and I cant deal with something like this. This black magic stuff. I got a family."

"Clarence —" Michael was shaken. What was he supposed to do?

"Maybe you should get that dirt checked out!" Clarence shouted over his shoulder as he left.

Michael could hear his grandmother babbling as he came up to the second floor. He raced to the room. Mickey-Gene was struggling to keep her in bed. "It's like in *Macbeth*," Mickey-Gene said. "The woods of High Dunsinane hill, coming against him."

"I knew he felt betrayed by all of us," his grandmother began. "But I didn't think he'd take it out on *them*."

Chapter Eighteen

THE TOWN WAS almost empty. It made no sense. They'd had the most gruesome murder anybody had ever heard of and the murderer in the local jail and the deputy scared to death of angry folks taking his prisoner and her daddy almost shot the most popular moonshiner in the county and there were two big families now that didn't know how to talk to each other and of course there was the preacher going a little crazier each day. Who walked around with a snake under his shirt curled around his chest and belly.

She'd have thought people would be in the street gossiping, hanging around for the latest development. Unless they were too scared to be. Unless they were hiding in their little houses waiting for it all to play out.

"We got to talk to the Grans," she told Mickey-Gene. "Are you coming with me?"

"Course I'm coming. With the preacher running around I cant let you go off by yourself. But do you think it's safe up there at the Grans? If we had to holler for help nobody would hear us."

"It cant be helped. I've got to *talk* to them! I took the preacher's Bible and he *still* did that thing to Jesse and, and to Lilly." She stopped, stared at the ground. "And maybe that was partly my fault, because he was so angry. There must be something more I can do. And I reckon maybe only the Grans will know what that is."

"Do we need his Bible?"

"There's no time. Besides, it's too risky to carry it round till we know what we can do with it. If we run into him before then, how could we stop him from taking it away?"

Maybe it was because she was so tired, tired of everything, like if there was just one more terrible thing she'd lie down in the dirt and let happen whatever was going to happen. It seemed to take a lot longer to get up to the Grans this time than before. The mountain seemed steeper, the sun hotter, and her legs weaker. Every once in a while she'd stop to catch her breath and she'd turn around to see how high they were and it looked like she was the highest she'd ever been. She would have loved to live up there, so that she could see things going on but she'd be enough above it to look toward the sky and still feel it was in her reach.

She had a sudden terrible thought that maybe the preacher had already done something to them. The way he'd acted at the birthday picnic, she'd been sure he'd meant them harm, but they were family, and the preacher worshipped family, or at least family blood.

Should she have talked to somebody about it? Was this going to be her fault? But she wasn't old enough for that kind of responsibility — they couldn't put all that on her and expect her to take care of things.

Granny Grace would keep an eye on them — she was sure of that. It was just the kind of thing Granny Grace would do. She clutched Mickey-Gene's hand and pulled, trying to hurry him. He was wheezing, but he was keeping up.

But once she reached the top of the ridge she was confused. The Grans had had a lot of junk lying around outside — parts of old cars, farm equipment, old steam-powered machinery, and a bunch of things big and small she had no idea what they were or what they did or how old they were. Now the ground was clear — hard-packed clay and limestone slabs and ugly little trees, a scattering of grass between. There were a few drag marks, and scattered ruts and holes and rectangular pits where heavy things had once stood, but no sign at all of the actual things that had once been here.

They walked around a small stand of cedars to get to the Grans' house, that little one-room shack that had been so full the personal debris had been spilling out of doors and windows. The door was wide open so already she could see the difference. The porch was empty, without even those old rockers they'd had. And there was nothing visible just inside the door.

"Do they really live here?" Mickey-Gene asked beside her.

"You've never been here before?"

"No — you're the only one I ever knew of to visit the Grans at their own place. Is it always so quiet and, I dont know, empty?"

"I only came the one time," she told him. "But no, it wasn't like this.

"Maybe they're visiting?"

"I dont think they visit. Elijah? Addie?" she called. There was no answer.

She started walking faster and jumped up on the porch. Mickey-Gene stumbled on the steps and swore. Then she was standing in the doorway, staring. Mickey-Gene came up behind her. "It's empty," he said.

"Completely." Although she wasn't sure she fully meant that, because the Grans had left something behind. She went in, Mickey-Gene close behind her.

The wooden floor was scrubbed and polished, without even a piece of lint or sliver of paper to distract from the beautiful red oak grain. The walls were painted with a continuous mural that wrapped completely around all four sides, with even the two windows and the door worked into the design. The mural obviously wasn't new — the colors were unevenly faded and there were scrape marks and some gouges where things had rubbed against or struck the plaster. But it was still in pretty good shape. Sadie figured that all the things stuffed into this house — she hadn't even been able to see the walls before — had served to protect it.

She wondered which of the Grans had painted it, or if both had. It was possible they'd had someone else paint it for them. But it seemed too personal for that.

Her eyes were drawn to the ceiling. It was such a dazzling white she almost expected a window there — it was like clouds that had soaked up the sun — or some kind of white fire (Was there such a thing? Maybe in the Bible.) Something was written faintly in the center of it. She kept moving around trying to find an angle where she could see it better. The lettering was pink-colored, and thin in places, as if there hadn't been enough paint on the brush so some of that improbable white shone through, like a ghost burning up through the skin that wrapped it, an idea which thrilled and amazed her.

Finally she was able to read it.

Psalm 139 - I will praise You for I am fearfully and wonderfully made.

The mural around the walls started with an obscurity and a heaviness down by the floor — dark browns and blues and blacks showing rocks and fallen trunks, old bones and what crawled beneath the bones, and a fluid that ran through part water and part oil and a melting of body fat.

In the layer above was the living soil, active with creatures and their burrowings, and a certain fire, a promising warmth that Sadie could not find specifically in either the colors or the shapes. Plants began there, forming a complex layer of green, the branches above in harmony with the roots below, and both resembling the engravings Sadie had seen of the circulatory systems of humans, and how lungs and hearts and brains were like the fruits, or the flowers of those systems, or the lightning bolts that branched out of the multiple layers of sky reaching for their opposites.

The sky of the mural went from white to blue to shadow and then to that unusually brilliant white of the ceiling. It wasn't the same in all places, which made it seem that much more real, that much deeper, so that she kept staring into it, expecting to find something in the distance.

The land, too, wasn't the same in all places. There were close hills and distant folds of mountains, flatlands and hollows, and even one flat ridge rising above the trees and populated with little crude houses and tiny figures she couldn't quite get the details from but which still seemed familiar.

Overlaying the landscape were large rough outlines of people spaced around the room, varying in size and slightly in shape but still recognizably human. These had no features but the colors that filled them ranged from that dazzling ceiling white to softer pinks and reds like floating mists of pastel lights, soups of chemicals and human beings turned spectacularly into gas. And despite their lack of detail Sadie was convinced they were still supposed to represent specific human beings and when she stepped up to one it was almost a perfect fit. It was like her shadow but more like her shadow's opposite.

"It's like a church," Mickey-Gene said beside her, and although she agreed with him she thought it was certainly unlike any church she'd ever been in in her part of the country and obviously it was much more.

Another Bible passage was written into the sky of each wall:

> *Isaiah — They shall mount up with wings like eagles, They shall run and not be weary, They shall walk and not faint.*

And,

> *Corinthians — Now we see things imperfectly as in a cloudy mirror, but then we will see everything with perfect clarity.*

And,

Corinthians — we fix our eyes not on what is seen, but on what is unseen. For what is seen is temporary, but what is unseen is eternal.

And right above the door that led in and out of the house,

John — Greater love has no one than this, that he lay down his life for his friends.

Sadie thought about that as she left the Grans' house for the last time. She had so many questions for the Grans, but now she really didn't expect to see them again. How long had they sat in that house, painting and then gazing at that mural, before filling up their house and hiding it? Did they just forget it was there, or did knowing about its secret existence only make it more powerful? Of course she had no right to the answers to any of these questions, and maybe that's why it had been hidden. What's theirs was theirs — they didn't owe anyone answers.

"Sadie, slow down! You're going to hurt yourself!" That was poor Mickey-Gene shouting behind her, scared to death himself but still trying to keep up, still trying to protect her. But she was sure they couldn't have much time. Maybe it was that urge she'd had just to stay up there on the mountain, maybe even move into the Grans' old house, and not worry about what was going on with the rest of her family, or with anybody else down in the hollow. She could be above all that. She was just a child really, and she wanted a child's life.

But she couldn't let any more people die, and she could feel it in her body all the way to the ends of her nerves that more people were going to die if the preacher wasn't stopped.

"We need to look at the preacher's Bible!" she shouted back to him. "Maybe Granny Grace already has it figured out and she can tell us what we can do with it!" He was yelling things back but he was so out of breath she couldn't understand him.

She stumbled a few times, but still kept her feet. Her stomach dropped so rapidly in her descent she had to fight sickness. She was worried maybe she wouldn't be able to find Granny's place on her own. She might need extra time for that. Mickey-Gene would just have to keep up best he could.

She was about a hundred yards ahead of Mickey-Gene when things started flattening out a little, coming up to the edge of her grandpa's old farm. Her need to go over and talk to him about everything that had happened since his death, to talk to him about anything, was overwhelming. Grief seized her face and turn it into a mask he would not have recognized.

The trail off the mountain disappeared into the curve of the dirt road running past his house. The barn was still as tall and as red as ever, the finest barn in three counties. Two wagons were pulled up along the side of the house facing the road, the first full of furniture and the second mostly empty, horses hitched to both. Her mother had told her the Simpson clan was returning to Wythe County that morning, saying that Morrison had gotten a little too "rough" for the likes of them. The farm would be put up for sale, and they'd given Momma the pick of whatever was left in the house before the sale went through. But they should have left by now. They were for sure going to have to ride over some difficult mountain road in the dark if they left this late in the day.

No one was in sight. As she passed the entrance to the farm she kept turning her head trying to get a better look. That was how she saw the big, sloppy lettering almost the color of the barn up on the side of Grandpa's pretty white house. She turned around and trotted back, just as Mickey-Gene reached that point in the road.

"Sadie, the preacher's Bible…"

"Wait a second. We need to check on things here." She ran past him and went through the gate. When she came up beside the wagons the horses jerked their heads nervously. She checked the wagon beds — one was full of Grandpa's best furniture and the other had a few piles of quilts and linens, some clothing, with some chairs and benches for passengers filling the rest of the space. "Hello!" she cried. There was no answer.

Mickey-Gene came up beside her. "What's that noise?"

She focused on sound: the horses flicking their tails around their hips, their occasional snorts, and the rapid pulse in her ear, the rise and fall of the flies' buzz. "I dont think…"

"The preacher's been here," Mickey-Gene said. He'd gone ahead of her to the side of the house where she'd seen that loose lettering.

The flies were a little louder in their complaints (or was it a celebration?) as Sadie walked up to him. Something red had been rubbed onto the clean white house to make the lettering. It reminded her of when some kind of meat would half fall out of Homer Goin's rendering truck and make a smear as it was dragged down the road. The flies were the same, too, spinning around and settling down to feed, then taking off again. Buzzing the whole time.

The smears had been pushed around to make letters, like a kind of rusty red paint with here and there lumps of fat or threads of skin to make the letters more physical, and unforgettable.

It said,

> Luke 21:16 — And ye shall be BETRAYED both by parents and brethren and kinfolks and friends and some of you shall they cause to be put to death.

Except some of the letters were broken and not all there and in a few sections a faint trail of blood was all that completed a letter, but Sadie could still read the message just fine. She looked down on the ground and saw the trail of blood leading around to the back of the house, punctuated here and there by a bloody boot print.

The flies were loud here, but not as numerous or as loud as they were somewhere else.

Mickey-Gene ran ahead and she tried to stop him. He was saying something but the flies were too loud in her head for her to hear him. She followed him and watched as he fell to his knees, his hands on his face, mouth open, repeating over and over something terrible and full of anguish and soul scouring but she couldn't hear a word of it because the flies were too loud in her head.

But she could follow his hand as he threw it forward in a gesture of surrender, the finger pointing, shaking.

At the end of the house beside her grandpa's back door they had left their dirty laundry, piles and piles of it fouled and smeared and layered with flies. It seemed like such a terrible and disrespectful thing to do, to leave such a thing for her mother to clean up. For a moment she just wanted to go to the back door and beat it down, scream at them to come out and take care of their awful mess. And she started toward the door to do that very thing, angrily waving the flies away as they seemed to be attacking her in waves.

Then she saw more lettering on the back of the house beside the door and it distracted her. She felt like she needed to read it just so she'd have some sense of the extent of their crime.

> *As it is told in Exodus — Thou shalt not suffer a witch to live.*

She gazed down at the bloody pile to the left of the door and discovered that the dirty laundry had faces. Hands and arms and legs as well, but it was the faces of all those Simpsons from Wythe County that bothered her the most.

And then she found the smaller pile to the right of the door, and spread over the top of that pile as if to protect what lay beneath her was Granny Grace, her clothing even more stained and ragged than usual, her arms fallen out from their sleeves, her legs angled too sharply from where they left the bottom of her torso. One foot was bare and torn; the other had a blood-stiffened sock hanging from the toes. Her eyes were as wide open as Sadie remembered them, and the wicked smile was there, but extended somehow, and the width of her face seemed wrong, and her neck lopsided.

More words had been scratched into the dirt below Granny Grace, deep, dry, uneven scratches as if the author of all these verses had run out of his red paint.

> *Suffer the little children to come unto me — for of such is the kingdom of heaven.*

That's when she saw the small arms and hands, tiny legs of those rude Simpson children and grandchildren, peeking out from under Granny's dress.

Chapter Nineteen

MICHAEL CAME OUT of his grandmother's story weeping and curled on the floor of her hospital room. He stretched his hands out and felt the tile, pushed himself up so that he could get a better look at his hands on the surface of the tile, feeling the smooth slickness. No grit, no dirt, no grass, no blood. He struggled to stand, finally managing by grabbing the hospital bed and pulling himself up. The room spun momentarily as his eyes tried to find his grandmother in the brilliant white sheets, thinking of that celestial ceiling at the Grans' house, and not being able to find her at all.

He looked around. There was no sign of his grandmother, but Mickey-Gene was sitting on the floor in the corner mumbling "tomorrow and tomorrow and tomorrow" softly to himself with his eyes closed. Michael was still seeing him as he had been in that vision of a long ago yesterday, brilliant and confused and scared.

Michael walked over and touched his shoulder, shaking him gently. "Grandpa. She isn't in the room. You need to help me." Mickey-Gene's lids shot open. He looked terrified, grabbing Michael's arm. "Grandpa, it's Michael. You're just coming out of her story. Everything's okay, but we need to go find Grandma. She's not in the room."

They ran to the nurse's station. The woman in charge said she had seen nothing. She got on the phone while Michael and his grandfather headed for the elevator. As it opened on the ground floor Michael saw his grandmother going out the front door still in her hospital gown, dragging her overnight bag by one strap across the floor behind her. They reached her as she stepped into the parking lot.

"Grandma, come back inside." Michael tried to grab the strap from her hand but she wiggled it away from him.

"We have to leave *now*." Her voice was firm, and clearer than he'd heard it in some time.

Mickey-Gene tried to get ahead of her, made sure she saw his face. "Where you going, Sadie? You're still in your hospital gown!"

"Going to that crate out in the field. *You* should know," she said. "You helped put it there." She kept pushing forward about as fast as Michael imagined her short legs could manage. They both were struggling to keep up with her. Mickey-Gene was carrying her bag now which allowed her to move even faster.

Michael's grandfather's face was pale, his eyes looking somewhere else. "You're *feeling* something?"

"I'm feeling that we've got no time for talking. We'll take your pick-up. Michael can drive while you help me get dressed."

"Grandma, Clarence says that whole area is under kudzu now. I dont think…"

"I *know* it's all under kudzu, and I know that nasty vine is growing ever-which-way out there. That's why we got to get out there, because I also know why it's happening!" She grabbed the side of Mickey-Gene's arm and started slipping out of her gown.

"Grandma!"

"If you dont want a public show then you better get me into that cab! Mickey-Gene, you still got that kerosene in the back of the truck?"

"Yes ma'am."

"And matches? An axe?"

"There's a bunch in the glove box. And yep, there's an axe in the truck bed, a little rusty I'm ashamed to say."

"It'll do. Get me to that crate, Michael!"

"*What* is it?" He felt a little childishly resentful about her bossing him around this way. "Do you need to get something out of that crate?"

"No, child. I'm trying to keep something in."

Chapter Twenty

Psalm 50:19 — Thou givest thy mouth to evil, and thy tongue frameth deceit.

It was written in dried blood on the floor of the millhouse with a scatter of yellow, white, and gold corn. The handwriting was thin, almost delicate. Sadie figured the preacher had cut open his own finger and used it to make the letters.

"He got his Bible back," Mickey-Gene said faintly. "I'm sorry — I must've done it all wrong."

"No. No. He has a sense for the thing, like a hound on the scent of what he's hunting. I think he would've found it no matter what."

"So what do we do now?" Sadie didn't blame him, but she really wished he'd stop being so scared, and confused, or whatever he was. She felt terrible and mean-spirited for thinking it, but there it was.

They'd gone down to the next farm and told the old man there what they'd found. His son rode out to get the deputy and then over to tell Momma. Sadie and Mickey-Gene had waited by the wagons until everybody got there. It took very little to convince Momma not to go around back. The deputy had just asked who they thought could've done such a thing and Momma hadn't even looked at him. She'd just stared at the ground and said, "The preacher. The preacher done it."

Nobody said a word for a little until the deputy just spat on the ground. "I think you're *all* crazy," he said. "All you Gibsons and half the other families in town, all you Melungeons with your weird churches and your feuds and all. You cant tell me one man did this without no help, without nobody else knowing about it, and a *preacher* to boot. Little girl, did you *see* the preacher anywheres around here?"

"Nosir." Sadie stared at him, mad, but what did she expect him to do?

"Then why does your momma think he done it?"

"It's hard to explain," she said quietly. Then she looked at him more directly. "It *cant be* explained really. You have to see for yourself, and ask yourself questions, like about how some things were even possible. Seen many folks in town today, deputy? Have you wondered any about why folks might be hiding out?"

"The law needs evidence, young lady. That's how it works. The sheriff'll be here in a couple of days. Maybe he can sort it out."

"Maybe," she said. "If it aint all done by then."

There had been nothing silly about his questions. Sadie just didn't know. It seemed unlikely the preacher trusted anybody enough to help with something so awful, but she couldn't see how he could have done something like this by himself, unless he had changed some. But she wasn't ready to believe that yet, because believing that made stopping all this seem impossible.

She told Momma she was going to take Mickey-Gene home. He hadn't spoken up while the deputy was there and no one would expect him to. Momma barely even raised her head to say goodbye.

"So what do we do now?" Mickey-Gene asked again.

"I dont know. I dont see any use of running, do you? Where would we even go? The deputy aint going to do anything, at least not till it's too late for us."

Mickey-Gene kept staring at the Bible verse painted in blood onto the millhouse floor. "Well, I dont think he wants us dead. He had plans for us, right?" He still didn't look at her.

"That's right," she said. "We're blood. So we get to play our parts. The preacher knows exactly what he wants us to do and say — he's got it all worked out. We just have to hope it all goes the right way. Maybe we can do and say things that are going to surprise him. You never know what's going to happen. But as long as you keep playing, getting up and going out and living, something might just go your way. And if we ran, or tried to run, what would happen to all these folks we left behind?"

"'One man in his time plays many parts'," Mickey-Gene said. Sadie stared at him, thinking how exhausting it would be to spend much time with this person. "What's that?"

"Shakespeare. His play *As You Like It*. It's from that. During your life you play many parts — a daughter, a mother, a grandmother, a hero, a villain. You enter people's lives and then you exit them. You say your lines — you inspire some people, and maybe some people hate you. And then, well, you leave the stage."

"You do the best you can," she said.

"Right."

"He wants us to continue the bloodline because we have this power, to see things, to feel things. So maybe that makes us safe, at least for a little while. Safe enough maybe to do what we need to do."

They got to Sadie's house after sunset. They came in the back. It was quiet, with only the one lamp on in the kitchen. It looked like her mother hadn't started supper, so maybe she was still over at Grandpa's farm. Sadie started to go into the living room and stopped. It was dark in there, but she could see a shape sitting in the old soft chair by the window. The room stank heavily of what at first she thought was that Minard's Rubbing Alcohol her grandpa used on his sore muscles, but then she realized it was something else. She turned around and grabbed the lantern off the table and motioned Mickey-Gene to join her as she entered the room. "Daddy?" she said. "Why are you sitting here in the dark?"

He blinked a couple of times, his face yellow from the lantern. He wore nothing but a stained undershirt and boxers. He raised the jar of moonshine to his lips and sipped, wincing, and then licked his lips. "Felt like it I reckon. Where you been? That the idjit with you?"

"Dont call him that."

"You makin the rules now?"

"Where's Momma?"

He jerked his head toward the bedroom door. "Missus Willis give her something to help her rest. Woman's been through Hell this week."

"Is she going to be okay?"

He shrugged. "She's a strong gal. Why I married her."

"Daddy, I need your rifle, and the pistol."

"Hell you say. You're just a kid." His wide eyes with the black marbles inside looked scared, not angry. But Sadie didn't need her eyes to tell her that — the fear rolled off him in waves.

"We're going for the preacher. We need some protection."

"Aint no job for the two of you!"

"Why, are *you* going after him?" He put the jar down on the table and stared off toward the corner as if seeking some kind of advice there. "Is that Lowell Jepson's shine?"

"Might be."

"I thought you hated him. Didn't you figure he'd poisoned Jesse into doing what he done?"

"Well, *you* said it wasn't him! So when we paid him to get me outta jail he offered me some and I cepted it."

"So you believed me when I said it was the preacher?"

He turned his head and looked at her calmly. But he was forcing himself. He wasn't calm at all. "I did. You *sense* things, I knowed that about you."

"So you're just going to sit here? You're not going to help?"

He picked up the jar again and started drinking from it. Then he said, "I cant leave your ma. And you two are gonna get yourselves killed."

"Well, if I *do* get killed you're *forgiven*. And if I *dont* get killed you're *not!*"

"Forgiven!"

"For what you wanted to do. For what you tried. For how you made me feel. You know what I'm talking about."

He sat there and neither moved or said anything more. Sadie went into the closet and got out a couple of coats, the rifle and the pistol, and she and Mickey-Gene left.

Chapter Twenty-One

MICHAEL FELT A peculiar resignation as they drove out of the hospital parking lot and through this flat and much sanitized version of Morrison. He supposed if you'd lived here a long time you became accustomed to gradual change, so you weren't shocked if any individual piece was shuttered, torn down, wiped off the map. And he supposed some might appreciate the easy access to gas, cigarettes, and snacks, and the larger roads quickly connecting you to distant cities. He probably could even have gotten cell service here, had he not misplaced his phone weeks ago. But he'd forgotten, as he'd forgotten most things that told him he was a young guy with an exciting life ahead of him.

He didn't want to be one of those who thought all change was a decline, but how could this simple layout of similar buildings be an improvement over the richly-detailed community of his grandmother's memories?

The lane up to that old and largely forgotten world was steep, warped and cracked, with tall trees both shading and threatening the shoulders. When they emerged onto the old main street it was as if they'd risen from the ground. Both his grandparents fixed themselves to the window then, as if they'd never seen the town before. Michael couldn't take his eyes off it either. It was a jolt to be yanked out of the bustling thirties of his grandmother's stories and into this almost abandoned, ghostly remnant of worn down brick and plank. Besides all the commercial buildings that had been torn down, the school up on the hill, the park, the houses close to town, all were gone.

"Not much left," his grandmother said. "The kids leave, the old folks die, and nobody comes back. Cept you Michael. You came back."

He'd come back, yet he'd belonged here less than most. And when this was over, however it was over, he'd be leaving. He hadn't realized that until this moment. He'd be getting on with the rest of his life.

His grandfather had been muttering since they'd left the hospital. For all the man's obvious intelligence he had a kind of weariness, and a mild befuddlement, that muted his ability to be present in the world. "Tomorrow, and tomorrow, and tomorrow," he repeated softly and constantly to the window.

Grandma kept patting Grandpa's leg. "It's his Shakespeare," she explained to Michael. "It makes him feel better."

As they left the old town limits Michael noticed the dark clouds out over the farms and fields. Not weather, too low to be weather. There was an agitation in them like the wings of thousands of insects, or bats, or birds, their sharp wings beating at each other.

But then he rolled down his window and sniffed the air. Smoke. A lot of something was burning. The world was on fire, or at least the world surrounding the Gibson family home.

A short distance outside town they encountered the first signs of what the kudzu had become. This area was, or had been, the Simpson farm owned by Michael's great-great-grandfather, a series of greats that might have relegated the man to some sort of genealogical dustbin, but because of Sadie's stories he was more vivid to Michael than his own father.

The white farmhouse had been torn down before Michael had lived with his grandmother as a child, but the red barn was still there, sold and resold over the years and used to store everything from hay to tobacco to antiques. It wasn't precisely red anymore, more a grayish color with brown rubbed on to it, but it was still large and still standing.

And now featured a great, flowing green wig, the ends of which dangled like bouncing curls in the wind, giving the illusion that the whole building was shaking nervously. As he drove slowly past Michael could see that the runners came together at the base to form a series of thick, parallel trunks that ran along the ground and disappeared under the barbed-wire fence, wandering off through the fields and occasionally resurfacing.

"Creeps, creeps," his grandfather muttered.

They travelled a little further down a series of sharp switchbacks that didn't allow a view of what lay ahead, until the last bend pointed them toward the Gibson home place again, and the giant green shapes walking across the road, towering above the fields, escaping toward some distant ridge.

"It's covered danged near everything," his grandmother said.

"This petty, petty pace," his grandfather said faintly.

The trees, the low hills, a few buildings were layered and mounded with the complex green leaves and runners of kudzu, the breeze making them shimmer and wave. Michael knew that the shapes he saw had little to do with the overgrown objects at the center of them — it was like interpreting the shapes in clouds. Still, some of them looked so specific, and nightmarish, it was hard to believe that some intelligence hadn't played a part. Growth in the image of a giant warrior fallen, arms flailing, blocked the lane. A grizzled old man in an orange road crew vest stood in front of the kudzu, waving.

"From day to day to day," Grandpa said.

"You cant get through here!" The old man waved his arms in the air, looking angry about the news he had to deliver. He approached the driver's side window, peered inside. "Oh, hey Mizz Gibson."

"Howdy, Tommy. How bad?"

"Afraid it's like this the next mile, nothing but this crappy vine. With this here truck you can go off cross that field there, about a mile, then straight again. Just watch for the ditch on that far side.

There's a path, but you have to look for it. And *be careful* where they're burnin! Some of these idjits dont know what they're doin! Gonna burn down half the county afore it's over!"

Michael got stuck a little when he first entered the field, but alternating forward and reverse a few times rocked him out of it. As he skirted the farthest reaches of the kudzu a wind-driven reach of the vine tried to snag him.

"To the last, the last," his grandfather wheezed.

They got back on to another dirt road that would join the one they'd had to detour off of. The fields here were burning, caught fire no doubt from the green figures erupting nearby. Several men in coveralls appeared to be both fighting the blaze and igniting more. Michael wanted to drive as fast as possible past the burning areas but the road was too rutted and uneven — if he wasn't careful he'd send them into a ditch.

A wall of flame rose behind the men, turning them into black silhouettes. He saw their arms go up, their legs moving as if they were dancing, but the joints too limber and improbably hinged, like marionettes. Igniting kudzu rose behind the flames and curled over, becoming burning streamers as they dropped toward the men.

At the last moment they danced out of the way but other runners on both sides were catching fire, hissing like vipers as the plants rose on the hot currents of air.

"Syl... syllable of recorded time." His grandfather was gasping and coughing now from the thick smoke, the stench of pulpy, burning vegetable matter. Michael recklessly pushed on the gas pedal, anxious especially to get his grandparents out of this.

They swung back onto the better paved road on the other side of the huge green figures, now bending, struggling to stay upright.

"... all our yesterdays have... have lighted fools," his grandfather continued, "the way to dusty death."

"So is his Bible in the crate?" Michael asked them. "That's why it's all bound up, strapped in iron?"

"Out, out, brief candle!" his grandfather suddenly shouted. "Life's but a walking shadow!"

"No, honey," she replied. "*He's* in the crate."

"He?"

"The preacher. And now that bastard's waking up!"

"… poor player that struts and frets…"

The overgrowth of kudzu had completely altered the landscape and Michael was quickly getting disoriented. The pavement had disappeared under a scatter of broken leaves and stems. Something had gone through here and ripped everything apart.

Something metal struck the left front fender with a loud clang followed by a terrible ripping sound. The truck rose up a little in front then slammed down.

"… and then is heard no more…"

"Stop here!" Grandma cried. But they were already stopped. They all stepped out of the truck. Michael crouched down near the left front wheel well. A heavily rusted metal post had gouged the fender, then fragmented into several pieces. Underneath it lay a corroded "Bird Sanctuary" sign.

"You aint the first," Grandma said. "They put it up in the Fifties, because we had so many damn birds! Nuisances, a lot of them. Then it started a few years ago — ever vehicle going by hit that sign, didn't matter where they were in the road they always managed to find it. Sign snapped off eventually, just leaving the post. The birds went away long time ago. You can't tell me that's a coincidence, the preacher being right there out in that field and all!"

She stepped over several thick kudzu runners and began wading through the stuff into the field. Michael picked up the longest section of the metal post and looked at it. Instead of snapping it had twisted and sheared along the rust lines leaving knife-like ends. He'd already cut his hand on one edge. He stuck it into his belt loop like a kid's pretend double-ended sword, the kind of toy some reckless kids never survived. Well, he'd *been* a reckless kid. It looked silly, but they might need it.

"Told by an idiot, told by an idiot," his grandfather muttered, and they both ran after her.

They followed her through torn apart vines and a choking cloud of green, finally joining her by the ruins of a shed. The filthy crate had been pulled out into the field and split apart. Inside were the skeletons of numerous snakes and nothing more.

"They were his'n," Sadie said, "so we put them in there with him. We best get to the house now."

"Why?"

"I hid his special Bible in there. He'll be wanting it."

His grandfather said, "The sound *and* the fury. Where'd you hide it?"

"Tell you true, I have no idear. It was a long time ago, and I aint bothered with it since then."

Chapter Twenty-Two

SEVERAL LAMPS BURNED in the preacher's house. Sadie didn't know why. She didn't know anybody who lit up their house like that — lamp oil was too expensive. She looked for movement, and occasionally there'd be a quick pass of something, like a wing across the moon, or someone dancing, celebrating. Then something narrow and windy against the shade — one of his snakes she guessed — looking huge because of the angle of the shadow.

"You think he's scared of the dark?" Mickey-Gene said beside her. "I mean someone like him?"

"I reckon we're all scared of the dark, given the right situation. He's a lot scared of something — I can feel it every time I'm around him. Maybe that's part of why he is the way he is — he's taking sides with it. I dont know. I dont really want to understand him — I just want to stop him."

"You think he knows we're coming?"

"He knows *somebody's* coming. You dont do something like what he done and not expect folks to come after you for it. It's kind of like an invite. Dont know that he'd expect it to be us though — we might be the last two he'd be expecting. But that's probably why all the lights are on — he dont want to be snuck up on."

"You think he'll be shooting his way out? Like that Dillinger fellow?" Mickey-Gene's eyes looked large in the reflected light.

"I dont think guns are his style, least I've never seen him with one."

"You think because he's a preacher he'll be throwing words at us?"

"Words will raise you up or bring you down. Depends on what you do after they've been said." She started toward the house, the rifle slung from its leather strap across her shoulder. "Careful you dont blow a hole through yourself with that pistol."

"Tomorrow, and tomorrow, and tomorrow," he said.

"What's that?"

"Shakespeare. *Macbeth*. The next lines go, 'Creeps in this petty pace from day to day, to the last syllable of recorded time...'"

"Mickey-Gene, that's kind of pretty, but maybe a little too gloomy for me right now."

They were almost to the porch when the gray women came streaming from hidden spaces around the house, blown about like damp sheets in the wind. Their mouths were all open, arms raised and pointing away from the house. Sadie couldn't see their eyes — that part of their faces was shadowed and blurred as if erased.

"Mickey-Gene? Can you see any of this?"

"I cant see the house too well. I think I've got something in my eyes."

"What are you feeling?"

"Like I dont ever want to go into that house."

One after another the gray ladies rushed up to her, their mouths open, showing her things she didn't want to see. "It's the gray women, warning us away."

"I guess they've seen a lot of women walk into this house," he said.

"And hardly any of them leave I bet." Sadie made herself move past the ghosts, apologizing quietly as she pushed them from her concerns. They smelled bad. Of old sweaty clothes and closed-up rooms, mold damage and rot, disuse and despair.

A lantern had been set in the middle of the front room, for them to use, she figured, so she used it. She carried it into the next room, and the one after that, moving it around so that she could see into every corner.

"What are you looking for?" Mickey-Gene was so close behind her they might trip each other up, maybe even one shoot the other.

"Snakes. I dont want to step on one." He didn't reply, but he moved closer. "Mickey-Gene Gibson, dont you dare bump into me while I'm carrying this rifle. I've never used one before."

"I've never used a pistol before, either."

"Then we're a pretty fearsome pair for sure. Preacher's going to give up without a struggle." Something about the house was nagging her. "He's cleaned up," she said.

"Looks pretty dusty to me."

"It's a showcase compared to when Granny Grace and I were here. There was grit everywhere from the crumbling walls, and he'd chopped up all his furniture — it was in stacks in these rooms."

"Chopped it up? Winter's not for a couple of months."

"I dont think he did it for fuel. I think it had something to do with something he'd read in the Bible. Forsaking the world's goods, that kind of thing. The man's crazy for them Bible verses. But look at these rooms—he's got some wallpaper hanging down in places, but it's all tidy and swept. It's like he's getting ready to move out."

She was nervous about guiding Mickey-Gene into the next room. That was the one that'd had all the women's clothing hanging up in it. And the underwear nailed to the wall. No telling how he'd react to it. But it was mostly bare like the others, except there was a homemade cross about two feet high leaning in the corner, and the room was well swept.

Before they had a chance to go into the next room the preacher's voice came out of it, clear and loud as if he were standing right there preaching to them. "You can come on in if you think you're right with the Lord."

Mickey-Gene stared at her. She shrugged. She had no idea if she was right with the Lord or not, although she suspected not. She went over to the corner and picked up the big cross. It was heavy and required both hands, and the rifle strap kept coming off her shoulder and she had to nudge it back. Mickey-Gene opened the door for her and she led the way in.

The preacher sat in a high-backed chair in the middle of the room. With a little hurt in her throat, Sadie thought of Grandpa's chair like that; she'd always thought it looked like some kind of throne. The Simpsons had had it on that wagon to take away.

Despite the hot night he was dressed in his long black coat, white shirt and tie, gray pants, and that huge black hat like some kind of weird pet pressed down on his head. He even had a little red flower in his lapel, but it was wilted, twisted, unable to tolerate the heat.

His Bible was spread open in his lap, a rattler curled up on the open pages. The preacher was perfectly still, watching them with a smile like a knife blade run through flesh, his eyes two cold wet pieces of coal.

The snake, however, was not still. Its huge head — much too large, she thought, for a rattler — floated up and floated down at the same time its body uncoiled and rose, passing side to side from one of the preacher's shoulders to the other. It looked as if it knew it was the most dangerous thing in the room and was ready to prove that at any sign of doubt.

A second snake unfurled out of the back of the preacher's hat, curling into ever-tightening circles over the brim and crown. Sadie heard a rocking, shaking noise, looked down and saw that the preacher had his feet up on a long wooden platform. Two snakes appeared over the edge and she realized it was the box the saints had carried into the church with his snakes in it. The snakes flowed over his dark boots, slithered up his pants, and curled around each leg.

"Uncle, how can we stop this?" She could tell he didn't like her calling him Uncle, but it was too late to take it back. "Terrible things are happening." With difficulty she shrugged the rifle back on her shoulder and raised the heavy cross over her head with both hands and looked up at it. "That cant be what you wanted for your kin, the people, this town!"

"You aint no little girl no more, darlin! You had your bloody time, so I aint gonna talk to you like no little girl. Course there are turrible things happening in this town — *I'm* the one doing those turrible things! But sometimes you got to use the power you got to change things. Sometimes you got to make that iron fist. Do you think the Lord Jehovah didn't know he was doing a turrible thing when he killed the first born Gyptians? And in Deuteronomy didn't he order the killing of all the men, women, and children of sixty cities? Blood of the lamb, Sister, blood of the lamb!"

"But you cant just *murder* folks!"

"*Sacrifice*, Sister, that's what it be! The Lord requires his sacrifice so's he knows you will honor him above all the others! I'm the oldest one of my generation of the family and I have to lead them out of this wage bondage, this coal bondage, this race bondage we been subject to since the first Gibsons came off that mountain! We got our future writ right in this here Bible!" He suddenly raised his Bible high in the air. The snake tumbled off, hissing and striking at empty air. "And it's a powerful one — you'll see!"

"But the Grans..."

"Open your eyes, Sister! Do you see the Grans round here? The Grans dont stay — they always leave when the blood starts flowing! But me, I say *born in blood!* That's the way it's always been and always will be!"

"But you made Jesse kill Lilly!

"My brother had to *learn*. The fool had to sober up. He needed a *strong* lesson! And that woman of his, well, if she'd been strong enough she would've protected herself!"

"And those young women! We know you've been gathering them up, satisfying your lust with them, and *murdering* them after!"

When the preacher stood up the remaining snakes flew off his body like living lightning. He shook his fist at Sadie. "I'm just a man, Sister, with a man's lust and thoughts of revenge. Some things just cant be helped! I could no more deny my natural power over women than a polecat can deny its stink! But when this is all over, I'll be a better man for all the sinning I done!"

"What about the Simpson family? And Granny Grace? They were innocents and you butchered them!"

"Enough! Aint no innocents in this world — aint you learnt that yet? Maybe in the next. And maybe that can be *arranged*." She struck him with the cross then, opening up a large gash in his forehead. The blood rapidly painted his face a muddy red. He stumbled back and sat down in his throne. "Kill me then," he said. "Kill me now! Put me in that there box and bury me out in the field!"

Chapter Twenty-Three

IT WAS AT this point in his grandmother's story that Michael became terrified.

He felt it at first as a pressure in his head. His eyesight narrowed and his vision was affected. He could barely raise his eyes, was compelled to watch his feet as he carefully stepped over the withered vines of kudzu. He looked at where the crate had been ruptured, the force that must have been required to splinter oak and shatter iron, the trampling on the vegetation around it as either a thrashing or a celebration had taken place, the long, twisted skeletons of the once vibrant snakes stomped into the pulpy ground.

Off to his left he could see where whatever force had been contained by the crate had torn through the vines and pushed through the tightly-packed woods. On the other side of those woods was his grandmother's house. And all around him the smoke gathered and descended, and beyond the trees on the other side of the road the flames climbing higher than the trees. And still he could see untouched kudzu around the margins of his vision, and he could hear the distant shouts of the people trying to contend with it all, and almost as frightened as he.

It was one thing to see calamitous changes in the world — plants or fires or a disappearing town — because these were the inevitable ravages of nature and there was no understanding the ways of nature.

And it was one thing to listen to an old lady's ravings, and even to believe them, to see them acted out right in front of you as if you were watching a television show.

It was one thing to go crazy and hallucinate these wonders yourself.

But to *truly* believe it, to face it in your own time and in the flesh? Impossible. It would be like having a face to face meeting with Frankenstein or Hannibal Lecter. Such meetings did not take place in the real world. He should never have stayed. He should have gone off and found some plain, explainable, less interesting place to live.

Once they got back in the truck he could feel his grandmother's eyes on him but he could not look at her. He drove slowly and carefully. Fallen vine and burnt vegetation lay everywhere, threatening to stop or overturn the vehicle. Along some portions of the road the flames were quite close and posed a real threat to the truck. All his familiar landmarks were gone. He knew the relative length of this stretch before the turnoff for the farm, but he'd become completely disoriented — nothing looked as it should. For all he knew the turnoff had been obscured by fire, vegetation, or both. She kept looking at him and he kept looking away.

"Tomorrow and tomorrow and tomorrow," his grandfather muttered.

"Hush, Mickey-Gene," Grandma said, patting his grandfather's leg. "It's not a good time."

"You know it seems like the preacher wasn't that much of a threat to you that night," Michael said. "After he killed all those people. Slaughtered them. He knew you were coming. Obviously he was just waiting for you. From what you've said, it looks like he gave himself up pretty easily. Did he even put up a fight? Did you even raise your gun?"

"He might have," she said. "His falling back like that, all helpless like in his chair, that might have been a trick. He might have been trying to catch us off guard. But then that's when they all came into the house."

*   *   *

"KILL ME NOW!" the preacher said again. "Put me in that box and carry me out to the field! That's what you want to do, aint it? Go ahead and do it!"

Sadie raised the rifle. "Just you shut up! Shut up now! We got to think about this!"

There was a pounding on the front door. Then the thunder came in, a roar and a knocking around that swept through the house, bringing the angry voices with it. Mickey-Gene, standing in front of the door to this room, looked at Sadie. The snakes were in a frenzy. She ran over to pull Mickey-Gene out of the way.

The first one through the door was Sadie's mother, her hair sticking out, face a wild mask. She carried a double-barreled shotgun, firing one barrel immediately into a cluster of snakes that had gathered on the floor nearby. The preacher moaned.

"Tell me one reason I shouldn't let you have it with the other barrel, take your head clean off!" she shouted.

The preacher just grinned. In a county where folks couldn't always afford good dental care the preacher still had all his teeth.

Daddy came around Momma carrying a pitchfork. He drove it through the preacher's hand into his open Bible. Sadie noticed that the hand was the one with the dark poison spot. The preacher didn't make a sound.

George Mackey pushed through the people jamming the door, towering over everybody. He carried a short, thick piece of wood. He nodded once at Sadie, then swung the stick and hit the preacher full in the face with it. The preacher's head jerked, blood and a few teeth spilling to the floor. Mackey stooped and picked up the teeth before leaving.

Several folks crowded in then, so many there was considerable pushing and shoving, with Mickey-Gene stepping in between Sadie and the more aggressive members of the crowd. She wanted to tell them to wait, there was something wrong about how the preacher was being and they needed to just stop awhile and figure it out. But there were too many of them, and they wouldn't have listened to a girl her age anyway. Several had been drinking besides her daddy. As places were sorted out Will Shaney ended up at the front with several other members of the preacher's congregation, including two tall men Sadie recognized as part of the preacher's troop of saints, their faces calm, their eyes moving back and forth over the crowd. Mr. Shaney carried a heavy-looking hammer in one hand, a cluster of long nails in the other. Sadie's mouth went suddenly dry. "Mickey-Gene," she whispered. "This is getting out of hand."

"We trusted you," Mr. Shaney said, "we all did. You were our preacher. You read that there Bible to us. And after what you done, well, I dont know how, but you killed my boy didn't you, or you were part of it?"

Someone in the back yelled, "Go on! Shoot him!"

"Shooting's too good for him," one of the two saints said. He laid his hand on Mr. Shaney's shoulder. "I know how you feel, sir, but *Christ* was crucified. It would be a sacrilege to use them nails on the preacher, givin that polecat the same treatment as our lord Jesus!"

The other saint walked over and kicked the box under the preacher's feet. The snakes inside jerked and hissed, making the box buck. "Be a shame to separate the preacher from his pets!" he said.

There were shouts of agreement and several people grabbed the preacher. He didn't struggle. The two saints pulled some poles out of the corner with hooks on the ends and stood by the crate.

"Well, aren't you gonna say somethin?" someone shouted. "You're a preacher, so preach!"

There was a moment of silence. The preacher looked at them all and smiled, but only with his lips. His eyes remained cold and dark. "Well, you folks should at least know your Ecclesiastes," he said. "Remember there's an appointed *time* for everything! There is a *time* for every event under heaven!

And I know when *my time* has come! And some day so will you!" Then he looked directly at Sadie and Mickey-Gene. "At least I see you two are together."

They pried off the lid of the crate then, the saints holding down at least a dozen snakes as the people threw him in with them. Sadie saw that the snakes were biting him already, and although his body jumped a little with each bite he didn't make a sound. "He's tryin to get out!" one of the saints cried, but Sadie didn't think it was true. That saint took out a fresh-looking wooden stake, and grabbing Shaney's hammer from him, drove that stake right between the preacher's shoulders. Even the eager ones in the crowd shouted and drew back from that terrible act.

Then the saints crashed the lid over the preacher's flailing body, and they helped Will Shaney nail it down, spacing the nails only a few inches apart all around the rim. They argued over who got to carry the crate out to the field, and eventually they decided they would all take turns, and a bunch of people lifted it and carried it through the door, Mickey-Gene trailing behind.

The ones that stayed back looted the few belongings left in the house. Sadie saw several older women walk out carrying crosses, including the one she'd hit the preacher with. They went through the house like banshees, yelling and screaming and taking everything.

Daddy was the first to come back, sweaty and out of breath and stinking of hooch. He put his pitchfork down and leaned against the wall, grinning sloppily at her. "You shoulda been there, darlin. We made him a little bitty grave house just like he was a decent person, put the crate in there and threw a little bit a dirt on it. But he *was* my brother, so he oughter had *some* kind of grave. You know there was still thumpin on the inside of that crate, the preacher or them snakes or both, hard to say."

"Where's Momma?"

"She's still all wound up, bout Lilly and her Simpson kin and all. She's just runnin around out there in circles, pretty much. You know what she said when we threw on the dirt? She says 'Now he's partly above ground and partly below. Just like a snake! He's just some kind of animal,' she says, 'that dont deserve neither heaven nor hell!' I just about bust a gut!"

"So you've done what needed to be done?"

"I reckon I did."

"Then you got to go, Daddy! You got to go away from here and never come back! I cant be worried about you messing around with me no more!"

"Now listen here, girl! Who do you think's the man, the *father*, goddamit!"

She raised the rifle and pointed it at him. She tried to ignore the shaking barrel. "Too late. Too late for that! Now git before I pull this trigger!"

He stared at her for a little while, his drunkenness draining away. Eventually he went out the door. She would never see him again. Her mother would never mention it. It would be as if he had never been. Over the next year she became the mother Sadie had always wanted and they eventually moved into the preacher's house. It would have some terrible memories of course, but you never turned down an inheritance in 1934 in Morrison, Virginia.

Chapter Twenty-Four

MICHAEL MOVED THE pickup gradually down a tunnel of green. He couldn't see the road bed. It was matted with crushed vine and layered leaves. The leaves appeared wet, as if the mass of kudzu had created its own weather. He could feel the tires slipping, the manual transmission trying, and failing to find purchase. Afraid he was going to slide them off the road, he barely pressed the gas pedal.

"So he let himself get caught," he said to his grandmother. "He could have gotten away. He could have killed you both. But he didn't."

"No, he sure didn't."

"And you knew something was up, I got that. I was there, in that way we have of being there. For whatever reason, he wanted to be buried that way, alive."

"No, Michael. Not buried, exactly. His saints, it was supposedly their idea to put him in the box with his snakes. *That's* what he wanted."

The truck was moving so slowly it was almost at a stop anyway, so he made it complete. His grandfather was nodding slightly, rocking, his eyes half-closed. "He also wanted the two of you together. And you knew that."

"I knew that," she repeated, "but I was just a girl. Mickey and I came together years later, after Momma died. I made myself believe the preacher was dead — why wouldn't he be? I didn't think it mattered anymore. He wasn't in our lives anymore, he just wasn't. But then we had our son, your father, and later you were born, and Mickey and I, we could see it."

"See it?"

"Our part in it. Your granddad here was always quoting that play, about how everybody has many parts to play…"

"*As You Like It*," he said.

"Yep, that's it. And how you say your lines. Everybody has their lines, everybody has their parts."

Michael started moving the truck again. The green tunnel trembled. "Just like I have my part," he said.

"Yes, baby."

"The preacher was waking up again. Somehow I must have known. It was time to play my part. I got myself injured, trying not to come back here, trying not to play my role."

"Yes, baby."

"But I got back here anyway. I guess it was in the blood. I had to come back."

"All these people. All these innocent lives."

"I dont know any of them," he said. "I dont know them. I shouldn't have had to come."

"If you hadn't come he would have killed everybody here anyway, and still gone looking for you, and he would have killed people along the way you might have cared about."

"All our yesterdays," his grandfather muttered. "The way to dusty death."

"Hush, Mickey. Hush," Grandma said.

"But what does he expect of me?" Michael gripped the wheel angrily, trying to keep the pickup from sliding off the road. "What can he possibly expect?"

"That you'll be like him," she answered. "But you aren't like him." And then she stopped. "Are you?"

They came out of the green tunnel before Michael could answer. He pulled over and got out of the truck. He had some difficulty orienting himself within all the layers of what he was seeing, but as best he could determine the house and lawn were now entirely contained within walls of flowing and mutating kudzu. Even the sky had been obscured behind a lacy baffle of vine and leaf that moved to let in light, then floated closed and tinted everything in variations of green. The rest of the space was filled with the intricately imagined grounds and structure of what Michael thought might be a wealthy Victorian-era estate. But the style of it kept changing, so sometimes he thought he was seeing Roman features in the design, and sometimes Egyptian.

Of course it was possible that it was all his own imagination creating the effects, because the entire thing was made from kudzu — he couldn't even see the original underlying house and trees anymore — so what he was actually looking at were sometimes geometric and sometimes amorphous cloud shapes abstracted from masses of pulpy green leaf, blossom, and vine.

Smaller mounds of kudzu rose and collapsed within this more or less level part leading up to the house. Sometimes these shapes resembled the statues of lions you sometimes saw as protective figures on either side of entrances to large houses, but other times they were more bear-like or even bird-like, giant hawks or swans. He led the way forward to the first "lion" and tried to look it more directly in the face: the eyes were hollow green shadows, and inside the roaring green mouths there were still more layers of deepening green, a leaf or two stirring like a tongue.

He insisted that his grandmother and grandfather stay behind him as he moved past these figures. He could tell how much trouble they were having maintaining their balance on the constantly shifting vegetation. The grand doors of the green mansion yawned just ahead, and as they approached he heard the figures move behind him. He glanced back and watched them as they first appeared to run, then dissolved into the floor of green.

"Did you ever know the preacher to have this kind of power?"

"No! I think this must have come to him while he was in that crate," Grandma said. Michael flashed back to that image of the saint driving that fresh-cut wooden stake into the preacher's back.

Above the entrance and stretching across the entire front of the house, an elaborate balcony was decorated with twisted vine and leaf filigree. He saw just a brief moment of white there, followed by folds of rushing gray. He knew immediately these were the gray women he'd seen in his grandmother's memories, but in person they were even more chilling, their faces translucent enough to show jaw muscles and necks stressed to the extreme, the tongues inside ragged with decay. They paced the balcony with confused, awkward movements. At the front left corner of the kudzu house was a circular room — maybe a music room — that extended up into a kind of tower, except the top appeared unfinished, the runners and topmost leaves waving about aimlessly. There were more gray women in the tower, dancing with each other. Michael thought about kings, and the brides of kings, and wondered if maybe these dead women were all the preacher's brides frozen in their youth.

The leaves on the tower suddenly started fluttering like thousands of green butterflies. The tower itself began to spin, and some of the gray ladies were momentarily caught and torn apart by the force of it. The green tornado twisted out a minaret at the top. Green buttresses flew out of the walls to join other parts of the building. Michael rushed his grandparents inside.

Inside the viridescent interior, walls of vine separated and some ceilings lowered while others expanded into leaf domes. Long strands of vine hung down from the ceiling and swept through the space touching the leafy floor. Michael considered how far they'd walked already and decided they still hadn't even reached the original house. So far everything they'd seen was mounted on nothing but madness and imagination.

Here and there Michael was finding Bible pages caught in the vine and leaf tangle. He collected them, trying to keep them in order. Mickey-Gene started doing the same, now and then handing over what he'd picked.

"Is that the preacher's Bible you two are picking up?" his grandmother asked. "Dont keep nothing from me now."

"It's the very one," Mickey-Gene said. "That Bible isn't something I'd likely forget. I recognize some of the pages, especially the painted ones. Excuse me if I dont ever want to study them again, but I recognize them alright."

"Then he was able to find it. He had that damned Bible," she said. "So why'd he tear it up? Leaving it lying around like trash?"

Michael picked up some more pages. These were from Revelations. One passage in particular had been underlined and decorated with crude renderings of kudzu leaves. He wasn't sure what had been used to create the drawings. It wasn't pencil. It might have been a dirty fingernail.

> *there the tree of life, which bare twelve manner of fruits, and yielded her fruit every month: and the leaves of the tree were for the healing of the nations*

Filling the next page was an attempt at a painting of a tree. Long curving lines of vine had been drawn and painted with what might have been crushed kudzu leaves, crowning the tree and traveling back across previous pages. The brown of the bark might have been dried blood.

"I'm thinking he just doesn't need to refer to it anymore," Michael said. "He knows it all too well. And I think he's living the parts he believes in most."

"Sound and fury…" his grandfather muttered.

"I feel bad he found it so easily," his grandmother said. "I didn't remember where it was. He must have torn the place apart."

They soon found themselves in an overgrown area littered with debris. A shattered window frame hung off an upturned spur of kudzu. Nearby lay a pile of fractured wood, some of the pieces only a few inches long. There was molding, bits of floorboard, baseboard, a small section of door panel, and random splinters of plaster lathe, wall rubble and horsehair still attached. Most he could not tell where they'd originally been from, but some still bore the specific paint colors of particular rooms.

He could hear Grandma sobbing softly behind him, his grandfather's mumbled condolences. Michael had never owned much of anything, certainly nothing as substantial as a home, so he couldn't imagine what she was going through. She gathered what she could of some shredded family photographs, stuffed them into her pockets. She picked up a handle from a broken china cup and asked Mickey-Gene to keep it for her. Over the next few yards she picked up silverware, a scrap of wallpaper, a child's bright yellow spinning top, keeping a few things, dropping others, crying, spitting, cursing. Sometimes Michael's grandfather would pat her. Other times he kept his hands away as if afraid.

After Allison's grandparents died there had been an estate sale. She'd dragged Michael to it even after he'd attempted several excuses. For once she wouldn't take no for an answer. It had been held in their empty house, soon to go on sale, their last remaining things that hadn't gone to relatives spread out over four folding tables, things like silverware, un-matched dishes, some gaudy jewelry, an antique doorknob that had once opened an unknown door, books by old authors he'd never heard of, a jar full of buttons, a jar full of random parts to random things.

He'd wandered around the house for a bit, looking out of windows, imagining sights, viewpoints they might have had. He'd sat and watched Allison sell the last few items for dollars, quarters, and dimes. Then half a table's worth of items shoved into a trash bag which he took out to the can by the alley. Then a few hours patting and kissing Allison, comforting her ineffectively, just as his grandfather was doing now. After a couple of months she didn't mention her grandparents to him again. That's what it came down to — all that was left was what they'd done for each other, for friends, for family, for strangers. What they had done. Their story. Was his story going to be bigger or smaller than that?

To add to the insult of the destruction of his grandmother's possessions the kudzu had been used to duplicate the destroyed rooms, even down to vague representations of the pictures that had once hung on the walls. There were even crude approximations of the old furniture, emulations of the old views out the windows recreated in embossed green.

The farther they went in to the overgrown ruins, the larger were the broken pieces, until finally there were several rooms that appeared more or less intact — some of the old bedrooms toward the back of the house, and a couple more Michael didn't think he'd ever been into. He assumed that the preacher must have found his Bible at this point, and that was why the destruction had stopped.

Something tall and sinewy was moving between rooms, passing in and out of walls of kudzu, observing from shadow, but only briefly, because this was something so incredibly tired of being fixed in one place.

"Michael…" His grandfather pointed at something behind him.

Michael supposed the figure might have been considered naked, which would have shocked the preacher's conservative congregation. But the body was so different he didn't know that standards of nudity would actually apply.

There was exposed bone — a great deal of it — especially in the lower legs and rib cage, and on the back part of the head where pale flesh and a little bit of hair blended into the dingy off-white exposed skull. The preacher turned slightly as if showing himself, as if posing. Where his saint had driven in the wooden stake an irregular patch of old and woody vine had sprouted into two vaguely cloud-like shapes. To Michael they resembled a crude framework for wings, if the wings had developed malformed and nonfunctional.

Of course there shouldn't have been any flesh at all but there was a great deal of that as well, in the cheeks and neck and shoulders and upper thighs, and partially wrapping the arms and hands. In fact the preacher still had that ugly twisted place on his hand where he'd been bitten, and the flesh at its center was as dark as coal.

The preacher looked strangely muscular, and the muscles moved, or slid. Michael realized then that much of the preacher's flesh and muscle was actually snakes, rattlers and copperheads which had worked their way through his body, and were as improbably vibrant and well-preserved as he was. So his slim muscular calves were made out of yellowed rattlesnake hide with dark V-shapes all up and down them like tattoos. His biceps and some of his abdominal muscles had these brown hourglass shapes on them and when they started moving around his body it became clear that these were, or once had been, copperheads. A black, fuzzy, gauze-like material appeared to be trapped in the transitional spaces and margins between snake and human, decayed remnants of the preacher's black suit.

Michael closed his eyes, sick to his stomach. He opened them again and peered at his grandmother, who knew, who must have known, and still had allowed Michael to be here, had not tried to drive him away. She stared at him silently, but he could see the sorrow and feel the regret.

The figure in the doorway made a loud snorting noise as if trying to take in every last smell in the room and analyze it. Even though as far as Michael could tell the preacher no longer had a nose. "At lasssst…" The preacher spoke, lips ripping open as the mouth stretched wide. A second jaw within the mouth and behind the initial row of teeth was narrower and sported fangs. The snake came part way out of the preacher's mouth and both mouths said together, "the lasssst one." The preacher's throat made a bubbling, choking sound and two more words, "maahh blood!"

"Grandma!" he cried, feeling like a little kid. "Tell me what I'm supposed to do!" He was crazy, of course. All those times he'd gotten high, or so emotional he imagined he could feel his own nerves ache had taken their toll, driven the real world from his head.

"If he gets outta here he'll take the world with him!" she cried. "He wont stop at this town, this county! All those innocent people! All them murdered babes! All he is anymore is that bloodlust!"

"But I wanted…" Michael couldn't finish, because he'd never actually known what he'd wanted.

"It's a *curse*, Hone   y! I'm sorry! There's *nothing* I can do. All these years, it's been coming toward this day!"

His grandfather pushed in front of her, getting between her and the impossible thing they'd all come after. What had any of them been thinking? Everybody had nightmares, and everybody knew you just had to endure them the best you could. You couldn't just stop them from coming. When had the Gibsons become so stupid?

A rosy glow was creeping through the gaps in the curtain of kudzu hanging behind and overhead. The old house had no roof anymore, and only part of its outside walls, so the kudzu was the only barrier between them and the rest of the world. The leaves were curling, the vines twisting. What was the preacher doing now? The glow began to redden, and Michael wondered if maybe they had lost all time, they had been here all night, and now what was coming down was the dawn.

"People need filling, son." Michael turned and looked at his grandfather, who had a knife in his hand. He'd been like that all his life, always hiding in plain sight. "And if they cant fill up with love and joy, they'll fill up with something other." His grandfather ran into that abomination with his knife raised. The snake came out then and bit him, and the arms came down and broke him.

"Mickey!" Grandma tried to pull Mickey-Gene's body out of the preacher's embrace.

"Didn't *waaant* to do it, Sadie! Mickey-Gene is blood! But the snake in me! Aint gonna let me die!"

She continued to struggle with him, and the preacher kept saying "Nooo! Sa-deee, nooo!" in that new choking, stuffed throated way of his, until finally the snake pushed its way out of the preacher's mouth again, coming down and clamping on her throat.

"Sadie!" the preacher screamed, in a voice now much like it had been in the past, and Michael's grandparents lay together in a writhing layer of kudzu, as the preacher shook his head side to side and raged.

Michael raised his hands up in front of his face, wanting to grab onto something but having nothing to grab onto. He felt the first ice of despair, and waited for it to rip him apart. When it didn't he let his arms fall to his sides, felt the bit of post he'd fixed to himself like a sword earlier. He pulled it out and swung it about foolishly, shouting "Ha!" and wondering if he might finally be losing his mind. He cut himself again on one edge.

While the preacher still raged Michael tried to find the tears and the deep well of sadness he knew to be there for the loss of his grandparents, the loss of everyone he had ever loved. But it was all just words in his head. He found his deep well, but it was full of family blood, and the knowledge of what he would someday be able to do, as he could hear the voices of the snakes whispering to him.

The initial flames burst through the kudzu above his head. Strands of it melted and dripped smoking to the vines and leaves below, and they too ignited. The preacher didn't seem to notice. Now he stared at Michael with those shining, black coal eyes, both of his mouths grinning. "Blood." He reached out his arm of snake and bone.

It was possible the fire would get to them both before either of them could run, that the last vestiges of family blood might be destroyed without Michael having to make another decision.

But he could not take that chance, not with temptation slithering through his brain. He placed one sharp end of the post below his sternum and ran. There was an explosion in his head as the two of them came together, and he desperately embraced what had once been a man. The snakes came out and bit him, and the preacher filled the air with words, but Michael was not listening as the final curtain of flame came down.

Chapter Twenty-Five

SOMEWHERE NEAR THE middle of Kansas Addie cried out and slumped forward in the passenger seat. Elijah glanced over but didn't stop. It had been a long day, and he had several hundred miles more to drive before they rested. He hummed a little tune he half-remembered had been a favorite of hers from back before the Civil War. He stroked the few remaining colorless hairs on her head. She had been quite beautiful, but quite old even back then.

It was possible she was dead. Death was always possible, even for the likes of them. He hoped she wasn't, because he loved her dearly. He'd never thought to swap her, but the universe didn't much care what an old person thought, or what anyone thought for that matter. He sure didn't want a change now. Change was hard.

Something bad had happened back there. Addie had felt it more than he and that's what put her down. Feeling was a burden, but it made them a might better than snakes in the ground.

In a few hours he would stop and try to wake her. He would bide his time until then. And then he would find out if he was the last one.

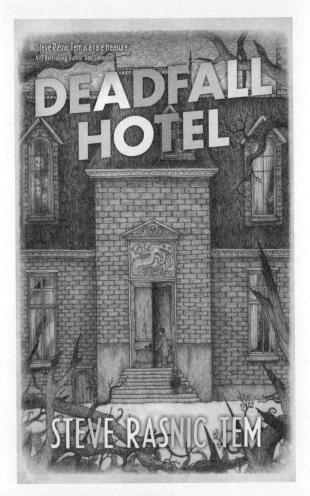

THIS IS THE HOTEL WHERE OUR NIGHTMARES GO...

It's where horrors come to be themselves, and the dead pause to rest between worlds. Recently widowed and unemployed, Richard Carter finds a new job, and a new life for him and his daughter Serena, as manager of the mysterious Deadfall Hotel. Jacob Ascher, the caretaker, is there to show Richard the ropes, and to tell him the many rules and traditions, but from the beginning, their new world haunts and transforms them.

It's a terrible place. As the seasons pass, the supernatural and the sublime become a part of life, as routine as a morning cup of coffee, but it's not *safe*, by any means. Deadfall Hotel is where Richard and Serena will rebuild the life that was taken from them... if it doesn't kill them first.

A Dark Novel of Possession

THE Waking THAT Kills

Stephen Gregory

When his elderly father suffers a stroke, Christopher Beal returns to England.

He has no home, no other family. Adrift, he answers an advert for a live-in tutor for a teenage boy. The boy is Lawrence Lundy, who carries with him the spirit of his father, a military pilot – missing, presumed dead. Unable to accept that his father is gone, Lawrence keeps his presence alive, in the big old house, in the overgrown garden. His mother, Juliet, keeps the boy at home, away from the world; and in the suffocating heat of a long summer, she too is infected by the madness of her son.

Christopher becomes entangled in the strange household, enmeshed in the oddness of the boy and his fragile mother. Only by forcing the boy to release the spirit of his father can he find any escape from the haunting.

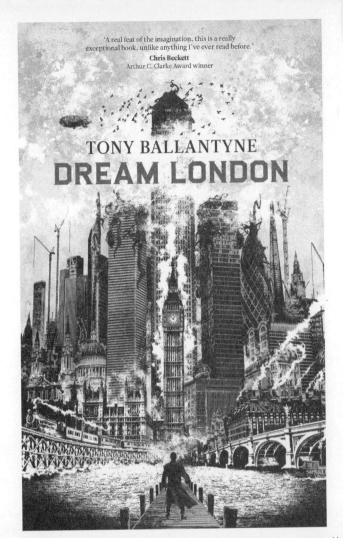

'A real feat of the imagination, this is a really exceptional book, unlike anything I've ever read before.'

Chris Beckett
Arthur C. Clarke Award winner

TONY BALLANTYNE
DREAM LONDON

Captain Jim Wedderburn has looks, style and courage. He's adored by women, respected by men and feared by his enemies. He's the man to find out who has twisted London into this strange new world. But in Dream London the city changes a little every night and the people change a little every day. The towers are growing taller, the parks have hidden themselves away and the streets form themselves into strange new patterns. There are people sailing in from new lands down the river, new criminals emerging in the East End and a path spiraling down to another world.

Everyone is changing, no one is who they seem to be.

 WWW.SOLARISBOOKS.COM

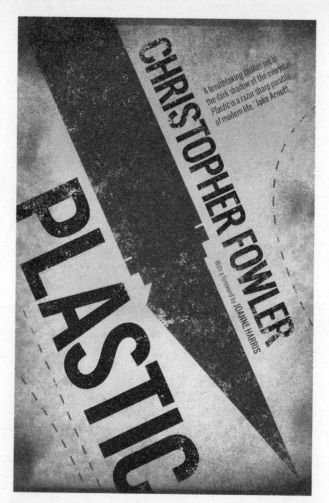

A breathtaking thriller set in the dark shadow of the everyday... Plastic is a razor sharp parable of modern life.' Jake Arnott

CHRISTOPHER FOWLER

PLASTIC

With a Foreword by JOANNE HARRIS

June Cryer is a shopaholic suburban housewife trapped in a lousy marriage. After discovering her husband's infidelity with the flight attendant next door, she loses her home, her husband and her credit rating. But there's a solution: a friend needs a caretaker for a spectacular London high-rise apartment. It's just for the weekend, and there'll be money to spend in a city with every temptation on offer.

Seizing the opportunity to escape, June moves in only to find that there's no electricity and no phone. She must flat-sit until the security system comes back on. When a terrified girl breaks into the flat and June makes the mistake of asking the neighbours for help, she finds herself embroiled in an escalating nightmare, trying to prove that a murderer exists. For the next 24 hours she must survive on the streets without friends or money and solve an impossible crime.

 WWW.SOLARISBOOKS.COM

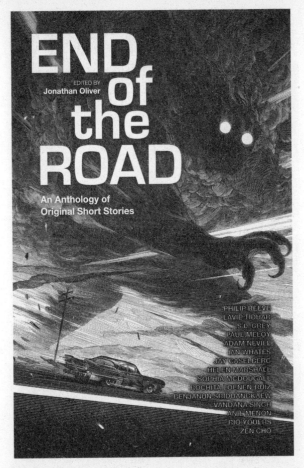

END of the ROAD

EDITED BY
Jonathan Oliver

**An Anthology of
Original Short Stories**

PHILIP REEVE
LAVIE TIDHAR
S.L. GREY
PAUL MELOY
ADAM NEVILL
IAN WHATES
JAY CASELBERG
HELEN MARSHALL
SOPHIA MCDOUGALL
ROCHITA LOENEN-RUIZ
BENJANUN SRIDUANGKAEW
VANDANA SINGH
ANIL MENON
RIO YOUERS
ZEN CHO

On the road to nowhere each step leads you closer to your destination, but who, or what, can you expect to meet along the way?

Here are stories of misfits, spectral hitch-hikers, nightmare travel tales and the rogues, freaks and monsters to be found on the road. The critically acclaimed editor of *Magic*, *The End of The Line* and *House of Fear* has brought together the contemporary masters and mistresses of the weird from around the globe in an anthology of travel tales like no other. Strap on your seatbelt, or shoulder your backpack, and wait for that next ride... into darkness.

An incredible anthology of original short stories from an exciting list of writers including the best-selling Philip Reeve, the World Fantasy Award-winning Lavie Tidhar and the incredible talents of S.L. Grey, Ian Whates, Jay Caselberg, Benjanun Sriduangkaew, Zen Cho, Sophia McDougall, Rochita Loenen-Ruiz, Anil Menon, Rio Youers, Vandana Singh, Paul Meloy, Adam Nevill and Helen Marshall.

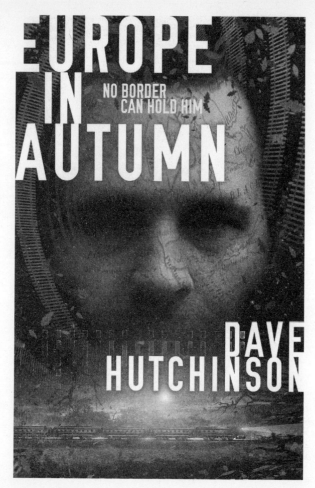

EUROPE IN AUTUMN

NO BORDER CAN HOLD HIM

DAVE HUTCHINSON

Rudi is a cook in a Kraków restaurant, but when his boss asks Rudi to help a cousin escape from the country he's trapped in, a new career – part spy, part people-smuggler – begins. Following multiple economic crises and a devastating flu pandemic, Europe has fractured into countless tiny nations, duchies, polities and republics. Recruited by the shadowy organisation *Les Coureurs des Bois*, Rudi is schooled in espionage, but when a training mission to The Line, a sovereign nation consisting of a trans-Europe railway line, goes wrong, he is arrested and beaten, and *Coureur* Central must attempt a rescue.

With so many nations to work in, and identities to assume, Rudi is kept busy travelling across Europe. But when he is sent to smuggle someone out of Berlin and finds a severed head inside a locker instead, a conspiracy begins to wind itself around him. With kidnapping, double-crosses and a map that constantly re-draws itself, *Europe in Autumn* is a science fiction thriller like no other.

 WWW.SOLARISBOOKS.COM

Follow us on Twitter! www.twitter.com/solarisbooks

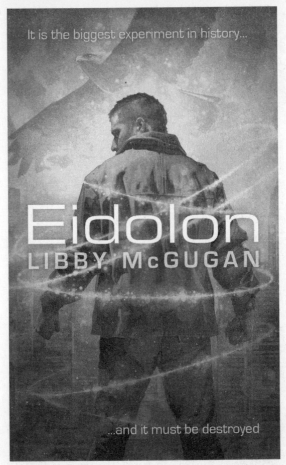

It is the biggest experiment in history...

Eidolon
LIBBY McGUGAN

...and it must be destroyed

When physicist Robert Strong — newly unemployed and single — is offered a hundred thousand pounds for a week's work, he's understandably sceptical. But Victor Amos, head of the mysterious Observation Research Board, has compelling proof that the next round of experiments at CERN's Large Hadron Collider poses a real threat to the whole world. And he needs Robert to sabotage it.

Robert's life is falling apart. His work at the Dark Matter Research Laboratory in Middlesbrough was taken away from him; his girlfriend, struggling to cope with the loss of her sister, has left. He returns home to Scotland, seeking sanctuary and rest, and instead starts to question his own sanity as the dead begin appearing to him, in dreams and in waking. Accepting Amos's offer, Robert flies to Geneva, but as he infiltrates CERN, everything he once understood about reality and science, about the boundary between life and death, changes forever.

Mixing science, philosophy and espionage, Libby McGugan's stunning debut is a thriller like no other.

 WWW.SOLARISBOOKS.COM

Follow us on Twitter! www.twitter.com/solarisbooks

a
nightmarish
otherworld
of
fathers and
sons,
hopes
and dreams,
love and
death.

Regicide
Nicholas
Royle

NON STOP.
ONE WAY.
STRAIGHT
DOWN!

HELL TRAIN
CHRISTOPHER FOWLER

Bizarre creatures, satanic rites, terrified passengers and the romance of travelling by train, all in a classically-styled horror novel!

'The very British spirit of Hammer Horror rises from the grave in Christopher Fowler's rattling, roaring yarn.'
- Kim Newman, author of *Anno Dracula*

 WWW.SOLARISBOOKS.COM

Follow us on Twitter! www.twitter.com/solarisbooks

n